Clara's Return

Suzanna J. Linton
9/22/19

Clara's Return
by Suzanna J. Linton

Copyright 2016 Suzanna J. Linton

All Rights Reserved. No portion of this book may be copied or used without permission from the author.

Other Works

Stories of Lorst
Clara

The Lands of Sun and Stone Series
Willows of Fate

For M., on her special day.

In Loving Memory of Ignatius, the best kitty mascot for which a writer could ask.

Acknowledgements

A lot of hard work went into creating this novel, which is true of all novels, really. I want to thank the creator of NaNoWriMo for coming up with Camp NaNo. If it hadn't been for that, it probably would have taken longer to get the first draft onto paper. I also want to thank the Florence Chapter of the South Carolina Writer's Workshop for giving me the first critiques and letting me know what made no sense and what made them cry. Finally, I want to thank Libby Copa of Sherman Writing Services (I loved your margin rants), my other beta readers, Fiona Jayde for the cover, and Julia Gibbs for proofreading.

Most of all, I want to thank my husband, who didn't mind that, sometimes, I forgot to cook supper, feed the animals, and clean the house. He made sure I actually left the house on occasion and knew better than to try to read over my shoulder. Thanks, honey.

Table of Contents

Prologue 1

Chapter One 13

Chapter Two 27

Chapter Three 38

Chapter Four 70

Chapter Five 94

Chapter Six 116

Chapter Seven 136

Chapter Eight 160

Chapter Nine 170

Chapter Ten 191

Chapter Eleven 193

Chapter Twelve 211

Chapter Thirteen 236

Chapter Fourteen 244

Chapter Fifteen 247

Chapter Sixteen 271

Chapter Seventeen 289

Chapter Eighteen 320

Chapter Nineteen 337

Chapter Twenty 351

Chapter Twenty-One 364

Chapter Twenty-Two 384

Chapter Twenty-Three 392

Chapter Twenty-Four 401

Chapter Twenty-Five 425

Chapter Twenty-Six 446

Epilogue 456

Letter to the Reader 476

About the Author 477

Prologue

Each stride down the snow-covered, darkened streets threatened a broken leg. Valiance ran anyway. His black cloak billowed behind him like crow's wings and the tails of his scarlet surcoat flapped against his legs. Underneath the fabric, his chain mail made soft chinking sounds.

He turned with a jerk of the hips, slipping on a chunk of ice only to catch himself at the last moment, and bolted down a side street.

He was in the Middle Quarters, the area for markets and the homes of those not quite rich enough for the high houses. Lamp light spilled from windows of homes and, with the tall torches lining the streets, cast the city in a warm glow. Inside the houses, people celebrated Mid-Winter with food, drink, and games.

Valiance's mind was not on Mid-Winter. All of his focus centered on running as fast as he could without injury. Earlier that day, a sudden rain had coated the city in ice and on top of that, snow began to fall when the sun set. When Valiance begged for a horse, the stablehands refused.

"Too slick," the Horsemaster grunted, "and I don't give a damn if you're the Acting Captain. You ain't risking my horses."

So, Valiance ran. He didn't bother to change from his Palace Guard uniform and only barely remembered to put someone else in charge before he left. The whole Palace was in revelry, even the King cracked his face enough to smile, and he didn't expect there to be any trouble.

His family's home came into view and he slowed. The ice-ridden air knifed through his chest as he tried to catch his breath. A faint breeze cooled the sweat on his brow and he shivered.

He mounted the treacherous steps and let himself into the dark, warm house.

"Hello!" Valiance called, stomping snow and ice off his boots in the foyer. "Father! Mother!"

Footsteps thudded upstairs and a door

slammed. His mother, in a long shift and a heavy shawl around her shoulders, appeared at the top. Her iron grey hair fell over her shoulder in a braid.

"Thank the Mother," she said. "Come up quick."

He did, taking the steps two at a time. "Where is she?"

"Abelia is in her room."

"And Father?"

"His gout has flared up, so he took a tonic before going to bed. Nothing short of the house setting ablaze would wake him."

He started to brush past her when she grabbed his arm.

"She won't talk to anyone," Mother said. "She hasn't said a word since she came home, other than say that you had to come at once and it was an emergency. Something terrible happened, Valiance. Her dress was torn and her jaw has a scrape across it. She wouldn't let us call the City Guard. She only said to send for you."

If someone had stolen away the honor of his baby sister, he would kill them. Slowly. And with imagination.

He left his mother and walked to his sister's room. As he drew closer, he heard soft weeping. He knocked on the door.

"Go away," croaked a voice he recognized as Abelia.

"Abbey, it's me," he said. "May I come in?"

No answer. He opened the door and stepped inside.

Like many girls her age, Abelia surrounded herself with pretty things. Little trinkets made from lace, ribbon, and shells crowded shelves, while a small case guarded a few precious gilded books.

A gown she was supposed to wear to the big Servants' Ball at the Palace the next day hung on a rack beside her wardrobe. The product of months of Abbey's patient labor, it was decked in bits of lace, ribbon, and a string of pearls Valiance had given her as an early Mid-Winter gift.

She sat against her headboard, her feet tucked under her, and wrapped in a flannel robe. Her wool tavern maid dress lay on the floor where she dropped it. He stepped over it and sat on the edge of the bed.

"Tell me what happened," Valiance said.

"Master Andrew let me off work early," she said, wiping tears from her face, "so I was coming home when-when the men came."

Valiance clenched one hand in a fist. He kept his voice calm. "Men?"

"They asked if I was your sister. When I said I was, they-they pushed me around-and tore my dress-and-" She gasped out a sob and crumbled into tears.

Valiance scooted closer and pulled her into an embrace. He wasn't that much older than her; he'd always been her protector and comforter.

Years ago, if any other children bullied her, Valiance was the one who bloodied those children's faces. And if they were at a dance where no one asked her for a turn, he would dance with her. And if Abbey and her mother fought, then Valiance settled the dispute and invariably took Abelia's side.

The fact that men attacked her because of her connection to him made his sight nearly go red with rage. He held it in. Abbey needed him.

When her tears eased, she pulled away.

"Abbey, I have to ask." He took both of her hands in his. "Did they, um." Damn, he didn't know how much their mother told her about what happened between a man and a woman in the confines of a bedroom. And he didn't want to be the one to explain. "Did they lay on you? Did they push your skirt up?"

She shook her head. "They threw me down and laughed. They laughed and tossed me a letter and said if I didn't get it to you right away, they would kill you. Then, they walked away."

Confusion replaced some of his anger. "Letter?"

Abbey drew it out from under a pillow. On it

was written Valiance's name in elegant script. He turned it over to scrutinize the seal only to find a blank dot of red wax.

"Val," she whispered, "what's going on?"

"I don't know." He broke the seal and unfolded the letter.

In the same elegant hand was written,

To Acting Captain Valiance of the Palace Guard

Greetings.

I hope this letter finds you healthy and happy, though perhaps the same cannot be said of your sister. I am truly sorry about that. Innocent women should never be harmed no matter their class or nationality. However, I wanted you to know how very serious I am.

If you do not wish for worse things to be done to her, you will remain in your home for the next two candlemarks after reception of this letter. That alone will not buy her safety, however.

Next week, at dusk, be at the Anchor and

Crown for further instructions. Not only will these actions help to ensure Abelia's continued well-being, you will be compensated more than enough to cover certain debts I know your family owes and which currently endanger your family's status. If you inform anyone of the contents of this letter, you and your family's lives will be forfeit.

I look forward to doing more business with you.

The letter ended without a signature or any mark that pointed toward the sender. For a brief moment, Valiance wondered what Captain Jarrett would do. His fear quickly overrode that thought.

He had to protect his family, no matter the cost. As the only son, that was his obligation. Years ago, long before he was born, a grandfather nearly gambled away the family coffers. He watched his father work himself to illness and still there was debt.

When he got older, Valiance swore he would undo the harm. And the gambling houses were losing patience after all this time.

His father, the gentlest and most caring man to ever exist, did not deserve to die at the hands of thugs. Neither did Abelia or his mother. And they didn't deserve to be disappointed or harmed because of him.

Whatever this person wanted, it had to do with the King and the Palace. However, kingdoms came and went. Family was forever.

"Val?" Abbey asked. She laid a hand on his arm. "What's wrong? You're white as snow."

"You're not working in the tavern anymore."

"I have to. Father's business doesn't create enough profit anymore and Mother hasn't found a marriage for me yet. Is it the gambling houses? Are they threatening you again?"

"No."

"Then what is it?"

"Abbey, I need you to trust me. I love you and I need to protect you. To do that, you need to trust me. Will you?"

She searched his eyes. "You know I've always

trusted you."

"Good." He kissed her on the forehead. "I'll see you tomorrow, then, at the Servants' Ball. Get some sleep. I'll be downstairs for a bit."

"Don't they need you at the Palace?"

A twinge of guilt went through him. "It's all right. We've got plenty of people on guard. Just go to sleep."

He left her and went downstairs, where his parents waited by the fire in their parlor. Apparently, Mother had managed to wake Father and tell him what had happened. His face pinched with worry and fear.

"What's happened, son?" he asked. "Is Abbey all right?"

Valiance went to the fireplace and tossed in the letter. It flared in the flames.

"What was that?" asked Mother. "Valiance, answer us!"

He faced them. "Abelia is fine. She got away from the men. She only needs to rest."

"And that letter?" asked Father.

"It was something I had on me from the Palace that I needed to destroy. I think I'll stay here for a couple of candlemarks before returning to the Palace."

"Won't the King need you?"

"No. You should know, I've invested some of my pay. I think some of that money will make a return soon."

His father beamed. "Good boy. I always knew you had a sound head. I suppose it's toward the remainder of your debt?"

"Yes, Father. The rest I'll give to you."

Mother waved her hand. "You should be preparing for marriage. Keep it for that day."

"No. I want you all to have it."

"Why?"

He didn't know what to say. Valiance couldn't tell them the truth and if he uttered one more lie, his stomach would start to heave. The mingled concern and pride on his parents' faces were bad enough.

"You always said you wanted to move to

Mauvia City in Arvent," he replied. "This is your chance."

Valiance stared toward the large window that overlooked the street. Who had sent the letter? And what were they planning?

Chapter One

Four Months Later

Clara stepped out onto the balcony. The cold morning wind cut through the velvet and fur of her clothes and lifted the brown mass of her hair. Far below, chunks of ice floated down the swollen Braddock River. Trees bedecked in the first lacey green traces of spring edged the river's banks.

The river embraced the island on which sat Candor City before it broke into two. If Clara walked around the tower, she would see them, the Lyn Tone and the Lance, as they angled away into the forests and rolling hills.

Behind Candor's tall walls, chimneys belched the smoke of hearth and forge fires. She could see tiny moving specks of people, horses, and carts in the crooked maze of streets. The bright bells of the cathedral called the devout to prayer and sent a small flock of doves flapping into the early morning light.

To the north, directly before her, the Larkspur Mountains girdled the horizon, half-hidden in clouds. In her mind, Clara could see the last traces of winter snow on their rounded peaks.

At one time, she couldn't imagine a life beyond them. They were home and always would be. Even as a slave, when she used her ability to see the future to save her master's life, it never once occurred to Clara that she would leave the mountains.

Then Gavin, a spy guised as a minstrel, came to the castle and changed it all.

The hard tramp of boot on stone alerted her to someone coming up the tower behind her. She didn't turn.

"I thought you would be here, since you weren't in the library." Jarrett came to stand beside her and braced his gloved hands on the cold stone.

Silence lapsed between them and Clara watched a hawk. Gavin used a hawk to pass on messages. She'd always been too afraid of the creature to approach it. During the civil war, when he came to Candor City to spy for Emmerich, the Rebel General, the hawk had been killèd as it left the city to deliver a message to Emmerich. Clara didn't know that until after the war, when they buried Gavin's tortured corpse.

After a few moments, Jarrett said, "Lord Candor waits in the keep and the pack mules are nearly loaded. We should be underway in less than a candlemark."

The wind whispered over the stone and the ruff of fur on her cloak. The hawk drifted away.

Jarrett straightened. From his pouch, he drew out a folded paper, closed with red wax seal. "His Majesty sent a missive that I received late last night. In it was this for you." He held it out.

Clara took it and stared at the crest pressed into the wax.

Jarrett cleared his throat. "I'll leave you to read that, then. Like I said, we should be ready to go soon." He touched her arm, as if to convey reassurance, and she stiffened.

Years of being a slave meant she wasn't touched except in a rough manner and now, as a proclaimed noblewoman in a high station, no one touched her out of deference. Jarrett meant well but it only left her uncomfortable and confused.

Clara waited until the sound of his steps faded before she broke the seal and unfolded the paper.

Clara,

This morning, the larkspur in the Academy's garden bloomed and one of the Oldtimers told me that meant the mountain passes are clear enough for travel. I hope, then, that this letter finds you in Candor.

She smiled at the old wives' tale.

The Council will drive me mad. If it isn't about those damn aerials, it's about the increased sightings of Marduk's creatures in the eastern forests. Or, it's about marriage and an heir—and the question of your return.

On the last night we spoke, you said everyone

relies on me. That is not entirely true. There are those who value your advice and I am one of them. You did not often dispense advice but I feel the loss of it keenly. More importantly, I miss you.

Find what you seek and return to me. I have kept the Council at bay over the issues of my marriage and your return. I do not think I can keep that up beyond midsummer.

Keep a watch out. The creatures seem confined to our east; it doesn't mean they won't swing north.

May the Mother and Child be with you and Captain Jarrett.

Yours, always,

Emmerich

Clara's heart ached and she closed her eyes.

When she first met Emmerich, he was a boy, the son of the headsman of a caravan that wandered their country, Lorst. She met him on the same day her mother sold her into slavery.

It wasn't until many years later that Clara

learned he'd searched for her. He didn't discover she'd been sold to the lord of Castle Dwervin until the day he took it in battle as part of the civil war that rocked the kingdom of Lorst like a gale.

The civil war. She opened her eyes to stare off at the shrouded mountains.

King Tristan and his daughter, Monica, were killed and Emmerich blamed for both deaths. The rumors were only half right. Emmerich had been forced to slay Monica, his lover, in an act of self-defense.

A sorcerer called Marduk had, years before, slain Emmerich's family. When Marduk arrived at the Royal Palace, where Emmerich was the Captain of the Palace Guard, he pleaded with the King and Monica to dismiss Marduk. Instead, Monica became Marduk's apprentice and tried to kill Emmerich.

After the murder, Emmerich fled the capital city, Bertrand. Driven by anger and a need for revenge, Emmerich built an army from his military and Royal Guard connections. When Clara met him a second time, both of them grown into adulthood, she recognized him for his peculiar, gray eyes. Unfortunately, the familiarity ended there.

He'd become a different creature that wasn't above asking for her to join him, not for the sake of friendship or for the chance of a new life outside of slavery; no, he asked her because of her ability. She was his Seer and he depended on her.

So, she left her mountains and, for a time, the questions about her family and lineage. She passed from the familiar to monsters and an evil she could never imagine. Somewhere in all of that, in all of the lies and betrayal, love and friendship grew.

After the war ended and Emmerich sat upon the throne as the new king, old questions returned that she could no longer ignore.

Clara shook herself. She carefully folded the letter and tucked it into her belt pouch. She gazed out over the city and the mountains one last time before descending the tower steps.

The castle's keep swarmed with people. Vendors hawked wares to servants and nobility alike while a blacksmith plied his trade in a small smithy. The loud clang of his hammer banged a sharp punctuation to the duller roar of voices. Soldiers, dressed in Emmerich's green and brown uniform, laughed and gossiped. They admired passing women and bowed to the ones of rank. A juggler amazed a small knot of children and a bard sang while strumming a lute.

Candor City enjoyed a special position in Lorst. Its location at the feet of the Larkspur Mountains and at the spot where one major river split into two meant that every bit of wealth that streamed north to south, or south to north, went through Candor.

It was the unofficial capital of the mountainous northern half of the country and Lord Candor ranked just under the King in terms of power, wealth, and prestige.

It didn't surprise, then, that a great many soldiers stood shoulder to shoulder with merchants and nobility. Emmerich had appointed the new Lord Candor himself. That didn't mean he entirely trusted him.

Clara still remembered when Emmerich asked her, as his Royal Seer, if she could divine whether the new lord would ever betray him. And she had to reply vaguely because, ever since the war, she hadn't had a single vision.

Near the castle gates, Jarrett shouted and waved at Clara.

When Clara met Jarrett for the first time, she had been a willing prisoner of Marduk. Jarrett was the Captain of the Royal Guard and the two became friends while plotting Marduk's demise. When Emmerich took the throne, Jarrett remained Captain but was sent with Clara as protector.

Emmerich would have also liked to send a platoon of soldiers to guard her but she persuaded him that it would be best to move across the country quietly. No one could threaten a person they didn't recognize, after all.

Weaving her way through people, Clara tried to ignore them as they bowed or curtsied. The muttered words "Lady Seer" peppered the air. As she rounded a knot of ladies, she saw Lord Candor in his heavy velvet cloak beside Jarrett. Her stomach dropped even as she hiked onto her face her best false smile.

When she reached them, Lord Candor cleared his throat and bowed. Jarrett bowed with a cocky grin. Clara wished they would stop that.

Lord Candor said, "I am very grieved to see you go, Lady Seer."

"The winter snows have melted for the most part, my lord," she replied. "It's time we left."

"Could you not hold off until after the carnival?" He smiled. "I would be honored to have you upon my arm at the ball, your ladyship."

Jarrett coughed and rubbed his face. Clara shot him a glare. "I'm afraid I cannot wait that long. We really must be on our way, Lord Candor."

He sighed heavily. "As you wish, my lady. Does her ladyship have a good word before she goes? Forgive me if my question is impertinent, but her ladyship did promise she would have one before she left."

Jarrett suddenly became busy with the tack of one of the horses while Clara's mind raced for what to say. Despite her best efforts, Lord Candor cornered her every chance he could over the winter, either to pepper her with questions about her gift or smother her in flattery. She wasn't sure if Lord Candor wanted to marry her or keep her in a cage for study.

After a long moment, she said, "I believe your future will be full of peace and joy and profit."

"That is good to hear." He reached for her hand and Clara allowed him to take it. "You have been a wonderful companion through this dull winter, my lady. On your return to Bertrand, I hope to be blessed by your presence once more."

"Ah."

"My lady," Jarrett interrupted, "all is ready if you are."

The lord scowled as he released Clara's hand. "May the Mother and Child keep you." He bowed.

Clara smiled and allowed Jarrett to assist her onto her horse.

A few moments later and they crossed the bridge into the city itself. Clara, however, didn't relax until they left the city altogether and rode up the northern road.

Emmerich's letter still burned in the back of her mind. Was she doing the right thing? Should she turn back? Was it really so important for her to go on this journey in search of her origins? Her gut flipped as she remembered.

"Why are we even here?" Jarrett asked. "Not that I'm against getting out of Bertrand once in a while. It's only that King Emmerich needs you."

Snow flurries swirled outside the window. Clara hugged a heavy shawl to her shoulders.

"He needs a Seer," she replied, "which I'm not.

Not anymore."

He made a rude noise through his nose. "Even without visions, you are clever, and the King listens to you."

"I'm just a former slave."

"You know damn well that you're more than that."

Jarrett's voice brought her from her thoughts. "Clara?"

She lifted her head. "Hm?"

"I said I'm sorry Candor caught you off guard when he asked for 'a word'."

"It's all right."

"I tried to conjure up some excuse for him to go away. However, he felt it was his duty to see us off. And it was, actually, so my hands were tied."

"Don't worry, Jarrett. I understand."

"So, no visions at all?"

"No. Only strange dreams. I'm not sure they can be called visions."

"Well, we'll be passing shrines and

monasteries. Perhaps we can find someone who can help you."

"Perhaps."

He glanced over at her, as if he heard the doubt in her voice.

Remus watched them. Carefully laid spells kept the attention of others away from him. Their eyes slid away as if there wasn't anything there at all.

He followed Clara and her guardian as they wove through the crowds. He listened to them speak, cocking his head at the sound of her uncertainty, the doubt she carried in herself. Remus understood that doubt. He had carried that inside himself, once.

He stopped a few dozen yards from the gate, allowing the pair with their pack mules to carry on without him. He would catch up with them, but there were other things to do first, if the kingdom of Lorst and her king were to fall.

Chapter Two

Jarrett and Clara camped near a stream and Jarrett took first watch.

While he watched the night, Clara lapsed into an uneasy sleep. She ran through a maze of dreams, one moment in a sky scattered with stars, and, the next, she stumbled through a dark, thick forest. She glimpsed underground tunnels, lit by glowing moss, and sat in a great hall while a woman on a coral throne spoke to a man in a language Clara didn't understand. She saw things that terrified even while they filled her with an intense longing.

At one point, she found herself on the edge of a clearing. A caravan encircled a large fire that cast light and shadow over the wagons' brightly painted wood. Men, women, and children laughed and talked around the fire. One of the men picked up a lute and began to play. Another man picked up a flute to accompany him. The lute player broke out into a rollicking song about a shepherdess who fell in love with a blacksmith's son. Several couples stood and began to dance, the women's skirts flaring around them as they spun.

Out of the shadows of one of the wagons emerged a familiar figure. Clara stared at him as she tried to place where she'd seen that set of shoulders before. The figure took another step to reveal Emmerich.

Except, this was a different Emmerich: one without crow's feet emerging at the corners of his eyes. Emmerich laughed and clapped along with the beat.

She drew closer. Emmerich grinned when he noticed her.

"Wonderful evening, isn't it?" he asked.

"Aye. Why are you here?"

"I'm hoping a pretty lady will let me dance with her." He held out his hand.

"I don't know this dance."

"Just follow my lead."

Well, it's only a dream. She took his hand and

let him lead her out onto the grass. Emmerich drew her against him, one hand on her waist and the other held her hand, and he pulled her into a hopping, skipping, twirling dance that bounced strands of hair loose from her braid.

When the song came to a halt, they were closer to the fire. The couples pulled apart and applauded the players. Emmerich continued to hold Clara.

"You're not bad," he said.

The players struck a slower song. Clara didn't listen to the words. All her attention settled on Emmerich's grey eyes. Without breaking eye contact, he led her in the dance again. The steps reminded her of a court dance, except she spent more time in his arms rather than apart.

As she danced, the ground grew soggier and soggier. Thick mud caught at her shoes. "What—?"

Blood soaked the grass. She stopped.

The fellow dancers now lay on their backs, their bellies split open and entrails hanging out in long, glistening ropes. The flute player's instrument jutted from his throat while he continued to play it. And the singer continued to sing, even while his jaw lay against chest.

"No." Emmerich released Clara and turned in a slow circle. "No. Papa! Uncle!" He pressed his hands into his hair. When he drew them back, they were slick with blood. "No!"

He sank to his knees and the blood saturated his clothes.

"No!"

"Emmerich." Clara knelt beside him. It was obvious now whose dream this was. "It's not real. This is only a nightmare."

"I killed them. This is my fault!" Tears streaked his face as he stared at a nearby corpse. Clara followed his gaze and jerked back. Gavin sprawled out on the blood-drenched grass, his head lolling at an unnatural angle. Emmerich began to weep harder.

She gulped and grabbed him by the shoulders. "Wake up, Emmerich. It's just a dream! Wake up!" She slapped him.

In his bed chamber, hundreds of leagues away, Emmerich awoke with a gasp. His bedclothes stuck to his sweaty skin and he trembled.

In the camp she shared with Jarrett, Clara came awake with a small whimper.

"Are you all right?" Jarrett called from where he stood watch.

Slowly, she nodded even as she tried to make sense of her dream.

"You sure?"

"Aye." She cleared her throat. "Is it my turn to stand watch?"

"Not quite."

Clara sat up and scrubbed her face with her hands. "I think I might like to go on watch anyway." She doubted she would be able to fall asleep again.

"I see. Bad dream, then."

She shrugged and tossed the blanket from her legs.

"If you need to talk, I'm told I'm a good listener. I have bad dreams, too."

"You do?"

"Of course I do. What warrior doesn't?"

Clara thought of Emmerich at the Palace as she took Jarrett's spot on the edge of the camp. Had that really been his dream? And was he all right? She stared out into the dark and watched while her mind churned.

"We should trade in the horses at the next town," Clara said, "for mountain ponies."

Evening and another campsite. Jarrett sharpened a dagger in practiced strokes. The sharp rasps made a counterpoint to the crackling fire.

"You've been quiet all day," he said, "and the first thing you say is about horses."

"It's the first thing worth talking about."

"Hm." He tested the edge with his thumb. "Our horses should do fine." He went back to sharpening.

"For the foothills and for the first few passes. Bluebell is in the far northwest, where the ground is rougher. I'd feel safer on a mountain pony that can handle the terrain."

"People use horses up there."

A flash of memory: a young boy and his friends on horseback and dressed in bright, festal clothes, speaking with a shrewish woman. She pushed it away. "Aye. People also use ponies or mules. Even donkeys, in a pinch."

"Why in a pinch?"

Clara scowled. "Because they can be stubborn asses, like a certain Captain of the Guard."

He grinned. "Hee haw."

She stood. "I'm going to bed."

"No, no!" He put the knife and whetstone down. "Sit down. Sit. It's a good idea. And, you're right, I'm stubborn."

She sat and regarded him with suspicion. "You hate agreeing with me."

Jarrett rolled his eyes. "Will you stop that?"

"Stop what?"

"Always being dissatisfied and suspicious. Can't a man just admit he's wrong?"

"I hadn't realized I did that." She brought her attention to the fire.

"I know you've had a hard time of it. General Asher told me a lot about where you came from."

"Where I came from?"

"Yes." He gestured with his hand. "The kitchens in Castle Dwervin."

"No. I came from Bluebell." She balled her hands into fists. "I was *enslaved* at Dwervin. I didn't just form out of the flour and grease of that place! I have a past. A family—"

"A family that sold you."

She twitched, as if he had moved to slap her. "You don't understand. Life was hard."

"So hard that they sold their only child? Clara, they may not want to see you. Hell, they may be dead! This is a white hart chase when you should be back at the Palace, where you belong."

"I have a right to go back home. I am a free woman." Tears stood dangerously close to falling and she widened her eyes, afraid to blink. "And Emmerich charged you with getting me to Bluebell safely, so stop arguing."

"I just don't understand—"

"Da wouldn't have sold me!" The tears rolled down her cheeks. She wiped them away. "Da was passed out when Haggard took me away. He loved me. I have a right to see him again!"

Silence filled the small clearing, broken only by the crack and pop of the fire.

Feeling oddly naked, she wrapped her arms around her waist. "And there have been some remarks that I have Tieran features. If I have more family, or if I was adopted, then I'd like to know."

After a pause, Jarrett said, "So. Mountain ponies, eh? I'm sure we can trade in your mount but I'm rather attached to Heartsblood. He's surefooted. I'm sure he'll do fine. Besides, the Palace Horsemaster would have me strung up by my toes if I sold or traded him off."

"Suit yourself."

Another bit of awkwardness passed between them. Jarrett broke it with, "Do you want to learn how to punch?"

"What?" Clara's brows rose.

"Since we're journeying into the wilds of the North, it might be good if you knew how. What if you have to, I don't know, defend your honor?"

She snorted. "Isn't that what you're here for?"

"Still⋯" He rolled his wrist, gesturing as if to a crowd of miscreants standing before them. "I have to go to the latrine at some point."

Perhaps it was his way to diffuse the tension. Perhaps he really did think it was a good idea. Whatever the reason, Clara couldn't think of a reason to say no. "All right."

He led her over to the side of the fire. "Make a fist."

She did. He took it in his hands and rearranged the fingers so that the thumb curled outside the fist, just under the knuckles.

"The trick," he explained, "is to swing from your hips up. Though you don't have a lot of muscle, you can still make it count if you twist your body into it, from the hips up. Watch."

He took a stance not unlike the one Emmerich had shown her when he taught her how to wield a sword. Jarrett punched into the air, his body twisting into the blow.

"Keep your fists in front of you, slightly higher than chest level. Your turn."

Clara mimicked him. For the next while, he corrected her stance and swing. By the end of it, she could do what he termed a "passable uppercut".

"Catch a man unawares," Jarrett said, "and you'll knock him flat on his ass. Hopefully, you'll never need to use it."

Clara laughed. "Knowing myself, I'll probably find a reason."

Jarrett rolled his eyes and that only made her laugh more.

Chapter Three

Emmerich scrubbed his face with both hands and yawned. Someone knocked on his door.

"Come in," he called and pushed aside his breakfast plate. He glowered at the pile of missives that waited to be gone through.

The door opened and General Asher, as refreshed as a spring dawn, entered. "Good morning, Your Majesty. I trust you slept well?" He bowed and held up a sheaf of papers. "I have the latest reports."

For a brief moment, Emmerich thought of soft hands and warmth and music. There was a dark memory of blood and he shoved it to the side. "I slept well enough. Have a seat." Emmerich picked up a teapot and refilled his cup. "Tea?"

"No, thank you." Asher sat at the table across from him.

"The Tieran diplomat introduced me to this 'black tea'. It's very invigorating in the morning."

"I'm sure it is. And, forgive my saying so, I

think you need it."

Emmerich ignored that and sipped from his cup.

"Maybe His Majesty should see a healer—"

"I'm fine, Asher. Really. Just a little sleeplessness. Show me those reports."

The general handed them over. "I did as you asked and collected all the sightings of Marduk's monsters. Their locations are plotted on this map. Some of the stories are obviously false and I didn't include them here. However, a good many I can't prove to be false. So far, it seems that Marduk's monsters remain in the woods to the east. Many of the towns and villages have requested help. If we sent a squad to every one of them, we wouldn't have much of an army to protect Bertrand."

Emmerich studied the small map and silently cursed Marduk. The madman had taken people and used an ancient artifact to twist them into monsters. And then he tried to use Clara to unleash the full power of that artifact onto the world. It had been a near thing to stop Marduk. Emmerich still had nightmares about the sorcerer's lair.

He pushed the memory aside and said, "Local lords usually maintain their own militias."

"Yes, sire, but most of those lords keep their militias close to home. And you did pass a law regulating militia size. In some cases, the militias are too small to cover the entirety of the lord's fiefdom. I have a map of the fiefs here, beneath the first."

"I see it." He scowled as he held the two up side by side and studied size of the fiefdoms against the number of sightings. "Suggestions?"

"His Majesty could allow for larger militias to be raised, though with a traitor on the loose, that may not be the wisest course."

He laid the papers on the table. After the civil war, while Emmerich tried to decide what to do with the monsters locked up in their underground menagerie, someone killed the guards and released the monsters. The creatures cut a bloody swath through the city before escaping. It was a traitor's work, yet the traitor's identity remained a mystery. It irked him every time he thought about it.

Emmerich said, "The most we could do is have a platoon sent to each baron's castle, rather than to each lord. That way, the barons can determine how to augment the militias of the lords under his domain."

"Will you grant a special exemption to lords in greatest need, so they can raise larger militias?"

"No. I passed that law to keep barons from amassing their own personal armies that could challenge my own. Someone might decide now would be a good time to grab for power. The last thing Lorst needs is another civil war."

"Very good, sire."

"And send out a call for more recruits for the national army."

"Yes, sire."

"Any word on the search for the traitor?"

"Lord Bruin has shortened his list of suspects but we're no closer to an arrest."

Emmerich grunted and picked up the thick stack of missives. He began to go through them.

"Any news from Captain Jarrett or Lady Clara?" asked Asher.

"No. By now, they've left Candor, I'm sure."

"What do you think the Lady Seer hopes to find?"

He tossed the missives back onto the table. "I don't know." He took another sip of his tea.

Another knock came from the door and Emmerich groaned.

Asher smiled. "Perhaps you should issue an edict about office hours."

Emmerich gave a crooked half-smile. "Now, that's a thought. Come in!"

The chamber door opened and Emmerich's secretary, a portly fellow in rich robes, entered. He bowed. "Good morning, Your Majesty. I wanted to speak to you about the agenda for today's Council meeting."

"Ah, yes. Come and sit."

Asher stood. "With the King's permission, I must go see about some new horseflesh for the cavalry."

"See you at dinner, tonight?"

"Yes, Your Majesty."

Asher bowed and left, and the secretary took a seat. "Now, Your Majesty, the first item on the agenda will be the Tieran diplomat's offer of a union of marriage between you and one of King Precene's daughters."

Emmerich groaned again and rubbed his aching eyes.

"Bran!"

The young boy, his tunic flapping loosely, stumbled to a stop. He faced the thin woman as she rushed toward him.

"You're not fully dressed," she chided, and knelt in the dirty street to fasten a brown belt around him.

"Ma, I'm going to be late," he said. "It's

assignment day!"

"I know, and you should be presentable." She adjusted the tunic until King Emmerich's symbol, blue and white starburst, lay perfectly in the center of his chest. Bran's mother smiled at him. "You know that, no matter what, I'm proud of you?"

"Yes, Ma."

She kissed him on the cheek. "All right. Off you go."

Bran sprinted away up the crooked, cobblestoned street. Bran didn't really understand everything grown-ups did. However, he did understand why his mother was so nervous. Bran was nervous, too.

King Emmerich opened ten slots in the page roster for any boy, no matter the rank. All he had to do was pass a test. Bran went every evening for a month to study with Presbyter Cyril to get ready for the test and it was the best day in his life when he passed.

Turning a corner so fast he nearly tripped,

Bran left the Low Quarters, with its stink and filth, and ran as hard as he could to the Palace. He dodged merchants and servants on their early morning errands with quick, nimble steps.

Bran paused only once at a fountain in the Jeweler Market for a gulp of water. From there, he sucked wind like a racehorse as he ran all the way to the Palace's main gate. His new tunic stuck to his back and sweat slicked his face. A stitch cramped his side and he pressed his hand against it.

"Assignment day?"

He straightened at the deep voice. A man in the scarlet of a Royal Guard smiled down at him. The sunlight glinted off the chain mail on his arms and the blade of his halberd.

"Yes, sir," Bran replied.

"Thought so. You're the third boy to run up here as if the hounds of Hell were on his heels."

"I came from the Low Quarters," Bran gasped.

"And ran the whole way?" The guard smiled at his partner. "Maybe we should take this one for our ranks."

His partner chuckled. "He's a bit young, I think."

"You might be right." The guard jerked his head. "Go on, boy, or you really will be late."

"Yes, sir. Thank you, sir." Bran jogged through the open gate and up the hill. The Palace, with its grand steps that swept up to meet golden double doors, sat upon the city's tallest hill like a bone-white crown. Its spires and towers pierced the sky while soldiers patrolled the surrounding walls' crenelated parapets.

As Bran passed through the double doors, he felt like he entered a fairy tale. He had been there before, for training and to be measured for his uniform, but it still struck him. Beautiful ladies in bright, embroidered gowns walked with men in vividly colored tunics. Men in scarlet surcoats covering chain mail patrolled. Even the servants, in their bright livery, suggested another world. Bran tugged on his clothes and felt like an impostor.

"You there! Page!"

Bran gaped at the tall, blocky man striding to him. He remembered to bow a heartbeat too late.

"Bran," he said. "My-my name is Bran Weston. I'm here—"

"For assignment. I know. I'm to collect any stragglers. Come along."

The man didn't wait. Bran's aching legs stretched to keep up.

"I'm sorry I'm late, sir," he said. "I live—"

"In the Low Quarters. I know. We've made exceptions for you lot. Don't expect that to keep up. Be late again and it'll mean a lashing."

Bran flushed. "Yes, sir."

The man took him to a small room in the servants' wing, where thirty other boys waited. Nervous chatter filled the room as the boys tried to guess their assignments. The Pagemaster, a short bald man, stood by the door and peered down at a list.

"And this one?" the Pagemaster asked.

"Bran Weston," the escort replied.

The master made a mark on the list. "Still missing two. Go back to the main hall. If they show up, send them home."

"Yes, Master Thom." The man bowed and walked away.

Master Thom peered over the edge of his paper at the boy. "Well, son, don't gawk. Go on in."

Bran ducked his head and entered the room. He took a spot near the back beside his friend Robert. Slightly smaller than Bran, though the same age, and capped with a shock of red hair, Robert resembled an imp from fairy tales.

"Didn't think you were gonna make it," Rob whispered.

"Same here." Bran tugged again at his tunic.

"Stop that. You'll bust a seam."

Rob sounded so much like his mother, Bran giggled.

"Quiet, everyone!" yelled Master Thom as he moved through the room. "Everyone settle down." On reaching the front of the room, he addressed them. "Some of you are old hands to assignment day, but some of you—in fact, many of you—are new. This responsibility is more than simply carrying packages and messages. You will see and hear things no one else will. Gossip will not be tolerated. If we find any tale-bearers, that boy will be expelled from the program and his family fined. Heavily."

Bran gulped and thought about his mother's hands after a day of washing the laundry of merchants: red, chapped, and cracked. They could not afford even a light fine.

"Now." Master Thom consulted his list. "We've divided you lot into two groups, one for the Academy and the other for the Palace. As I call your name, line up at the door. There'll be someone to take you to the Academy for orientation and assignment. The rest of you will receive Palace assignments."

He began calling out names. Bran's gut clenched and he begged the Mother that it wasn't his fate to go to the Academy. The wizards in their black robes were frightening and mysterious.

"Robert Campbell," Master Thom called.

Rob made a noise of dismay but moved forward to take his position in line.

"Good luck," Bran whispered after him.

When Master Thom finished, a small whisper of relief went through him, despite being disappointed that he didn't get the same duty as Robert. He waved at him and Rob waggled his fingers back in a sign of good fortune.

Next came specific Palace assignments. As the Pagemaster worked through the list, Bran's gut knotted again. With each passing moment where his name wasn't called, he worried. Had there been a mistake? He didn't know what he would tell Mam if they sent him home.

Master Thom called a final name for Council pages and sent the assigned out to be shown their posts for the day. Once the green-tunicked boys were gone, it only left five of them.

"Come here, you lot," Thom said.

The five clustered around him. Bran recognized only one: a fellow low-ranker from the Quarters whose parents worked at a tavern. The other three came from nobility.

"You are on a special assignment," Master Thom explained. "You will work on a rotating schedule as personal pages to King Emmerich."

He paused and let that sink in. Perhaps he expected a burst of excitement. Bran didn't know about the other boys, but he could only stare in shock at the Pagemaster.

"Terrell," Thom said, addressing one of the experienced boys, "you'll take today. You'll find His Majesty in the Council chamber. The rest of you, go home and collect your belongings. You will room in the Palace, in the servant quarters near the Royal Wing. You'll find your rotation posted. Dismissed."

It wasn't until Bran finished packing his spare uniform and his only good set of clothes that the reality of leaving home hit him. He sank down onto his narrow cot and studied the one room apartment. Would his Mam be okay without him? Who would make sure she woke up in time for services on Temple Day? Who would fetch the morning bread or cook supper when she couldn't?

Who would comfort him when he woke up from a nightmare? Who would tell him what to do if another boy taunted him? Who would take care of him when he fell ill?

The more he thought about it, the more fear pinned him to the low bed. What did Presbyter Cyril like to say?

"The Child doesn't bless a coward," he told Bran. Well, the longer Bran sat there, the more cowardly he felt. So, he couldn't sit there anymore.

He gathered his bag and left the small apartment. First, he would stop at the wash house where Mam worked and then off to his new life in the Palace.

Emmerich tossed down the latest report on

the search for the traitor. Jarrett's sources, currently being cultivated by Valiance, his temporary replacement, hadn't found any rumors or any indication of who released the creatures.

"Almost like he doesn't exist," he muttered.

He checked the candle clock. Sleep was probably the best thing to do so late at night: the candle was half-spent. He drummed his fingers on the table as he weighed his options and then stood. He strode to the door and jerked it open.

A young boy, about nine summers, sat in a chair across from the door. The boy hopped to his feet and bowed.

"Who are you?" Emmerich asked.

"Bran Weston, Your Majesty." The boy shifted from one foot to another. "I'm one of your pages."

Was the Pagemaster aware of his late night errands and trying to anticipate his needs? Emmerich strode down the hall.

It wasn't long before he heard the patter of steps behind him. He stopped. "Why are you following me, Bran?"

An uncertain expression puckered Bran's brows. "Master Thom said I'm to accompany you everywhere."

"Even to the latrine?"

The boy blushed. "I can just wait outside the door, sire."

Emmerich smiled. "I'm only kidding. I do believe this is the first time I've had a page outside my door in the middle of the night."

Bran smiled a little. "Master Thom said my shift ends when you go to bed, sire. The other pages said not to worry about it, but I don't want to be expelled, sire."

Emmerich felt guilty at the thought of his insomnia keeping the lad up so late. "You should have listened to your peers. Go to bed."

Desperation filled Bran's face. "Please, sire. I'll be real quiet."

Emmerich's brows rose. "It means that much to you?"

"I want to be a good page, Your Majesty, so

Mam won't work so hard."

"And what does your Mam do?"

"Wash clothes, sire."

"Ah. I see. Well, come on, then."

Bran smiled. "Thank you, sire."

They left the Royal Wing, the guards at the door saluting as he passed, and walked through lantern-lit halls to another set of chambers. Emmerich reached to open the door but Bran scurried ahead, pulling it open for him.

"Master Thom spoke to you about secrets?" he asked.

Bran puffed up his chest. "Yes, sire."

"Good."

They entered a darkened sitting room. Emmerich lit a nearby lamp with flint and tinder, illumining a room decorated in pinks, greens, and blues. Several books sat on a table, as if waiting for their reader to return to them in the morning. An open door led into a bedchamber.

Emmerich walked through the room. Every few steps, he stopped and touched a statue and a wooden box and other personal items. She had decorated these rooms herself and had been proud of them. Now they sat dark and cold and he wondered if they would ever be alive with her presence again.

He didn't know why he was there. He never knew why he came. Sometimes, his visits sparked nightmares about the day Gavin died or that he would receive news of Clara's murder. And yet he still came. Had he become like one of those stupid romantic courtiers?

Mother Above, I hope not, he thought as he came to a stop at a window.

He crossed the room and snuffed the lamp. They left the chambers to return to Emmerich's wing. He peered over his shoulder at Bran, who wore an expression of confusion at his sovereign's behavior. He caught Emmerich's eye and smoothed his face to indifference. Emmerich chuckled.

They reached the Royal Wing when running boot steps approached. Guards pelted down the hall and skidded to a stop before the King. The men saluted.

"What is it?" Emmerich asked.

"Sire," said the leader, "there's a riot down by the river docks. General Asher and the City Guard Captain await in the Council Chamber to brief you."

Emmerich brushed past them and walked as quickly as he could, barely hearing the patter of Bran's steps behind him.

Had he raised taxes too high? Had he not set grain prices low enough? Were there bad working conditions he should have known about? His stomach curdled at the thought of all the mistakes that would lead to this.

Asher and Captain Tarsus stood and bowed as he entered. Emmerich planted his hands on his hips.

"Report," he snapped, going from king to rebel general in a smooth instant.

Captain Tarsus spoke first. "Men gathered at the taverns near the docks after work ended for the day, which is not unusual. My informants among the dock workers tell me that a group of men began stirring up the dock workers with stories about Marduk's creatures advancing on the city and that it would only be a matter of time before the aerials attack. They said that the King will do nothing to protect them and there's some grumbling about the height of current taxes."

Emmerich muttered a curse. "Asher, could this be connected to our traitor?"

"It's a possibility, sire," the general replied.

"What do we know about this group of men?"

Tarsus said, "They aren't from Bertrand. My informants didn't recognize them and said they had an accent they couldn't place."

"No chance they're Tieran?"

"No, sire. That would have been recognized."

"What's being done to quell the riot?"

"At the moment, it's contained in the docks. There is some damage being done to buildings. Several squads of men are on their way right now to put a stop to it."

"I will go as well," Emmerich declared.

Shock flooded Captain Tarsus's face while Asher's expression grew stony.

"Your Majesty—" Tarsus began.

"Don't bother, Captain."

"It's too great a risk—"

"Asher, get a horse and a small guard ready."

"Yes, sire." Asher saluted and headed out.

Tarsus paled. "Sire, I must protest."

"Duly noted. Now, you can either come with me or remain here. Your choice."

The captain gulped. "I'll saddle a horse."

"Good man."

Tarsus saluted and strode out.

"Any experience as a squire?" he asked Bran, who was watching the whole thing with wide eyes.

The boy shook his head. "No, sire."

"Well, now is as good a time to learn as any. Come along. We don't have much time."

The night air still carried a bitter bite of winter as Emmerich rode down the street. Behind him, Captain Tarsus rode on horseback while leading his contingent of City Guardsmen, who marched on foot in neat rows. Young Bran had tried to come along, suggesting that a page-turned-temporary-squire should be with the King, but General Asher sent him to bed.

Emmerich was amused, though, at the boy's enthusiasm.

It felt deeply right to Emmerich to be in the saddle again, the heavy weight of chain mail on his shoulders while the ringing of horse shoes and stomp of boots sounded around him.

There were no politics in this. No pride to be soothed or coddled. No protocol to be observed. Just action and reaction. For the first time in a long while, Emmerich felt alive. Blood rushed through his limbs, his heartbeat filled his mouth, and the colors of the night-washed world were brighter, sharper.

He heard the incoherent shouts of the rioters

while they were still a few streets away. Emmerich's left hand dropped to the pommel of his sword, his fingers curling around the familiar steel and leather.

They rounded two more turns and the incoherent formed into words:

"Death to the aerials!"

"Death to the King!"

"Defend Bertrand!"

Captain Tarsus began, "Your Majesty, please—"

"Don't bother to finish your sentence," Emmerich replied. He yelled over his shoulder, "Arms!"

The clack of cudgels broke out behind him as his men brought them up cross-ways against their chests.

"I hope we won't have to fight against our own people," he said.

"As do I, Your Majesty," replied Tarsus.

They rounded the corner and entered the street running along the river docks. Torches held by rioters blazed and threw flickering light onto the shouting men and women. In the center of the crowd, an effigy burned in a fire. Men looted a nearby store.

"Who's the effigy?" Emmerich asked.

"Probably you, Your Majesty."

"Well, then. Let's put a stop to this." He nudged his horse forward. Tarsus gave orders for the men to spread out and follow behind.

As they approached, people began to notice them. From somewhere in the center of the crowd, someone yelled, "They're here to push you down! Take your voice away! You gonna let them do that?"

The accent sounded crisp and severe. Perhaps the speaker came from Arvent in the south?

The mob answered the speaker with discordant cries and began to march toward Emmerich.

The same voice yelled, "Death to the King!"

"Death!" yelled the mob.

"Death to the King!"

"Death!"

Emmerich bellowed, "Silence!"

The mob shuddered to a stop as Emmerich reined in. About ten feet separated them.

"And who're you?" asked a man in a tanner's thick apron.

"Your King."

Whispers rippled through the crowd. Emmerich shifted in his saddle, moving his left hand from the pommel to his hip.

"Now," he continued, "I know that you're all afraid but you have nothing to fear. Marduk's monsters are not advancing on the city and the aerials are not going to attack." Emmerich looked over the crowd. "And I swear to you that I will do all I can to protect you. Now, return to your homes and no one will be charged with a crime, save for any caught looting."

People began to mutter among themselves. After a heartbeat, a few cautiously began to walk away. Emmerich scanned the crowd for the owner of the voice. However, he couldn't make out foreign features on anyone.

From the crowd flew a bottle and Emmerich brought his arm up. The bottle *thunked* against his gauntlet and spun away to fall harmlessly into a gutter.

What happened next, he wasn't sure of. One of the people in the mob fell back, blood pouring from his forehead, and then the crowd rushed them. The soldiers surged forward to encircle and protect their sovereign. From the other end of the street, the squads Tarsus sent earlier came running up with cudgels at the ready.

Later, Emmerich learned none of the soldiers had thrown anything, so how that first person had been wounded was a mystery. At that moment, however, he didn't give any thought to it.

Emmerich unhooked the cudgel from the horn of his saddle and brought it down on a heavyset man just reaching his side, one hand on his boot. The man dropped without a sound. The soldiers reached Emmerich and the man's body disappeared from view.

"Your Majesty!" Tarsus pushed through to his side. "You must return to the Palace!"

For a brief moment, he almost said no. His eyes swept over the mob, at the men in brown and green fighting the men in civilian clothing. These were his people.

A familiar scent (lilac and sandalwood) brushed over him. He turned his head as if someone called his name.

Clara, dressed in deep red riding clothes, stood by a shop door. She pointed out to the side, back toward the Palace. Her lips moved, mouthing the word *Go*.

"Your Majesty!"

He jerked around to Tarsus, whose frightened, worried eyes filled his vision for a moment.

"Aye," whispered Emmerich. "Aye!"

He yanked hard on the reins of his horse and twisted his mount around. Soldiers fanned out to push back the mob.

With relief mixed with guilt, he escaped the crowd and kicked his horse into a gallop down the street, back to the Palace. Shame burned in the back of his neck the whole way.

These are my people, he kept thinking to himself.

Clara woke with a start and strangled shout. She jerked upright.

"What's wrong?" Jarrett asked from where he stood watch.

She wiped her face with shaking hands and clasped them hard enough for the knuckles to turn white. She shook her head, over and over, as if she'd forgotten how to talk.

Jarrett came to sit next to her. He started to wrap an arm around her shoulder but dropped it away. "Hey. Everything is all right. What did you see? Did you have a vision?"

She dropped her hands to her lap. "Not exactly."

"Tell me about it."

Clara described the scene of the mob, of Emmerich seeing her, and of the man in a dark cloak who slipped into an alleyway.

"Is this something that's about to happen?" Jarrett asked.

"No." She rubbed her face. "No, I'm sure it isn't. It was like those times when I would see Emmerich in battle. Only, I didn't see all the possible endings of the event." *Thank the Child.* She wasn't sure she could handle that again. Actually, now that she thought of it, it reminded her of that dream where she had been in Emmerich's sitting room and they had been rather intimate. Her face heated and she hoped Jarrett didn't see her blush.

"And you said Emmerich saw you?"

"Aye. I pointed for him to go back to the Palace. I yelled but I'm not sure he heard me over the noise. And then I left that and went somewhere else."

"To see the man in the cloak. Can you

describe him?"

"Shadows covered his face. I knew that he wasn't from Bertrand. I just knew. For as much good as that can do."

Jarrett laid a hand on her shoulder and squeezed it before withdrawing. "Well, it's better than nothing. And it's a good sign, I think."

"Good sign of what?"

"That you haven't lost all your ability, that you still can do something. Maybe instead of the future, you can see the present now. Or go places with your mind. I think I read that in a story somewhere."

"This is not one of your copper-piece books that you pick up from a peddler, Jarrett." Clara paused. "Are you going to lecture me about returning to Bertrand?"

"Would it do any good?"

She gave him a long look.

He put his hands on his hips. "Clara, if they're rioting in the streets, then Emmerich needs you."

"To do what? Tell him what he already

knows?"

"Do you think he knows about this man?"

"What good would my telling him do? I didn't see his face!"

Jarrett scoffed and stood. "I'm going to go back on watch."

She didn't stop him, just scowled into the fire and pictured the Palace. In her mind, she carefully recreated the layout, decorations, and the color of the banners hanging in the main hall. She stretched her mind, mentally searching for that spark of ability that allowed her to see the future or other places.

However, the heart of the fire only held flames and a dull pain grew behind her eyes. With a groan, she lay back down. Sleep, though, did not come.

Chapter Four

The town of Hernesferry bustled with the excitement that came whenever a caravan visited. Traders came through it regularly on their way to Candor City. Jarrett sensed this was the first caravan since winter closed the passes.

Windows and doors of home and shop alike stood open while vendors lined the main street with wares and food. A man ran up beside Clara and held up a selection of beaded strands.

"Lovely bauble for lovely lady!" he cried.

She shook her head, smiling, and the man backed off, turning to another woman. Children ran, squealing and laughing as they dodged the crowds, to the booth selling small jam pies. Clara watched them with an expression equal parts of envy and longing.

Jarrett was struck, again, by all the contradictions packed into this small woman. One moment, she was as stubborn as a mule and the next, she envied children going after sweets.

Her childhood had been frittered away in the bowels of a castle, so should he really be surprised?

Clara caught Jarrett staring at her. She formed a question with her brows.

He replied, "I guess I just get reminded some days that you didn't really have a childhood."

Some of her budding good humor faded from her face. "Well. It's nothing to go on about."

They stopped at the large horse barn and dismounted. A man in traditional mountain clothes of a sleeveless tunic and shirt with trousers made of thick cloth came out of the large building to meet them.

"How can I help ya?" He smiled, his eyes disappearing in a crinkle of laugh lines.

"We need mountain ponies," Clara said.

"Just one," Jarrett interrupted. "For her."

The man replied, "Happy with your mount, eh?"

"Oh, yes." He patted Heartsblood's neck. "I think he can take me where we plan to go."

"And where's that, may I ask?"

"Bluebell."

The smile faded on the man's face. "The horse may get you there and the lady will need something other than a palfrey."

Something unspoken hung in the man's words. Jarrett hooked his thumbs into his belt. "But?"

"We've been hearing strange stories about things from up that way. Not raiders, mind. Strange stories about some of the Old Ones coming back."

"Old Ones?"

"Trolls and giants and the like. That caravan came down from Bluebell way and they've got all sorts of tales of oxen going missing and strange sounds in the night."

"What would wake the Old Ones?" Clara asked.

Jarrett snorted. He wasn't sure who or what the Old Ones were. It sounded like another backwards mountain tale.

"I don't know," the man replied. "The rumors say it's because of that Sorcerer King, that he stirred them up with his spells. It's a good thing our King Emmerich came along or who knows what trouble we'd be in by now."

"Yes," interrupted Jarrett, before the man launched into a rambling speech about the King and the recent civil war. "We still need a mountain pony for the lady here."

"Well, then. My name is Jack and I'm happy to help. Come right this way." He gestured.

Jarrett leaned close to Clara. "Can you handle this?" he whispered. "I can haggle the price but I'd like you to pick out the pony."

He knew she had probably never judged horseflesh but he could see the bullish need to prove herself at every turn come alive in her eyes.

"Of course," she replied.

He patted her on the shoulder. "Clara here knows what she wants. I'll just stay here and mind the horses and luggage."

Jack went into the dark barn. Jarrett gave Clara an encouraging smile. She narrowed her eyes before vanishing into the barn.

The man that had been trailing behind them stepped out of an alley and approached Jarrett.

"She's pretty," the newcomer said.

"You've seen her before, surely."

"At a distance. I can see why His Majesty favors her. Those eyes can really draw a man in."

"It only begins there." Jarrett studied the man, who wore peasant clothes like everyone else. He casually strolled to the side of the barn door so Clara couldn't watch them. "I worried you wouldn't be here."

"Why? I don't have to be concerned with ordinary means of travel. A few of Marduk's portals are still in good order. In fact, the last one in the northern part of Lorst is near here."

The portals provided wizards means of traveling across the kingdom in a heartbeat. Jarrett asked Lord Bruin, the head of the Academy and one of King Emmerich's advisors, how the portals worked. Bruin rambled on about "tears in the fabric of space and time" and "magic providing safeguards to allow safe passage" until Jarrett's eyes glazed over.

Jarrett pivoted and put his back to the barn, as if observing the crowd. "What news do you bring?"

"A riot broke out last night down on the docks."

"Then the lady dreamed true."

"She dreamed it? Before it happened?"

"No. During."

"Ah. That must have been when the King saw her while he was in the Low Quarter."

"Yes. That stupid bastard."

"Perhaps." The wizard shrugged, as if the vagaries of kings were a matter beyond him. "His presence almost calmed the crowd until someone threw a bottle at him. It all went downhill from there. Captain Tarsus of the City Guard got him out and they quelled the crowd. However, it cost the City Guardsmen a man and I think three of the dock workers died. No one is sure who started it, only that it was a foreigner. The King thinks an Arventi."

Jarrett sighed. "I hoped Clara had a nightmare."

"The King and Lord Bruin had a long discussion about her mysterious appearance."

"And?"

"It's not normally associated with Second Sight, so Bruin has no idea why it happened, or why it only seems to happen with the King."

"So, you're here to tell me what I already know and that you can't provide any good explanations?"

The wizard smirked. "Not entirely."

"Oh?"

"Lord Bruin has suspected for some time that the traitor could be one of the apprentices, perhaps even one of the adepts. Now, anyone from Arvent is suspect."

"The two could be unrelated."

"It's a possibility but I doubt it. We have five

students from that region and they're all under watch. Secretly, of course."

"I suppose that's progress."

"In a way. Has her ladyship had any visions of the future?"

"Not that I'm aware of. I'm not entirely sure, though, that she would tell me. She likes to keep some things close and her visions are a tender topic."

"Mmm. Any news we wish for me to carry to the King?"

"Only that if her ladyship continues to be stubborn, I might pitch her into a mud puddle."

"I'll be sure to mention that." He walked away to meld back into the crowd.

Jarrett considered this news. As Captain of the Guard, his instinct was to rush back to King Emmerich. Valiance, his lieutenant, was a good man. His only fault was his lack of experience. Besides, King Emmerich didn't know and trust Valiance like he knew and trusted him.

During the usurper Marduk's short reign,

Jarrett had been the Captain of the Palace Guard. When he saw what Marduk did to people, using magic to turn them into monsters, he joined the Rebellion in Bertrand.

He tried to be a good Captain. He did all that Marduk asked of him, which was a guilt that still burned despite how he watched for a moment when he could betray Marduk for the good of the kingdom. When Clara arrived and Marduk began acting like a tomcat who just caught his prize, Jarrett knew he had found his chance.

He protected her and introduced her to the Rebellion. He stood up for her when she suggested a mad plan to assassinate the usurper during a ball in Clara's honor. The assassination attempt failed but Jarrett used the confusion to turn the Palace Guard against Marduk and made way for the Rebel Army.

Emmerich, after his coronation, rewarded Jarrett by allowing him to keep his position as Captain of the Guard. The King even took Jarrett into his inner circle. When Clara insisted on this adventure, King Emmerich entrusted her to his care.

Jarrett owed the King everything he had.

Footsteps alerted Jarrett to Clara's and Jack's return.

"Found something?" he asked.

Clara's gaze went from him, to the crowd, and then back again. The expression in her eyes said that she had a few questions for him. Instead of asking, she only said, "I found a nice one that I think will do."

"Well, then, we can get to haggling." He grinned and leaned closer to Clara. "And perhaps then we can see about a jam pie."

Clara fought it but a smile formed on her face. "We can do that," she replied.

By the time Jarrett finished haggling for the pony and suitable tack, the sun had drawn to the center of the sky. Jarrett wanted to continue. Clara wouldn't hear of it. She wanted to see some of the wares the caravan brought.

It baffled Jarrett at first until he realized it probably reminded her of some happy moment of her childhood. And there had been so few of those. So, after buying a pair of small jam pies, they strolled along the lines of temporary stalls the traders erected along the main road through the village.

"Who was that man you were speaking with?" Clara asked casually before biting into her pie.

Jarrett felt his gut trip over itself as he stepped around a man trying to sell a brace of roasted chickens. "I don't know what you mean."

She tossed him a sarcastic glare and took another bite of her confection.

He rolled his eyes. "A wizard from Bertrand. He met me here to let me know how things in Bertrand are doing and ask if you've had any visions." He licked some blackberry jam from his thumb.

"How would he know we were here?"

"Lord Bruin has ordered we be scryed once a day, to keep a watch over us."

Clara scowled. "I don't like that."

Truthfully, Jarrett didn't like the idea of a wizard using a bowl of water to spy on them, either. It felt disloyal to King Emmerich to say so, however. "Emmerich's only worried about you. No one can hear what we say, only see where we are, and only that for a moment."

Silence lapsed between them. Jarrett finished his pie; Clara continued to savor hers. She stopped to admire the items on display in the window of a milliner's shop.

"Was I right?" she asked.

He didn't need to ask about what. He could tell by the set of her shoulders. "You were."

"Is Emmerich all right?"

"He's fine."

"Do they know who started the riot?"

"An Arventi, they believe, but they haven't caught him." He repeated everything his contact had said. "If you want, we can turn around. If we take a boat on the Lyn Tone, we can be there inside of a week."

"You know the answer to that." She finished her pie and carried on, stretching her legs to get a few paces ahead of Jarrett. Dust from the road puffed up around her ankles. He let her go.

Remus watched Clara and Jarrett discreetly from a stand selling toys, games, and other trinkets. He had worried he wouldn't be back in time but the man he hired had met with him as appointed. Thank the gods for Arventi punctuality.

"Everything is going fine," Vitus had assured him. "The people are easy to manipulate. Marduk left a lot of fear in the shadows and this Emmerich—he does not do all he could to quell it. He lets those feathered lizards fly free, and so the people have a constant reminder of the usurper, no matter how pretty they are."

They stood in a boarded up building in the outskirts of Bertrand. Behind Remus, etched deeply into the stone, was a ring of sigils. During the time of Marduk, it had been used as one of the many portals in Bertrand that could convey a wizard nearly anywhere in Lorst.

Now, there were only a few left. King Emmerich had many of them destroyed. He must have feared what men could do if they could travel across the country at will and at the wink of an eye.

It was dangerous for only one wizard to use a portal. Ideally, it took three, one at the destination and one at the departure point. They kept the tear in space and time steady while a third made his passage, maintaining the road as he went and guiding a passenger if he had one. A misstep could mean injury, landing in the wrong place, or disappearing altogether.

Remus was willing to take the risks.

"Very good, my friend." Remus tossed him a pouch of coins. "And the Acting Captain? Is he still on his leash?"

"He hates every minute of it but he won't throw it off."

"So, he'll be ready when I return?"

The mage light Remus had cast to light the room threw hard, cold luminance and made the Arventi's eyes seem darker and deeper. Vitus smiled.

"Oh," he said, "Valiance will be ready."

Clara suddenly walking away from Jarrett, passing Remus close enough for him to feel the breeze of her passage, ended the memory. Jarrett was distracted by a juggler. Remus slipped into the crowd to follow her.

The pair apparently felt that by traveling in such a small group, Clara would be safe under the cloak of anonymity. Remus admired the cleverness of that and the good fortune. If their party had been bigger, he would not be able to approach.

There was no sense or logic in approaching her. He simply wanted to talk to her.

She stopped to peruse a bookseller's wares. He watched her for a moment with hungry eyes.

They were of a similar height, with the same dark hair. He knew her eyes were hazel while his took after his father's blue. From his observations at Emmerich's Court, he knew they sometimes used the same expressions. For a brief moment, he feared she would recognize her face in his and it would ruin everything.

"You might as well come over here," Clara called out to him. "I'm not blind."

Surprise snapped through him but he tucked it away quickly as he strolled over to join her. "How did you see me, my lady?"

"Captain Jarrett told me he met with you earlier and King Emmerich was having us watched. It made me notice you."

For a brief moment, Remus was confused. He wasn't dressed as a wizard, having eschewed his dark robes and blue and white belt for peasant's attire.

She looked up at him. "Don't stare at me like that. I noticed you following me right away. If you aren't Jarrett's contact, then who are you?"

Clara is making an assumption, he realized. In Remus's fascination with watching his half-sister, he forgot to better cloak himself. Jarrett's encounter with a wizard earlier had made her more paranoid and more likely to spot him.

"I'm sorry, my lady," Remus replied. "You just took me off guard."

She snorted. "I do that, I've noticed."

And he felt angry all over again at Emmerich and his Court. Remus had come to the Academy many years ago to perfect his magic, leaving behind a family that tried to smother him in protocol and expectations. In Bertrand, he rose in the ranks quickly. As the child of minor nobility and a talented wizard, he knew esteem, even if it was from those he despised. Lorst had caused a lot of destruction in Tier, and Remus still remembered the mud huts where proud homes once stood, built on the sooty remains left by Lorstian armies.

But even if it was from those he despised, he welcomed the esteem. It irked him deeply that Clara was not showered in praise and respect as well.

When the woman he immediately recognized as his half-sister came to Court, recognized because of what his mother had told him about her, he wanted to run up to her and embrace her. In a family of mediocrity, here was someone bright and talented, nearly as talented as him. He didn't have to be alone anymore.

And it wasn't only that. Clara had survived slavery. She, too, knew what it was like to suffer at the hands of Lorst. Clara would understand Remus.

But it wasn't time to embrace her, to spill his soul out to her. Remus swore to bring her to his side after he had his revenge on Lorst. He kept his distance. He wanted everything to be just right before he revealed himself.

"What's your name?" Clara asked.

"Remus, my lady."

"Stop calling me that, Remus. We aren't in Bertrand."

"Of course."

"Did King Emmerich give you any more

instructions about following us?"

He shook his head. "No. I'm to go on a research trip after I report in, actually."

Playing along as Jarrett's contact was a great deal of fun. It was like they were children, playing make-believe. For an instant, Remus could feel like a little boy with a friend and not someone consigned to feeling outside of the family because he was different. Their mother, Thalia, was a witch of small power but not even she knew how to relate to her son.

"Research?" Clara asked. "Into what?"

"Alchemy. I'm one of Lord Bruin's chief alchemists."

Her brows rose. "You look young to be a chief alchemist."

Remus beamed, glad that she noticed. In fact, at twenty, he was two or three years her junior. "I'm very good at it."

"Well, I hope you do well." She looked back at the books and picked up a blue one embossed with gold vines.

"Thank you, my—I mean. Thank you, Clara. Is-is that Marrione's *Verses*?"

"I believe so." Clara scrutinized the binding. "It is. Do you know it?"

"I love it." He took it, letting his fingers brush hers for a moment. His heart jumped at the brief contact. "My favorite is Sonnet Twenty-Nine." Remus flipped to the correct page and showed it to her.

Clara leaned close to read the first few lines. She smelled of horses and lilac. "It's beautiful."

"I'll purchase it for you if—"

"No, that's not necessary."

"I insist. It will keep you company on your long journey."

Remus felt nearly giddy with happiness as he paid for the book. Smiling, he presented his half-sister with her first gift from her brother, even if she didn't know who he was.

"Thank you, Remus," Clara said. She glanced over her shoulder at the swarm of people filling the side street.

"Looking for Captain Jarrett?" he asked.

"He's probably looking for me."

"I should let you go, then."

"Thank you again, Remus."

"Hopefully, I'll see you soon in Bertrand. If you don't mind, I can show you my research."

Clara gave him a thin smile and walked away, disappearing back into the crowd.

"See you soon, sister," Remus whispered after her before walking away. He needed to reach his own destination by nightfall and there was still some ways to go.

Rain poured from the sky and lightning cracked the horizon. Lightning's brother, thunder, rumbled after it. Clara and Jarrett huddled around the small campfire near the cave's entrance. Their animals were tied up at the back of the cave.

"I hate rain," remarked Jarrett.

For a time, neither of them spoke. Clara fed slivers of wood to the fire while he riffled through some of the food stores. He took out a bag of dried fruits and held it out to her. She shook her head.

A bellow boomed through the night and both of them jerked to their feet. Heartsblood, trained for combat, only flicked his ears but the pony reared on its feet, snorting.

Jarrett rushed to the pony and held its halter. Rubbing the nose, he asked, "What the hell was that?"

The ground shuddered at regular intervals, as if something gigantic walked toward them. With a gasp, Clara began to kick dirt onto the fire.

"What are you doing?" Jarrett demanded.

"Quiet," she hissed.

Dirt extinguished the last flame and threw the cave into darkness. Outside, water continued to rush down, splattering on the rocks outside the cave. It seemed to her that the panicked gait of her heartbeat was louder even than the enormous sound of footsteps.

The steps grew louder and louder and *louder*

until they filled the world. Blindly, she backed up until she felt Jarrett behind her and grabbed his tunic. He wrapped a comforting arm around her shoulders.

The footsteps passed the cave outside and slowly began to fade away. Before long, they became as distant thunder.

"What in the name of the Child?" Jarrett's voice wobbled slightly.

"A giant," she replied. "The old folks used to tell stories about them when I was a child. I'd never seen or heard one before but what else could it be?"

"That's mad, Clara. Giants are only in stories."

"Well, what else could make footsteps that loud?"

"Was it heading to Hernesferry? We need to warn them!"

"It won't do any good. It will be there long before we could find our way there in the dark."

Silence, broken by the patter of hard rain on earth and stone, swamped the cave. In the distance, another bellow erupted.

Jarrett said, "I think we can do without the campfire tonight."

Chapter Five

Emmerich watched the winged figures wheel in the blue sky above, long blue and red tails trailing behind them. Wind slipped through the trees and the sound almost covered the brush of someone's feet over grass as they walked toward him. He smiled at Lord Bruin.

"Taking a turn in the garden?" he asked.

Lord Bruin opened his hands, palm out, as if to embrace the space. "Sometimes, my office in the Academy feels too small. I saw Your Majesty standing all alone." He tilted his head at the guards nearby. "Or, as alone as you can be outside your quarters."

"And you thought to keep me company?"

The young man smiled pleasantly as he came to a stop by Emmerich. "Among other thoughts."

"Other thoughts?"

Bruin tilted his head back to watch the aerials. "I also thought about the incident down by the docks."

"Do you plan on lecturing me about how stupid it was for a king to have gone?"

"I don't know. Do you plan to listen?"

Emmerich laughed. "No."

Lord Bruin smiled. "Then I won't waste your time."

Emmerich returned his gaze up to the aerials. They had soared away. He started across the small field back to the garden path. Bruin followed.

"Lord Bruin," he said, "do you fear the aerials?"

"No. I trust the Lady Seer's assessment."

"Even though she is a former slave who couldn't read two years ago?"

The wizard gave him a sidelong stare. "That's a rather harsh thing for His Majesty to say."

"It's one of the objections my Council members bring up." He pitched his voice higher. "Your Majesty, she is a former slave! She probably thinks the world is round." He made a sound of disgust.

"The problem with people of the southern portion of our nation, as opposed to the north, is that we've lost an appreciation for the mystical. Yes, we have the mystical in our worship, but many of us try to confine it there. That's also why Marduk's monsters terrify us and why the aerials are becoming more of a concern. They are a physical reminder of the mystical and cannot be contained. To Lady Clara's northern-nurtured mind, the mystical need not be feared right away. It is a natural part of our lives." Bruin smiled. "And the world is round."

"Well, don't let Lord Barkeley hear you say that. And I think you're right. In my travels in the north, and what dealings I had in Tier in my youth, I noticed that people were more willing to accept things like fairies and seers. And wizards. Some southerners have taken to referring to you and your kind as 'natural philosophers' because it's easier to think of you dealing in nature rather than magic."

"Magic is a part of nature, Your Majesty."

"Well, I meant tangible."

"I know what you meant." Bruin smiled at the King.

They reached the garden path and Emmerich stopped. A small frown played on his brow. "The Council is considering purging the city of all aerials, in order to calm the people's minds."

"That would be a mistake. There's a very good possibility that they are protecting us, just as they came to General Asher's aid outside the city when Marduk set his monsters on them." He crossed his arms, tucking his hands into his large, black sleeves. "And it may confirm to some that they are dangerous."

"So I told the Council. They requested time to consider the proposal."

"Who proposed it, Your Majesty?"

"Lord Barkeley."

"This isn't the first time his name has come up in our conversations."

"No." Emmerich turned to him. "He's become a very vocal opponent to all things magical. He led the debate against increasing the Academy's coffers and his faction in the Court grows larger. I want you to investigate the chance that he is the traitor or is behind the traitor."

Bruin bowed his head. "Yes, Your Majesty. Chances are, he's simply a stubborn man, afraid of what magic could do to our country after witnessing Marduk's evil."

"True. Yet, I don't want to take any chances."

"Consider it done, then."

Emmerich started to walk away, back to the Palace.

Bruin called out, "Your Majesty."

"Yes, Lord Bruin?"

"Any word from the Lady Seer?"

"Only that she has passed through Hernesferry, which you told me."

"Yes, Your Majesty. I wondered if she sent you any correspondence or if you'd seen her, as you had the other night."

Emmerich shook his head. "I will let you know if I do."

"Thank you, Your Majesty."

"Have you made any progress into what it could mean, her appearing to me?"

"We're still searching, Your Majesty. We don't think it's bad or harmful."

Emmerich's face darkened. "Not yet, that is."

Bran reached under his bed and pulled out the errant boot. As he stood, two of his fellow pages entered the dormitory. The boys, Bartholomew and Xavier, grinned when they saw him. Bran's gut dropped.

"Low-boy," Xavier said, "if you're cleaning, perhaps you can do my area as well."

"Yes," chimed in Bartholomew, "and mine, too."

"We're sure you're used to that."

"And once you're done, our clothes could use a wash."

"Your mother taught you how, right?"

The boys laughed. Bran flushed, picking up his brush and tin of polish. He sat on the bed and tried to ignore them as he began to polish the boot.

Xavier sniffed loudly. "That's an awful smell, isn't it, Bartholomew?"

Bartholomew made a show of sniffing the air. "It is."

"It's that Low Quarters stench. We need to get a maid to take the trash out." Xavier walked over to Bran and knocked the boot from his hand. "You hear me, Low-boy?"

Bran stood, brush gripped in one hand and the other balled into a fist. "Leave me alone, Xavier."

"Or what?" He shoved Bran in the shoulder. "You low-rankers think you belong here, but you don't." He shoved him again. "You're stupid." Shove. "And ugly." Shove. "And you don't have any business here. You should be home, with your whore of a mother."

With a yell, Bran tackled the taller boy. The tin flew to the side as both of them fell against a bed. Bran used every dirty trick he learned on the streets: kneeing Xavier in the groin (he missed and got him in the thigh), yanking his hair, biting and scratching him. Xavier screamed and tried to cover his head with his hands.

Large hands grabbed Bran's shoulders and wrenched him off the boy.

"What in the Nine Hells is going on?" shouted a guard.

Xavier, snot and tears running down his face, gained his feet. "This *bastard* attacked me!"

"You started it!" Bran shouted. He yanked against the guard's grip with no luck.

"I don't give a damn who started it," the guard replied. "You there!" The guard pointed at Bartholomew, who watched the fight with eyes the size of serving plates. "Go to the King. He needs an extra page in the throne room. Well, go on!"

Bartholomew turned on his heel and ran out. The guard grabbed Xavier's shoulder.

"And the two of you," the man said, "are coming with me to see the Pagemaster."

Xavier protested, yelling something about his father's rank. The guard ignored him. He half-dragged them out of the dormitory and down to the Pagemaster's office in the same wing.

Master Thom scowled as he listened to the guard's account, and the scowl only grew darker when Xavier jumped in with his story before Bran had a chance. Bran stood by the guard, arms crossed and torn between rage and fear.

"Xavier," Thom said, "don't bother coming to dinner this evening and don't try to have it sneaked to you. Dismissed. You may go as well, guardsman."

The guard saluted and left with Xavier, who shot Bran a murderous look.

Thom sat back in his chair. "I told the King that this new program wouldn't work out. Sit down, Bran."

Bran obeyed. With head bowed, he stared at the toes of his boots while he waited for the expected dismissal.

"Bran, there are always scuffles among the

pages. Jockeying for position and the like. Lately, however, I've had more complaints about fights between high-rankers and low-rankers than I care to handle. And I don't want to see it among the King's personal pages. You lot have to be ready to serve at a moment's notice and I can't have you serving if you have black eyes." He tossed his pencil onto the desk. "Do I need to send you away and get a replacement?"

He jerked his head up. "No, Master Thom. I want to be here."

"Then don't allow yourself to be provoked." Thom pointed at the boy. "This is your only warning. Next incident like this and you're dismissed from the pages." He lowered his hand. "Now, I would do more to discipline Xavier, but his father is a Council member. You have no one to protect you and someone needs to be punished. From now on, you're on the night shift and are to take bread and water for your meals for the next two days. Understand?"

"Yes, Master Thom."

"Very good. I suggest you try to get some sleep for your shift tonight."

"Yes, Master." Bran stood and bowed himself out. However, as soon as he stepped into the hall, he ran out of the wing.

He didn't stop, dodging servants and guards, until he reached the small kitchen gardens. He dropped down next to a plot of herbs and burst into miserable tears.

Bran knew enough about bullies to know that Xavier wouldn't stop. Not if he thought he couldn't get into trouble. And if Bran fought back in the only way he knew how, then he would be dismissed the next time one or both of them arrived for duty bruised and bloody.

A shadow brushed over Bran. He jerked upright, expecting to see a maid or cook demanding to know why he was getting snot all over the mint. Instead, to Bran's surprise, an aerial that shimmered like a casket of jewels settled on the ground near him.

The creature tilted its emerald head to study

him. Its serenity clashed against Bran's fear at being regarded by such a strange thing. It was as if a dragon and a peacock had mated.

Sad boy?

Bran looked around for the source of the voice. The aerial shifted closer and poked its head toward him.

Sad boy?

A shock zipped down his spine. He heard the aerial!

"Y-yes." He sniffled. "I'm sad."

Why?

"Because they may ask me to leave."

A dizzying array of colors and an image of flying against the wind spiraled through Bran. It took a moment before Bran realized that they came from the aerial, showing its confusion.

So, he tried his best to explain the fight and what Master Thom said. The aerial listened, as still as stone, as if it took all of its energy to understand him.

When Bran finished, a picture filled his mind.

A large battlefield spread out beneath him. Vertigo rocked his stomach as the land tilted and grew closer. Below him, a man in chain mail fought snarling cats the size of carts. The image faded and he sat again in the garden.

"What was that?" he asked.

The aerial only stared, as if waiting for him to work it out.

And Bran thought about it. He tackled it like he did his sums under Presbyter Cyril's tutelage. It dawned on him that the aerial compared Bran's problems with a great battle. And, maybe what Bran saw was the memory of the great battle waged on the plains outside the city.

"I guess it's a battle. Xavier doesn't like me and I have to defend myself. I have to do it without getting in trouble. I don't know how to do that."

The aerial came closer and Bran tensed. The creature, as large as a mastiff, could hurt him easily. He noticed it smelled like almond flowers.

It blew in his face.

No sad anymore.

Joy filled Bran like wine overflowing a goblet. The aerial stepped back, opened its wings, and heaved into the air. Wind and leaves coursed over Bran. He scrambled to his feet and watched the aerial fly away. Once it faded into the distance, he went back inside.

Why had he felt that way?

He put the mystery out of his mind. Master Thom was right, after all. He did need some sleep before his shift that night.

"A giant?" Emmerich stared at the emissaries. "Please tell me that this is someone's idea of a prank."

Soft mutters and a fluttering of giggles rippled through the throne room. Emmerich had been hearing the day's large number of petitioners when the black-robed men swept through the crowd. Courtiers and petitioners alike edged away from the magic workers and it wasn't Emmerich's imagination that the guards stepped closer to the dais where he sat.

"I wish it was, sire," replied the spokesman, named Benjamin. "Our contact for Captain Jarrett barely got out before the giant destroyed Hernesferry. And as soon as he passed through, the portal ceased to function. We have wizards trying to repair it now."

Cold washed over Emmerich and his chest tightened. Marduk's portals granted instant travel from one place to another. Only a few still worked and the last one to the north existed just outside of Hernesferry.

If there were no other operational portals to the north, then he had no way of getting help swiftly to Clara if she needed it.

Gavin's broken, bloody body flashed through his mind and that sense of helplessness washed over him again. Gasps and talk erupted in the throne room as everyone speculated and panicked in turns. Emmerich barely heard them. The Acting Captain, Valiance, stepped onto the dais and took a cautious step toward his sovereign.

"Your Majesty?" he asked.

Emmerich jerked.

Valiance bowed apologetically. "Shall I clear the throne room, Your Majesty?"

"Yes," Emmerich bit out.

The Acting Captain stepped down from the dais. He jerked a hand at the Master of Ceremonies. The elderly man rang a hand bell. Guards opened the doors. Obeying the signal, albeit slowly, the courtiers and other petitioners filed out. Once the last person left, the guards swung the tall doors closed.

Emmerich stood. "What of the Lady Seer and the Captain?"

"Our contact has already met with them."

"Where are they now?"

"Well, according to him, they were still en route to Bluebell. We don't know if they still—"

"Then find out!" shouted Emmerich.

Benjamin winced. "Yes, Your Majesty."

Emmerich clenched his jaw, trying to gain

control of his temper. "And why didn't your man try to stop the assault? I want to speak to him."

"Your Majesty, our contact is currently at the House of Healing or he would be here. He relates that he couldn't stop the giant. It appears they, or this one at least, are immune to magic."

Emmerich tensed. "You said it appears? Are you saying you didn't know before?"

Benjamin clasped his hands. "Until today, sire, the official stance of the Academy was that giants didn't exist and if they did, surely they died out long ago. Anything else was mountain legend and superstition."

"I suppose it's safe to say you've changed your stance?"

"Yes, Your Majesty."

"And where is the giant now? Where is it going?"

"We don't know, sire."

"How in the Nine Hells do you lose a thirty foot tall man?"

The wizard paled, probably deeply regretting

agreeing to be the bearer of news. "We can't scry it, Your Majesty, and our man didn't see where it went before he escaped."

Personally, Emmerich wanted to charge the wizard with cowardice and desertion. However, if he hadn't left when he did, would he have lived to tell the tale? It bothered Emmerich more, though, that the wizards couldn't call up the giant's image in water.

He stepped down off the dais. "Scry for the Lady Seer and report back to me. And I want messages sent to Candor and every castle and town in that area. Warn them about this giant and tell them to hide. Seek shelter in the forest and mountains. Scry surrounding areas. If we can't watch it, we can at least map out the damage and track it. Perhaps if we know where it's been, we can guess its destination. Then, we can surprise it with a platoon of soldiers. Let's see if arrows have a better chance of success than spells."

"Yes, sire."

"Dismissed."

Mother Above, he thought. *Is Clara all right?*

For moment, Emmerich felt guilty for not worrying over Jarrett's well-being. He'd known the man for years, ever since he joined the Royal Guard out of the army while Emmerich was still Captain, before Monica's death.

Emmerich knew better than anyone how well-trained Jarrett was and how seriously he took his duties. Emmerich knew how deeply Jarrett's sense of honor ran. Jarrett could take care of himself and keep out of trouble.

Clara, on the other hand, would run headlong into danger if only to prove her worth.

The bitter scent of smoke met them long before Jarrett and Clara reached Hernesferry. His gut clenched, the smell triggering memories of battles that still plagued his nightmares.

They reached the river crossing that gave the town its name. Jarrett rang the bell hanging from a pole on the bank. The bright chime rang over the rushing water and was met by silence from the cottage on the opposite side.

The dock that should have jutted out from their side of the river was gone. All that was left was a lone piling leaning over the roiling water. It would probably be gone in a day or two.

He could make out churned up mud on the far bank and an enormous footprint. Pieces of wood were strewn over the bank, possibly the barge that had been tied up near the cottage. The dock, too, was gone, but the cottage stood intact. Smoke rose in a large column from behind the trees, melding with the heavy grey clouds.

"How are we going to cross?" Clara asked.

"I'm not sure we can. It's leagues and leagues to the next crossing. And the river, look at it." He waved a hand at the swollen, swift water. Foam flecked the water and small whirlpools danced around a nearby clump of rocks. "Yesterday was rough enough. But last night's rains combined with snow melt are going to make ferrying across even more dangerous. Other crossings may not be in operation at all by the time we reach them."

"No chance we could swim across, then?"

"I wouldn't try it."

"What if someone needs help?"

He sucked his teeth. "Clara, what do you want me to do? We can't get to Hernesferry, not unless we go miles up or downstream. By the time we reach the town, anyone in need of help could already be dead."

"Shouldn't we warn someone?"

"There's a very, very tall man wandering the countryside. He's his own warning, I think. Besides, I'm sure the wizard I spoke with escaped and has returned to Bertrand. And if he didn't, the King will wonder why he hasn't gotten a promised update and he'll send someone to investigate. Besides, someone could need our help from where the giant came."

They watched the smoke billow into the air from behind the trees.

Clara said, "My Da used to tell me stories

about giants dancing in the mountains. He used to say that was where thunder came from."

"I rather don't like the idea of that thing having a dance partner. Come. We still have a long way to go." Turning Heartsblood, he went back the way they came. "You couldn't have prevented it, you know."

"I should have known it was going to happen," she replied, her voice angry and bitter.

Chapter Six

Bran took his seat across from the door of the King's private chambers. His stomach rumbled but he tried his best to ignore it. A large bruise had blossomed on his jaw at some point while he slept. He hoped the King wouldn't notice.

The door to the King's chambers opened, spilling light into the dim corridor. Bran stood and clasped his hands behind his back. A man in black robes, wearing a wizard's blue and white belt, came out of the room.

Bran recognized him as the mysterious Lord Bruin. All the pages learned to recognize the members of King Emmerich's inner circle. Lord Bruin was supposed to be just under his fourth decade, but to Bran, his eyes looked far, far older.

Lord Bruin passed the page without taking notice of him. Bran sighed in relief and took his seat again.

The door creaked open a second time and he scrambled to his feet. King Emmerich leaned out.

"Bran, come in." He stepped back into the room. "And close the door behind you."

Bran obeyed. The King stood with his back to the page, facing his desk, and Bran heard the rustle of papers.

"I want you to deliver these for me." Emmerich rolled the papers into a tight bundle. "Take these to—what happened to you?"

Oh, no, he noticed. "Your Majesty?"

"Your jaw. It's bruised like you've been in a fight."

He could feel heat creep up his face and knew he was blushing. "I did get into a fight, sire."

"I hope it was over something good."

"Another page insulted my mother, sire."

"I see. And I take it the Pagemaster is aware of this incident?"

"Yes, sire. I'm on bread and water for three days."

Emmerich cocked a brow. "Who was the page?"

Bran dropped his eyes. "His name is Xavier,

sire. He's the son of a lord on the Council."

"Oh. I see." He held out the rolled sheaf and Bran took it. "I hope next time you have the sense to duck."

"Yes, sire. Where should I deliver these?"

"General Asher. He should be in his quarters in the barracks. You know where to find those?"

"Yes, sire."

Bran bowed and jogged away out of the Royal Wing.

The General was a strange man. He could have had the best quarters in the Palace, almost as good as the Lady Seer's. Instead, he chose to stay in the second floor of the barracks, with the other captains. Bran wondered what he would do if he was general of the King's Army. Would he stay in the barracks or in the Palace?

Palace, he decided, as he crossed the large courtyard between the Royal Wing and the barracks. Frogs and crickets sang in counterpoint to the laughter and conversation of some soldiers clustered nearby. As Bran always did when he stepped outside at night, he paused to find the North Star. Presbyter Cyril said that as long as he could see it, he could never get lost at night.

Smiling, Bran jogged on to the barracks, a three-story building on the far end of the courtyard. He entered and dodged a pair of soldiers to go up the narrow stairs to the second floor. He reached it in time to nearly plow into another page.

"Oh, sorry!" he cried.

One of the older pages, almost too old to be a page, ducked his head and muttered, "S'alright." Brushing past Bran, he hurried down the stairs.

Bran hurried down the hall and to General Asher's door. He knocked.

"Come in," came a muffled voice.

Bran opened the door and entered a neat room without much decoration or furniture. Just a bed, a writing table, and a washbasin on a stand. A trunk stood against the foot of the bed and a sheathed sword leaned against the head of the bed. A cloak hung by a peg. Beside it, on another peg, hung a cudgel. The general, stripped to just his shirt and trousers, stood by the table as he read a piece of paper by lamplight. Bran bowed.

"From the King, sir," he said, holding up the rolled sheaf.

Asher took the sheaf and unrolled it, reading the papers over while Bran waited. His curiosity got the better of Bran and he looked around the room. Now that he paid closer attention, he could see some things of beauty: a polished knot of wood laid on the table, a small framed painting of a lady hung on a wall, and a few books were stacked on the floor.

"This doesn't require a reply," the general said. He tossed the papers onto the small table. "You may go."

"General, I had a question."

"Yes?"

"Master Thom said that pages, at the end of their service, are el-el—"

"Eligible?"

"Yes. Eligible for special privileges. Like seats in higher school. I wondered if that meant a spot in the army?"

Asher smiled. "Any able man can join the army. To be an officer requires a commission, which requires a lot of money. A few pages have used their good reputation to find someone who sponsored their commission."

Bran nodded, thinking that over.

"You wish to be a soldier? I see you've already got the marks for one. Nice bruise."

He could feel the flush trying to come back. "It was a mistake, sir."

"That's what youth is for: making mistakes. Is that all?"

"Yes, sir. Thank you, sir." He left the general, pulling the door closed behind him, and walked with a quick step down the stairs and out. He didn't dare dawdle to listen in on the conversation of nearby soldiers, in case the King needed to give him another task. But his ears did itch with curiosity.

As he crossed the courtyard, movement on the edge caught his eye. Bran stopped. People in the halls and courtyards were normal at the Palace, no matter the hour. However, something felt strange about the way this indistinct lump moved in the dark.

The lump lurched into the torchlight. Bran gasped. The page he ran into earlier stumbled toward Bran with his arms wrapped around his middle. His foot caught a broken flagstone and he fell.

Bran knelt beside the fallen boy. "Are you all right?" He rolled him onto his back. The arms fell away, revealing a jagged, bloody tear in the page's tunic. The boy's sightless eyes stared up into the star-strewn sky.

"Help!" screamed Bran. "Someone, help! He's dead!"

"You don't know his name?"

The pageboy shook his head. "He's older than I am. I think he served the Academy."

Asher sat back in his chair. He hoped to be asleep by now and Heavens knew he needed his rest. Rubbing his eyes with his fingers, Asher tried to think of questions he should ask. "Do you know who he had come to see?" He dropped his hand and stared at the nervous boy.

"No, General. I just know that I ran into him when I came to deliver the papers to you and now he's-he's dead."

The boy's ashen face worried the general but he had refused offers of food or drink. Asher practically forced him to sit on the bed. He wasn't sure whether to admire the page's fortitude or be exasperated by it.

"Master Thom is being roused right now," Asher explained. "He'll be able to tell us the boy's name. I only hoped you knew him. And you didn't see anyone else with him?"

"No, sir."

Just as Asher formed another question, someone banged on his door. The boy flinched, while years of unpleasant surprises had hardened Asher. He only said, "Come."

The door opened. Valiance, Jarrett's replacement, came into the room. He bowed. "General. I was just informed of the murder. I will be more than happy to take the boy in for questioning now."

Asher stood. Palace gossip ran at a horse's pace but he couldn't see how Valiance learned so quickly about it. "Since the murder occurred right outside the barracks, Captain, I would think I had jurisdiction."

"General, it happened *outside* the barracks to a servant of the Palace. That puts it in my jurisdiction. Of course, I will keep you informed of what we find."

Asher narrowed his eyes, weighing the pros and cons of arguing. He was the son of minor nobility, so Asher understood the value of a well-placed word and the danger of an ill-timed dispute. Ever since he became general of the entire army, Asher had become more sensitive about what he said and how he said it.

There was much he wanted to say to Valiance at that moment, but he decided perhaps it would be better to watch this from a distance. It would give Asher a chance to see if Valiance was as duplicitous as he feared.

Besides, a giant on the loose required his attention.

"Please do so, Captain," Asher finally said.

"Page, come with me."

The boy obediently stood and began to cross the room. Asher caught him on the shoulder. "Young one, do you have any experience in the sword or the stave?"

"No, General."

"If you wish to one day have a commission in our ranks, you should have the knowledge. Come here in your spare time and we'll work on that. And your name again?"

A grin filled his face. "Bran, sir. Bran Weston."

"Off with the Captain, then, Bran."

Bran bowed and left with Valiance, who shut the door firmly behind him.

Asher didn't trust Acting Captain Valiance. His intuition, honed from battles and politics, warned him that something could go very wrong while Valiance escorted Bran. As their only witness, the boy was invaluable. And after talking with him, Asher felt very protective in a way that surprised him.

He swiftly reached for his cudgel. Asher listened at the door until the footsteps had receded into silence. Slipping out, he took the servant stairs down and out the back of the building.

He came around in time to see Valiance escort Bran across the courtyard, past the small knot of people crowded around the corpse. Asher recognized Thom's stoop as he stood by the body. Keeping to the shadows, Asher rounded the courtyard.

Bran and Valiance had already reentered the Palace by the time he reached the appropriate door and a lump lodged in Asher's throat. He entered the hall and relaxed when he saw the pair a few yards ahead.

Keeping a discreet distance the whole way, he followed the pair until they reached the doors to the Royal Wing. There, the pair stopped and Valiance spoke a few moments to Bran. Asher waited.

As soon as he finished speaking, Valiance left the boy and walked toward Asher. Asher stepped out of the shadows and blocked Valiance's way.

Valiance stepped back. His gaze flicked to the cudgel before raising it to Asher's face. "I see you still don't trust me."

"And I wanted you to see that," Asher replied.

"Why, General?"

"Sometimes an unveiled threat is better than a veiled one."

"General, with all due respect, just because I wasn't in the rebellion doesn't mean I wasn't against everything Marduk did. Jarrett told me of what he saw, the people that monster changed, and what he changed them into. If Jarrett trusted me enough to leave me in charge while he is away, then why can you not trust me?"

"Because I still remember Emmerich's poisoned cup and the fact that no one could find you."

Anger flared in his eyes. "That was a mistake. I had nothing to do with that! I told you. I was seeing to a family emergency and my family vouched for me."

"If you were investigating the King's near assassination, which you should be doing, wouldn't you suspect such an alibi? Because family will lie to protect their own."

Valiance's jaw flexed and his hands curled into fists. "Are we done here, General?"

"We are, Acting Captain."

With a jerk, Valiance turned on his heel and stalked off. Bran still stood at the door of the servants' wing, eyes wide. Asher waved for the boy to go on. With a quick bow, Bran opened the door and slipped away.

Asher took his time to walk back to his quarters. Many unanswered questions filled his mind.

Yes, the murder occurring outside the barracks made it Valiance's jurisdiction, but the way the Captain pressed his point made Asher's instincts clamor.

Why would someone want to kill a pageboy? If someone needed to send a missive of great importance, the kind that provoked murder, it wouldn't have been entrusted to a page. And Asher would have been the only person to send or receive such a missive.

And who would dare commit murder in the Palace itself?

The questions carried him outside, where he met Thom on his way back. Behind him, men carried the shrouded body on a stretcher. A healer stood next to it.

"General," Thom said, pausing to bow before heading on.

"Master Thom, wait a moment."

The Pagemaster did, raising brows over grief-smudged eyes. "Yes, General?"

"Who is the boy?"

"His name is-was Matteo Havens. My nephew."

"My condolences. Do you know who would have harmed him?"

"No. Matteo was a good boy. An excellent page. He had many possibilities before him."

Questions crowded Asher's tongue but he didn't want to stir up scandal by appearing to infringe on Valiance's territory. "I'm very sorry, Master. Please, let me know if there is anything I can do."

"Of course, sir." He bowed and watched them leave with their sad burden.

During the civil war, Emmerich had put a lot of trust and faith into Asher. When he was crowned king, Emmerich didn't set Asher aside but continued to rely on him. Asher could have just been another soldier but Emmerich saw his value, something for which he never stopped being grateful.

As Asher returned to the barracks, he quietly

renewed his vow to not disappoint his King.

Valiance strode down the Palace halls, taking turns almost at random and moving from servants' areas to public with the ease of a man who knew the Palace better than his own quarters. His long, winding route brought him to the Academy.

He paused at the edge of the courtyard. As best as he could tell, General Asher had returned to the barracks after his threat. The courtyard was empty and he didn't see movement in the shadows.

He crossed the courtyard to the main Academy building, glancing over his shoulder at about halfway. The courtyard behind him was empty.

The apprentice on duty at the desk curtsied when he entered and returned to her book. Apprentices were used to seeing Captain Valiance come and go, even as late as this.

Valiance strode up the stairs to the quarters

for the full wizards. Most of them were instructors and so were already asleep. He walked with soft and slow steps down the hall to the next to last door. Taking his glove off, he scratched at it.

Someone moved in the room and opened the door. Valiance pushed in, grabbed the man by the throat, twisted, and shoved him against the door, both closing it and pinning the wizard.

"What is the matter with you?" he hissed.

The wizard, a pale man from the North named Harold, raised an eyebrow at him. "You seem upset, Captain."

With a growl, Valiance released him. "I just had to kill a page for you. Damned right I'm upset. What are you doing using a page? You know we were instructed to keep all communication face to face."

"Our pages know better than to read correspondence. I thought sending a note to our compatriot would be safe enough. He needed to know where we were in the timeline and there was no easy way to plan a meeting. Why did you have to kill him?"

"I saw him read the note just before he delivered it. The boy planned to become a diplomat's aide. Of course he read every scrap of correspondence handed him. We of the Royal Guard have been watching him closely. If you'd asked *me*, I would have been happy to deliver a message. I am Acting Captain. I go where I damn well please."

Harold paled, making the dusting of freckles on his nose stand out more. "You saw him read it?"

"You're lucky I was coming down the hall behind him. And you're lucky he chose to deliver the note instead of going straight to the King. That was probably his next destination."

"You said you killed him. So what—"

"He was found almost immediately, before I could dispose of the body." Valiance scowled. "General Asher is interested now."

Harold fell into silence. Valiance put his fists

on his hips and fumed. He wanted to punch the stupid man but settled for a glare.

"General Asher is in charge of the investigation?" Harold asked.

"No. I am. And thank the Divine Child for that small mercy."

"Then it should be all right."

Valiance shoved a finger into the man's chest. "I am only a part of this to clear my family's debts. If you make another mistake, I will leave you for Asher to find. No. I will leave you for the King. I'm sure you've heard of his temper."

Harold's mouth worked before he forced a grin. "Our master wouldn't be happy about that."

"He isn't here to complain, is he?"

"No. He is on the way, though."

Valiance scowled, angry at Harold for being smug and angry at himself for the fear that sentence provoked. When a wizard approached Valiance with a way for him to clear his family's debts, left behind by a gambling grandfather, the acting Captain had jumped at the chance. He'd only thought it was passing bits of information or helping one of the Court factions in a meaningless power struggle. He'd thought the poisoned cup was a warning, meant to be discovered by a wizard like it was.

By the time Valiance learned the truth, it was too late.

He growled, "Just be more careful next time." He reached behind Harold to open the door.

The wizard moved nimbly out of the way. "You be careful as well, Captain Valiance."

Valiance shot Harold a glare fit to kill and left, trying not to think about how easy and simple was the road that led to treason.

Chapter Seven

They followed the giant's tracks until they vanished in a scree about half a league from the cave where they spent the night. Sheer rock face loomed above the slope of loose stones.

"Where did it come from?" asked Jarrett. He studied the swath of stones. "It's almost as if it had jumped down from the cliff above to the stones below. Except you would think that would leave a dent in the ground."

Clara dismounted her pony. She carefully stepped out onto the scree. The rocks crunched and shifted beneath her feet. She cast around, trying to find some sort of sign of the giant's passing.

"I don't know," she said. "I've always heard that the mountains birth the giants. Maybe this *is* where it came from."

"Clara, I'm willing to believe in giants because one walked past our campsite. And I'm willing to believe in magic because of people like Marduk and Bruin. But you can't expect me to believe that a giant rock gave birth to a giant man."

"Then what do you suggest?" She picked her careful way back to Jarrett. A flat rock slid beneath her. Clara caught herself and continued.

"I think it might have come down from that way." He pointed up to the top of the cliff.

"Didn't you just say it should have left a hole in the ground? It's not like it could have climbed down. That's sheer rock."

"You're right. Maybe a giant bird dropped it off here in return for some favor?" He grinned at her as she climbed back onto her pony.

Clara snorted and smiled a little. "You'd rather believe in a giant bird, then?"

"Of course. Think of the eggs." He nudged his horse down the narrow path that skirted the stones. "I love a good scrambled egg."

She laughed. "Are we going to find a way to the top of that?"

Jarrett studied the cliff face. "Is there a way?"

"Maybe."

"Well, you find it, mountain girl."

"What makes you think I've ever climbed?"

"I thought all mountain folk did."

"You really should do something about those preconceptions, Jarrett." Clara studied the scenery. Trees and vines sloped down on either side of the rock wall and probably hid a climbable path. "I think we could climb it. We'd have to leave the mounts behind."

"We're a ways from the watchtower. There might be bandits."

"Fine. You stay and I go."

"I don't know about that."

"Do you want to know where this thing came from or not? Or would you rather go, city boy?"

Jarrett made a sound of frustration. "If you take too long, I'm coming after you."

They pulled off the path when the side of the mountain leveled off enough to allow it, and they dismounted.

"It might take me a bit," she replied. "If I don't come back by sundown, then you may worry."

"I'm already worried."

"Well, worry more so than usual." She left him to his worries and began hiking through woods and underbrush. When her skirt snagged on a bush for the third time, she turned back.

Jarrett said, "That was quick."

"I'm not going to make it in this." She gestured at her clothes. "Lend me your spare pants and a tunic."

"Are you serious?"

"Aye."

Heaving the groan of the long-suffering, he dug into his pack and pulled out clothes. She took them behind a thick clump of holly bushes and changed. The trousers were too long and had to be rolled up. She cinched the belt tightly to keep the trousers up and the tunic from billowing.

Jarrett laughed when she came out. "You look like a boy wearing his father's clothes."

Clara ignored him as she draped her clothes over the pony's back and got her water pouch.

She slung it over her shoulder. "See you this evening."

"Good luck."

Going back into the woods, she began the climb at an angle along the mountainside.

Clara couldn't remember the last time she climbed like this. The comforts of noble living had softened her muscles. After a short while, she was winded and her back and legs ached. Gritting her teeth, she carried on. She grasped rocks and limbs for balance and to haul herself forward as the side grew steeper.

The day was more than half gone when she paused at a cluster of boulders. Clara sat on a flat one and fluffed the tunic to fan some cool air down her back. Strands of hair fell loose from her braid. She tucked them behind her ears. Unstopping the pouch, she sucked back some of the water.

Despite her fatigue, it felt good to be alone. She propped her elbows on her knees, stretching her aching back, and didn't wonder whether someone thought her posture unladylike.

Eerie silence covered the mountainside. The chorus of birds heard so clearly down on the path were distant here. She worried that she somehow missed the edge of the rock face they had seen earlier. It felt as if she should have reached it by now.

Throwing off the worry, she slung the pouch back onto her shoulder and carried on.

About a candlemark later, the trees fell back and the ground leveled off. The edge of the mountain peak dropped off into nothing a few yards away. She put down the water pouch and walked over to the edge, carefully getting on her knees.

Below, the swath of scree unfurled to edge the trail. She leaned further and saw Jarrett beside the animals. He waved at her and she waved back.

Clara got to her feet. From her vantage point, she could make out some of the giant's tracks below. In the distance, the column of smoke from

Hernesferry continued to scar the sky.

She re-entered the stand of trees crawling over the mountain peak. No tracks. No broken limbs. She doubled back and carefully inspected the granite rock. Light glinted off broken glass on the far side, which she'd first taken for crystal deposits in the rock.

She picked up the largest bit of glass. Thin as parchment and clear as water, it curved, as if once part of a bottle or globe. Who would shatter glass up here and why? From some of the prices Clara had seen at market, she knew that thin glass was far more valuable than thick. This shard alone held more value than Jarrett's horse. Clara carefully put it in her belt pouch to show Jarrett. Hopefully, it wouldn't break further on her way down.

She moved to the center of the peak. Around her, the horizon unfurled in a hazy field of lumps and plains. She gazed toward where they were going and more mountains reared, rounded backs like the whales she read about in books.

And, somewhere over the farthest ridge in the northeast, was Bluebell.

The sun cast rose and orange across the sky when Clara finally came out of the woods, hair mussed and twigs clinging to her clothes. The knot of worry in Jarrett's chest loosened.

It was stupid, letting her go on, but he would have just worried while he made the climb. He supposed he could have hidden their animals and packs. Good ideas always came too late.

"What did you find?" he asked.

"That's the strange part." She dusted her hands off and opened the pouch hanging from her belt. From it she drew a thin sliver of curved glass. He took it gently and cradled it in the palm of his hand.

"This was it? No footprints?" he asked.

"No broken limbs or trees. Nothing to suggest that a giant passed through." She drank from her water pouch.

"That is strange." He held the glass out.

She took it and returned it to her belt pouch. "Glass is so expensive, I can't imagine why anyone would want to break it."

"Yes. And what a giant could have to do with it." He put his hands on his hips.

"We should move on. Find a campsite before nightfall."

"All right. I'll wait for you to change."

She bit her bottom lip, eyes flicking from her pony and back at him. "Actually, I'd like to continue in this." She gestured at the clothes.

"What? Why?"

"It will feel better to ride astride than side saddle."

"That saddle is meant for a dress. Besides, those are my clothes and I might need them."

Clara scowled. He could see the stubbornness like clouds forming in her eyes. Jarrett crossed his arms, waiting for her to fold.

Honestly, he thought her rather comely in men's clothing. It hadn't escaped his notice that she always seemed ill at ease in finery. Her relaxed posture made her appear more attractive to his thinking, even though he preferred his women tall and swarthy.

Clara wasn't his to admire, he reminded himself. And he needed to think about propriety in case anyone recognized her. It would cause scandal in Bertrand if word reached the Court that the Lady Seer was running around the mountains in men's trousers.

After a long pause, Clara threw up her hands in defeat. She grabbed her clothes and stalked off to the bushes to change. When she returned, she said, "When we reach Bluebell, I will get a different saddle. And men's clothes." She tossed his clothes to him.

He caught them and rolled them into neat bundles. "And that will be your own business, but I think the villagers might be offended."

"Tierans allow their women to wear trousers and I remember some women in my village doing the same." She mounted her pony. "I really don't see what the problem is."

"I'm not arguing propriety with you. I'll go hoarse if I do so." He rolled up the clothes and tucked the bundle away before mounting Heartsblood. "Can we go on now?"

"Aye."

As they went on, he kept an eye out for both a good stopping place and more signs of the giant. It just didn't make sense. Where had it come from? What was an item as precious as thin glass doing there?

Clara appeared concerned as well. She studied the mountainside to the left and the rolling forests to the right, with a puckered brow. When they found a place to camp in a meadow, near a tumbling waterfall, they were no closer to an answer. Clara went off in search of firewood while Jarrett set up the camp.

"You know what else was strange?" she said when she returned with an armload.

"What?" He sat back on his heels next to the small fire pit he dug.

"There was no birdsong up there. It just felt

wrong." She dumped the wood next to the pit. "Like the air was heavy."

He began to arrange the kindling in the pit. "Do you think magic could have been worked there?"

"Perhaps. What sort of spell would bring a giant out of thin air?"

"I don't know. I'm not sure I want to know." With a scrape of flint on tinder, sparks flew onto the kindling and he gently blew on them until small flames began to eat up the wood. He carefully arranged larger pieces over it.

"Do you think Emmerich is in danger?"

The question startled him. Clara normally kept her concerns to herself. This evening, though, her arms were wrapped around her waist and her face held no anger, frustration, or cynicism. Her expression softened. The darkening night cast her eyes in shadow.

Jarrett stood. "Perhaps. He's already in danger because of Marduk's creatures haunting the woods and from intrigue at Court. Last I heard, the traitor that tried to poison him still hasn't been found or the one that released the creatures, if they aren't one and the same."

"Could this giant's appearance be connected to the traitors?"

"I hope so. A traitor with a giant is one thing. Traitors on one hand and giants on the other is too much to handle. Do you want to return to Bertrand?"

Clara pawed through the supplies for that night's supper of beans and salted pork. "I'm not of any use, Jarrett."

"What the hell does that have to do with anything, anyway?" All patience vanished under a wave of frustration. "We just saw a giant come out of nowhere!"

She threw a cloth-wrapped hunk of ham onto the ground. "Because that's all I am!"

"What?"

"Usefulness! That's all I am. All I ever was." She deepened her voice. "Clara, did you dream? What did you see?" She heightened her voice to an ear-splitting soprano. "And did the Seer have any interesting dreams the night before? I saw you staring out the window. Were you divining the future?" Her voice returned to normal. "All anyone cares about is what I can do, about whether I've seen the future. And when I haven't, I am mocked for it. And we're on this-this journey to see if there's more to me than being of use. If there is more to my past than parents who didn't care enough to keep me."

Silence came sharply at the end of her words. Wood snapped and sparked beneath the budding fire. Water gurgled as it splashed over nearby rocks.

Quietly, Jarrett replied, "I need to understand, Clara. I'm a soldier and I know soldiers don't have to understand. But this time, I need to."

She met his eyes, her shoulders square and tense. Her hands curled into fists. "I was a slave most of my life. It didn't matter if I wanted to go take a walk on a pretty day or if I'd rather bake the bread than mind the spit. It was whatever the

Cook said until I saved Lord Dwervin's life. Then it was whatever his lady said. Then Emmerich came.

"He offered me a purpose. A use. So, I went without even understanding what the civil war was all about. Then the war ended and I-I couldn't see the future anymore. And I couldn't give Emmerich any advice that his own Council couldn't give. And the courtiers mocked me for trying to be busy with my hands. I woke up one morning and realized I no longer had a use and it was the second worst moment of my life."

Clara's gaze went to somewhere over Jarrett's shoulder. "I spoke with the Tieran ambassador that same day. We met in the hall near the audience chamber. He offered to escort me and I let him because he was always kind. And he remarked, again, on how much I resembled his own people and he asked, again, if I had any Tieran relatives. And I couldn't tell him for sure."

She focused back on Jarrett's face. "That's when I knew I needed to go back to Bluebell.

That maybe it was there that I could find out why the ambassador kept asking about my lineage and if maybe I had another use and if my Da missed me. If he tried to find me. If he was sorry my mother sold me. If maybe there's something more to me than seeing the future."

Jarrett couldn't think of what to say to that. Her words made him reflect on his own upbringing. His parents still lived in Bertrand. His father, an officer in the army, continued to practice his swordplay. There was never any question that his sons would follow in his footsteps.

Jarrett never wanted anything beside that. He grew up on practice grounds and around soldiers. He couldn't imagine a life outside the military. He couldn't imagine not knowing what to do or be in life.

He asked, "You said that moment was the second worst of your life. Did you mean the first moment was when you were sold?"

"No. When I stood in that room with what I

thought was Emmerich's corpse. That was the worst moment of my life. I never want to experience that again. What can I do, Jarrett? What can I possibly do that would be helpful? Don't you see? I have no choice but to move forward."

"To find your use."

"Aye."

"To answer questions."

"Aye." An idea struck her. "You can go."

"What?"

"You can go back to Bertrand. You'll move faster without me to slow you down."

"Leave you in the mountains, with giants running around?"

"There's just one and it's already gone!"

"It's certainly not the only danger. Besides, Emmerich would kill me if I left you alone. He may not be as important to me as he is to you, but he was my Captain when I joined the Royal Guard. I learned everything from him. I cannot let him down, I cannot dishonor myself, because of your wild idea."

Clara snorted. "Will you just hear me out?"

Jarrett threw his hands up.

"If Emmerich is in danger, then he needs all the people he can trust. You're more use to him than I am. Besides, if I'm in Bertrand, he'll just worry about me. I'll be a distraction. He'll either keep me close and worry or send me away and worry."

"All right. I'll leave you in Candor and carry on to Bertrand."

"For all we know, the giant is going to Candor City. No, Jarrett, mine is the better plan. Bluebell isn't that far from here, anyway."

He raised a brow. "Really?"

"Aye." Her face looked entirely too straight.

"Clara, I've seen the maps. I know we've still got quite the journey."

"A journey I can complete more quickly on my own. Once we get deeper into the mountains, your prized gelding won't be able to keep up so well. My pony will climb better and faster. Once

I'm in Bluebell, I promise not to move until someone comes for me or I have someone to escort me back." She took a step toward. "Please. Don't let me relive my worst moment."

Jarrett considered her argument. If he pushed, he would be able to reach the next ferry more quickly than if he had Clara with him. And Clara wouldn't agree to return with him, even as far as Candor, without being tied down first. It occurred to him that she would just sneak off as soon as he left, anyway. She was right about her presence in Bertrand only serving as a distraction. Emmerich was damn protective of her, which is why Jarrett was ordered to escort her in the first place.

That brought him back to the reason why he couldn't leave her. Jarrett's sense of honor would not stand for it. He could not let down the King he admired and who entrusted him with his greatest treasure.

"No," he said. "Either I go with you to Bluebell or you come with me to Bertrand. Emmerich will worry for you whether you are near or far, so it's not a point even worthy of notice." Jarrett picked up the wrapped meat. "Let's have some supper."

Despite his resolution of the argument, a bad feeling plucked at the back of his neck all through the evening.

Jarrett awoke to the sound of birds and water. He cracked his eyes open and squinted at the morning light.

Why didn't Clara wake me for the last watch? he thought.

Fear and dread shot through him and he sat upright.

"Clara?" he called.

His eyes fell on the mounts. Only his gelding, Heartsblood, and a mule remained. Clara's pony and the second mule were gone.

He scrambled to his feet. "Clara!"

Only birdsong answered him. He took a step toward the road and his foot hit something hard. Her saddle, meant for riding aside, and a thick braid of hair lay by his pallet. Clara's hair.

A quick search through his saddle bags revealed that his spare clothes were gone. At some point in the night, during her watch, she had cut her hair, stolen his clothes, and left.

"Stupid girl!" he shouted, kicking the saddle. His toe complained and he swore, long and with imagination. He cursed himself for being fool enough to think she would let the argument go, and cursed any gods that listened for burdening him with the most bull-headed female to ever exist.

He knew he shouldn't be surprised. She was the same young woman who challenged a sorcerer without enough sense to be afraid.

Three men together couldn't have packed the camp as quickly as he did. To give himself more speed, he hid the burdened mule behind a stand of fir trees and bolted down the road on Heartsblood. The spirited war horse, happy to be going at a fast pace, stretched his legs easily under Jarrett's touch and bounded up a steep hill.

Clara had taken first watch, so she was candlemarks ahead. However, she had left in the night. It made sense that she would make camp around dawn.

Jarrett felt good about his chances of finding her until Heartsblood slowed.

"Hey, now," he said, digging in his heels.

The horse shook himself and stopped. Jarrett heard the labor of his breath. They'd reached the top of the hill but the energy it took left Heartsblood almost winded. The gelding was used to sprints across the flatland surrounding Bertrand, not the thrice-cursed hills of the North.

Jarrett growled in frustration. "How did King Emmerich march an army through this place?"

He looked ahead, hoping to see a stream of smoke from a campfire. What he could see of the horizon was empty save for clouds and random birds.

As he nudged Heartsblood forward, they went at a slower pace the horse could maintain. Jarrett could feel time slipping by like sand falling between his fingers.

About half a league after the hill, he came upon a fork in the wood where it split off into three directions.

One road went higher up the mountain while one went straight, probably to merge with the broader highway merchants liked to use when traveling through the Larkspurs. The third road angled off into the valley.

Jarrett studied the steeper road. There was no way he could get Heartsblood up that, which meant that had to be the way Clara took. It was also the sort of road she had warned him Heartsblood couldn't handle.

If he'd swallowed his pride in Hernesferry, he would be on a pony that could get him up that steep mountainside and closer to catching up with Clara.

He turned to the follow the road winding down further into the valley. Maybe he could find someone to trade with and then be able to chase after Clara, who went further away with each moment.

Jarrett felt a sinking sensation. Even if he found some poor farmer willing to trade a perfectly good mountain pony for a city-reared gelding that could barely run up a steep hill, Clara would be long gone. The only choice left, then, was to return to Bertrand.

Chapter Eight

Emmerich opened his eyes with a shuddering gasp for the third time that night. Heart thudding in his chest, he made himself listen to the scratch of mice in a wall and the distant sound of a night bird. He recognized the feel of the bed beneath him, especially that one particular lump under his hip.

This wasn't a cot but a bed. The sounds of mice in walls didn't happen in a tent. And that night bird Emmerich heard nested above his window; he knew its cadence well. Emmerich didn't hear the stamp and snort of horses tied up nearby, or half-drunk soldiers singing. He was in his quarters in the Palace, not on campaign.

He slipped out of bed and crossed the room to the window. Opening it, he let the cool night air chill the sweat coating his naked body. Emmerich braced his hands against the sill.

The same dream haunted him, over and over, with very little variation.

Emmerich stood in the center of a battlefield. He wore his mix of leather and chain mail and held a sword dripping with blood. Turning in a circle, he didn't see a single living person. Only corpse, after corpse, after bloody corpse. Limbs lopped from their owners lay next to guts and pools of gore. Crows blanketed the dead. They fed on eyes and exposed organs, screeching at competitors over the choice pieces.

Then she would arrive. Clara. Dressed in a slave's grey and wearing a leather collar, she watched him from across the field. Her mouth moved, forming the shape of his name.

He sprinted across the field of corpse. The bodies rose. Cold, lifeless hands grasped at him. They pulled him down while screaming filled his ears and dirt clogged his mouth.

Emmerich straightened and shivered off the remainder of the dream. Down below, torches lit the courtyard of the barracks. He chose these rooms as his bedchamber simply because of the view.

It felt good to be near soldiers, perhaps because he spent so much of his adult life near or in barracks of one kind or another. Memories of happier times among soldier friends stood closer to the surface, despite what nightmares came.

However, on this night, his thoughts took a more serious turn. The night before, a page named Matteo had died down there. Murdered. Many, him included, feared the murder was connected to the traitor somehow. Some Council members' minds were paranoid enough to connect it to Marduk's creatures and the giant as well.

Emmerich began to dress in the clothes he usually wore for sparring: black tunic and trousers with scuffed leather boots. He left his chambers while buckling his belt.

Young Bran's post stood empty, the boy having gone to bed when the King promised to do the same. At the doors to the Royal Wing, the guards saluted. One of them tried to follow him.

"No," Emmerich said. "Remain at your post."

The guard's face crinkled in concern even while he obeyed.

Outside in the courtyard, Emmerich walked over to the place of the crime. The blood had been washed away but Emmerich thought he could make out the stains in the flickering torchlight.

He noted that the darkness began nearby and couldn't make out the low hedge he knew to be only a yard or two away. That had to be where the killer attacked Matteo. However, Captain Valiance claimed a search didn't discover any evidence to point toward a killer.

Why would anyone kill a page on palace grounds? The question bothered him all day. And that Matteo's time of service had nearly ended made the whole matter worse. The Pagemaster said the boy had a bright future ahead of him as a diplomat's aide.

A chorus of laughter drew his attention to the far side of the courtyard. Something moved in the dark edging on that side. Another ripple of laughter and, this time, Emmerich heard a small squeal. He crossed the courtyard in long strides. As he drew closer, he could see a group of soldiers clustered around something.

One man saw Emmerich and nudged another. Soon, they all saw him and broke up their huddle just in time for Emmerich to see a soldier kick a small aerial in the stomach. The creature cried out, one wing flapping uselessly.

"Stop," barked Emmerich. The soldier who had kicked the aerial backed away. They all hastily bowed. "What is going on here?"

One of them said, "It's only some fun, sire."

"Fun? Torturing a creature that won't hurt you is *fun*?" He pointed to one of them. "You. Are you all in the same squad?"

"Y-yes, sire."

"And where is your sergeant?"

"In bed, sire."

"Fetch him. Now."

The soldier bowed and ran to the barracks.

"You." He pointed out another one. "Go fetch a healer from the Healer's Wing. Run, don't walk."

An awkward silence descended as Emmerich waited for the sergeant. Everyone ignored Emmerich, the aerial, and even each other. Flagstones, tips of boots, and the surrounding darkness became infinitely more interesting than the tiny aerial.

With each breath, it made small sounds of distress, and with each squeak, Emmerich's anger increased. How could anyone harm a defenseless creature?

The sergeant, hair in a tangle and surcoat askew, returned with the first soldier. The sergeant bowed. "Sire."

Emmerich pointed at the aerial. "Is this the behavior you allow in your squad?"

"No, Your Majesty." His jaw flexed, as if upset at the sight of the wounded creature. Emmerich wondered if he was more bothered about his men being caught.

"I want all these men, including the one I sent to get a healer, to be given twenty lashes tomorrow, in front of the entire company. Do you understand?"

"Yes, Your Majesty."

"You are all dismissed."

The soldiers left. Emmerich approached the creature.

It let out a pitiful cry as he settled down next to it. One of the beautiful, multi-colored wings stuck out at an odd angle. Patches on its jaw and belly were scraped raw. He picked it up as gently as he could, moving slowly so as not to jar it. The aerial whimpered and trembled. It was about as large as a six-month-old kitten.

"Shh." He cradled it against his chest. "You're going to be fine, little one."

Emmerich hadn't seen one so small before. Could this be a nestling that had left its parents for a night adventure?

The broken wing flopped over his arm and Emmerich could see small bones poking up through the feathers. A fresh wave of rage and disgust flowed over him. How could anyone do this to an animal so beautiful?

Increased trembling drew his attention back to the aerial. It watched him with a large, bright green eye. A sensation of terror spiraled through him and left him dizzy. And it came from the aerial. Belatedly, he remembered Bruin's report on the aerials' ability to receive and convey strong emotion.

"It's all right," he repeated and tried to think calming, soothing thoughts. He imagined lying in bed with Clara, his arms around her and her head pillowed on his chest. On nights when he couldn't sleep, this image sometimes lulled him.

The aerial relaxed slowly. He hummed a song he remembered his grandmother singing to him as a boy. The aerial's eye slid half shut.

When the soldier returned with the healer, Emmerich was running out of soothing songs to hum. Unfortunately, he knew more bawdy tavern songs than lullabies.

"Go to the barracks and report to your sergeant," he instructed the soldier.

The soldier bowed and jogged away. The healer, a thin-boned woman with black hair, knelt beside him. "This is it, Your Majesty?"

"Yes. I think it's just a child. A nestling."

"I've never treated an aerial before, sire. Perhaps we should take it to the Academy?"

"Perhaps. I hoped we could do something about that wing before we moved him overmuch."

The healer woman picked up the wing with her fingertips. The aerial awoke with a startled cry and struggled. Emmerich held it as tightly as he dared. He strengthened the soothing images and called up memories of watching his grandmother make the medicines she sold or with which she treated the members of the caravan. He thought about those times when members of his clan sang and played musical instruments around a fire.

After a time, the images penetrated the

creature's haze of pain and fear. It settled back into his arms again, though it still trembled beneath the woman's inspection.

"I can't set this here," the healer said at last. "And I wouldn't dare do it without a magic user to help me if needed."

"Then we'll go to the Academy and wake someone."

Chapter Nine

The Academy, a collection of buildings, stood on the far end of the palace complex. A tower rose from a wing of the palace on that side and, as always, its windows seemed to Emmerich to hold a malevolent glint. Dozens of sun catchers were found in the top of the tower when Emmerich's army took over.

Marduk had used the sun catchers to locate potential students for the Academy. Emmerich ordered them destroyed, to prevent such a powerful magic from being used wrongly.

Emmerich and the woman healer entered the main building of the Academy, where the offices, library, and teachers' chambers were located, as well as a few classrooms. A young apprentice sat at a desk just inside the entrance. She stood and curtsied, her head disappearing for a moment under the desk.

"Can I help you, Your Majesty?" she asked. With her grey apprentice robes and blonde hair, she could pass as a ghost. Her gaze flicked to the bright bundle Emmerich cradled to his chest.

"Are there any masters awake?" he asked. "We have a wounded aerial."

"I'm sure there is someone in the library, sire. It's this way."

She led them down the hall to the library, a vast three-story room packed with books and scrolls along the walls. At a long counter to one side, a woman in black wizard's robes sewed a binding onto a book.

Long tables and study carrels filled the rest of the room. A spiral staircase in a corner allowed access to the higher levels of books. It took a moment for him to realize, but no torches were used in the room. Instead, the sconces and lamps held strange, white lights that neither dimmed nor flickered.

Only one table was in use: a plump man with grey-streaked red hair furiously wrote in a notebook, open tomes scattered around him. His robe was open at the throat, revealing a green tunic beneath it. The girl led them to him.

"Master Amherst," she said.

"Busy," the man mumbled.

"Master, the King needs to speak with you."

His eyes widened and he dropped his pen. "Your Majesty." He stood and bowed. "To what do I owe this honor?"

"Master, I have a wounded aerial. This is Healer—" Emmerich realized he didn't know the woman's name.

"Healer Paula," she supplied. "It's a pleasure to meet you, Master Amherst."

"The pleasure is mine, I assure you." Amherst smiled. "So, a wounded aerial?" He stepped closer and peered at the creature in Emmerich's arms.

"Yes. I didn't want to treat it without a wizard's assistance. After all, these are creatures born of magic."

"Yes." He reached out and scratched the little one just about the eye. It made a weak sound of contentment. "I fear I'm not an expert on aerials. I'm more of an alchemist. However, our expert isn't available at the moment."

"Who is the expert?" asked Emmerich.

"Lord Bruin. He had some business to take care of in the city and won't be back until tomorrow."

"Do you know where we might reach him?"

Amherst shook his head. "I'm afraid he keeps such errands a secret. Not surprising, to be honest. What's a wizard without a touch of mystery, after all?" He chuckled at his own joke. "There is a laboratory nearby we can use. I may not be an expert but I still think I can help."

He led them out of the library and up two flights of stairs to the second floor. They turned into the third door on the right, entering a dark room. Amherst called up a mage light that flooded the laboratory with its cold glow.

Several long tables with chairs faced a chalk board. In the back were more long tables, crowded with glass tubes, beakers, dishes, and bowls. A dark glass cabinet in the back contained labeled bottles.

Amherst took them to the last empty table and nearest to the cabinet. "Well, then, let's have a look."

"Just a moment. Here, Healer Paula." Emmerich carefully gave her the aerial, who groaned at the transfer. He shucked off his tunic and made a bed with it on the table. Goosebumps rose up over his naked back at the chill in the room. "There."

Healer Paula laid the aerial on it. "Very kind of you, Your Majesty."

Amherst stepped close and Emmerich backed away, saying, "It's nothing."

"His breathing is very slow," Paula said. "I think he may be going into shock. Are aerials bird or reptile?"

"I do not think they fit into either classification," Amherst replied, running fingers over the broken wing. "I can feel his magic. It's strong. I don't think we're in danger of losing him."

"Him?" Emmerich asked. "You know that it's a

male?"

"Oh, yes. Aerial males are brightly plumaged while the females tend to be more simply colored. They stay close to their nests, however, and that is why they are not seen so often. I'm going to try something, Healer Paula. I'll need you to hold the little fellow down, just in case."

Paula did so as Amherst laid hands over the wing. He muttered and hummed for a few moments. The aerial began to pant and the room grew warm. The wizard dropped his hands.

"Not much change," he said. "His magic fought mine. I have calmed him some, so I think it will be easier to set it."

"No chance you'll do the healing for him?" Paula smiled at Amherst.

"I'm afraid not. And be glad. You'd hate for me to take your job, wouldn't you?" He winked at the woman.

She snorted softly. "We'll need a splint."

Amherst walked away to a cabinet and riffled through the supplies.

"Your Majesty," she said, "I'll need your help. Just put your hands⋯yes, like that."

He arranged his hands over the wing to keep it in place while she used her fingers to push and pull bones into place. The aerial screeched and struggled. Emmerich focused on soothing thoughts without effect. The screeching kept on until his head rang from it.

Pressure built up against his temples, as if two rocks pressed on either side of his head, and Emmerich clenched his jaw against it. A rending pain shot through his mind, blinding him with agony.

Aerial-Emmerich huddled in the corner of an alley, shivering, scared, and confused.

A few feet away, a group of men pounded something with clubs while another two stood nearby with torches. They shouted encouragement, pumping their fists in the air, but Emmerich didn't understand their words. And everything had a strange glow and was shaded in a blue-ish tinge.

The men slowly came to a stop. One of them laughed. Another spat. They sauntered away with clubs dripping with blue-green blood.

Aerial-Emmerich crept out of his corner to peer down at the bloody mess. Only the angular snout and mess of downy pale blue feathers hinted at its identity. The sharp scent of blood filled his nose and his gut clenched. He let out a cry and launched into the sky, beating the cold air with his wings.

With a start, Emmerich realized he was seeing what had happened with the aerial.

Fear, despair, and confusion roiled through the aerial, through Emmerich, in a torrent. He wanted to scream and to cry and to hide. He wanted to curl up against his mother—the aerial's mother—and cry into the soft down of her wings. But he couldn't. They couldn't. She was gone.

The distinction between minds grew too hard to maintain and they dissolved back one into the other.

Aerial-Emmerich flew blindly through the night, changing direction with quick jerks of his shoulders. His wings pounded hard, powering him through the night, until exhaustion seized him.

Down below, lights drew him. A large complex of buildings. A garden sprawled below and he aimed for it. In his fatigue, he overshot and came down on the edge of a cobblestoned area where men stood and talked. The aerial started to slink off to one of the bushes to wait until dawn when a shout startled him into stillness.

The men ran over. They said things he couldn't understand. They laughed. He looked up at them—Emmerich looked up at them—and mewed hopefully.

One of them drove a boot into his belly.

Aerial-Emmerich screamed and curled in on itself.

Another boot came down, slamming into his wing and breaking the fragile, hollow bones.

Aerial-Emmerich whimpered and tried to curl even tighter together. Everything hurt so much. Why were they hurting him? What had he done wrong? Had he been bad?

More blows rained down to shatter aerial-Emmerich's thoughts. He bounced across the pavement. More places hurt.

Then, a shout.

The men backed away.

More talking. Aerial-Emmerich didn't dare move. Didn't dare open his eyes until he felt someone approach. Cracking his eye open, he gazed up at a man all in black. A man with sorrow in his eyes and gentle hands.

"Your Majesty?"

Emmerich gasped and stumbled away from the table.

The aerial gazed at him with solemn eyes. Master Amherst and Healer Paula stared at him.

"Your Majesty," repeated Amherst. "Are you all right?"

Burying his face in his hands, Emmerich wept.

Emmerich hadn't cried that hard when Gavin died. He hadn't cried so hard since he found his family's lifeless bodies scattered like bloody leaves around their camp. All the old wounds from losing his father, grandmother, and all the people he grew up with, as well as from killing his lover Monica, bled anew in his chest. As he sobbed, his heart felt torn asunder.

Soft hands touched his shoulder and guided him into a nearby chair. Arms slid around him and held him close. He smelled herbs, with lemon balm the most prominent.

Eventually, the tears eased and the sobs faded. He opened his eyes and pulled away.

"Forgive me for the familiarity, Your Majesty," said Paula, "but I couldn't just stand there."

Emmerich cleared his throat. "It's all right. I'm sure you didn't think you were going to have to comfort your king tonight."

"No. I've learned not to frame expectations for how I spend my time." She drew a handkerchief from a pocket and offered it. Taking it, he mopped his face and blew his nose.

"If I may," Amherst said. "Your Majesty, what provoked such a response?"

"I saw what happened," he replied. "I saw the aerial's mother beaten to a smear on the pavement. I felt his grief and fear. His confusion. I saw what happened when he fled. I saw the soldiers set on him. I felt his pain. I felt every blow. I've never experienced anything like that before. Ever." Not even his nightmares had been so vivid.

"There have been a few, wizards mostly, who have forged a mind link with the aerials. There is one that Lord Bruin speaks with rather frequently. This is the first I've heard of one sharing memories and feelings. I wonder what's made the difference." Amherst stared into the distance, as if the air held the answer for him.

Emmerich stood and pocketed the handkerchief. "I didn't know that about Lord Bruin. I'll have to speak to him." He walked over to the nestling, who had fallen asleep. His bandaged wing hung in a sling projecting away from his body. With light fingertips, Emmerich stroked his head. "I want to carry him back to my rooms and have him tended there."

"Are you sure?" asked Paula. "It may be better for him to have constant care in the Healing House."

"He will have it. There's an empty bedchamber across the hall from my rooms. You'll stay there and will be able to check on the aerial constantly. Master Amherst, I expect you to also make regular visits." He lifted his head. "Unless you two have more pressing duties?"

"More pressing than tending a magical creature?" Amherst laughed. "I don't think so, Your Majesty. Healer Paula?"

"Neither do I," she replied. "I will be happy to tend to him."

"Very good." Emmerich returned his gaze to the little one. "I think we should call him Niall."

"That's a lovely name, sire."

With slow, careful movements, Emmerich lifted the bundle in his arms, being sure to support the splinted wing. "How long do you think it will take for that to heal?"

"I'm not sure. I'll have to ask some of the falconry masters."

Amherst said, "With all that magic coursing through Niall, I wouldn't be surprised if he healed much faster than a normal bird."

"We will see, then," Emmerich said. "Paula, I expect to see you tomorrow morning."

"Yes, sire," she said. "I would like to go with you now, if that is all right. You may need help settling him in."

"It's all right. Master Amherst, have a fine night. Be sure to apprise Lord Bruin on this situation. His insight will be invaluable."

"Of course, Your Majesty." The wizard bowed.

Emmerich and Paula left the laboratory. Amherst stayed behind to clean up any blood left on the table. The young apprentice still sat on duty at the desk. She hastily stood and curtsied when they passed.

The pair didn't speak on the walk to Emmerich's quarters. The guards outside the Royal Wing seemed surprised at seeing their sovereign return, bare-chested, with a small aerial and a woman, but they were trained well enough not to ask any questions. They saluted and opened the doors for him. Emmerich felt sure the story would run like wildfire through the barracks. Soldiers were the worst sort of gossips, after all.

Paula and Emmerich entered the chilled, dark parlor of his chambers. The banked fire glowed a dull red.

"I'll stir up the fire," she whispered.

"Good idea," he replied in an equally low tone. "Niall will probably want the warmth."

Soon, Paula had a fire going in the hearth and Emmerich came to sit in front of it with Niall in his lap. Paula settled down next to him.

"You don't think he'll get an infection?" asked Emmerich.

"I don't believe so."

"And all the kicking. You don't think he's bleeding on the inside?"

"It's possible, certainly. That takes time to show, however. Really, Your Majesty, we've done all we can."

They remained quiet for a few moments longer and watched Niall sleep. A sudden yawn overtook Emmerich.

"Excuse me," he said, blinking. "I must be more tired than I thought."

"Your Majesty could use the sleep. I'll leave you to rest." She stood.

"Wait." Emmerich laid the aerial before the fire and stood. "I'll show you those quarters I told you about." He picked up a lamp and lit the wick.

"Oh, no, that's not necessary—"

"I insist. It really is just across the hall." Without waiting for her to protest more, he crossed the room and opened the door. "You know it's a capital offense to disobey the King."

She smiled. "Well, then, sire, I suppose I have

no choice."

Together, they crossed the hall to another door. Opening it revealed a lavishly appointed sitting room. Bright red couch and chairs, tapestries embroidered with pastoral and garden scenes rendered in jewel tones, elegant cherry wood furniture, and an alabaster fireplace.

"Your Majesty," gasped Paula. "These are a queen's quarters."

"No, they're not. I don't have a queen. These are just empty rooms that the servants have to clean every few days."

"I don't think this would be proper. Surely there's another room nearby I can stay in."

"There is, but you won't be close enough if there's an emergency. I insist, Healer Paula, at least until Niall is recovered."

"Starting tonight?"

"Yes, of course. I understand if you need to return to your quarters for a few things."

"I suppose I could sleep on the couch, sire."

"The couch? There's a perfectly good bed in

there. I should know. I chose it."

If anything, that appeared to distress Paula even more. She played with a lock of hair.

"Please, Healer Paula," Emmerich said. "I want to make sure that Niall gets the best care he can."

She dropped her hand. "I'll be happy to stay here, Your Majesty. I would like to get a few things from my room."

Emmerich smiled. "I'll let the guards know. Unless there's more for you to protest, I need to go to bed. I'll leave the lamp with you."

"Of course, Your Majesty." She curtsied.

Emmerich left her, making a quick stop to let the guards know to allow Healer Paula through, and then returned to his rooms. Showing Paula the room reminded him of when the Queen's Quarters were completed.

"I'm going to show these to her tonight, after dinner." Emmerich smiled at Lord Bruin. A fire crackled behind him in the alabaster fireplace. "What do you think?"

Lord Bruin shrugged. "I don't know why His

Majesty is turning to me for advice. I know little of what women like in terms of decor and even less what Lady Clara prefers."

"I would ask General Asher. He has a sister, you know, and has more experience than either of us. However, he's out of the city, so I only have you. Do you think she'll like it?"

He smiled. "I think the Lady Seer will be pleased at your thoughtfulness. Your Majesty still has to propose, correct?"

"I'm sure she'll say yes. And if she tries to turn down the dinner invitation, do your best to persuade her."

"Yes, Your Majesty."

Emmerich dropped onto the couch and stretched his legs out.

"Do you love me?" he asked Clara. The dinner table stood between them but, with her hand on the door, it felt like a chasm.

"Yes."

"That isn't enough."

"No." She opened the door and walked out.

Over and over, Emmerich examined that conversation in his mind and tried to understand where he went wrong, why she had said no. Clara told him she needed to know who she was, if she really did have Tier blood in her like the diplomats had insinuated. Couldn't she have stayed and used the resources he supplied? Or was there more to it?

Closing his eyes, he tried to form the image of her in his arms. Instead of soothing him, it only made his heart ache. By the fire, Niall whimpered.

Paula picked up the lamp and used it to light the other lamps in the parlor. The room felt chilled, so she lit a fire in the alabaster fireplace. Though no one had ever used these rooms, a supply of firewood sat in a basket beside the hearth.

It felt so surreal and wrong. The richness of the fabrics and expensive materials of the furniture and decorations shouted at Paula that she didn't belong.

She fled. With long strides, she left the Royal Wing and didn't slow down until she was on the path to the Healing House. Beside a tall statue of a nymph, Paula stopped to catch her breath.

The cold night air cooled the sweat on her brow and she shivered.

People were going to get the wrong idea once word began to spread that she was staying in the Queen's Quarters. But the Master Healer, Master Valerian, was a sensible man. If Paula told him she was staying there to tend to a sick aerial, he would believe her and wouldn't tolerate any gossip within hearing.

But he couldn't control everyone.

She continued to the Healing House and scolded herself. Here was an ill aerial nestling who needed her help and she was worried about her reputation.

Chapter Ten

Bran ran down the back hall. His legs burned as he raced, the wooden floor echoing with each footfall. He clutched a message in his sweaty hand.

He rounded a corner, keeping tight to it so he could go around as quickly as he could. A dark shape burst forward from the shadows and slammed into his gut. As he bent, the air rushed out of him in a whoosh and grunt. He flipped over the object and fell hard on the floor, his head bouncing once.

Stars flooded his eyes as pain swamped him. Distant laughter followed by running footsteps. Then the hallway covered over with a blackness too dark to be normal sleep.

Bran awoke. His sheet stuck to his sweaty chest and the blanket, kicked off the bed, pooled on the floor. Lying back, he stared up into the darkness while he gulped in the cool air.

After a few moments, he sat up and sought

out the familiar glow of the candle clock. Soon, the other boys would get up for their duties. Bran didn't need to be awake for a while yet.

He pressed his hand to the back of his head. He felt no pain. No blood. No lump. Nothing to suggest that he had taken a fall. Had it just been a nightmare? It had felt so real.

A twinge went through his head, followed by a wave of fatigue, as if he really had run down a hallway. He lay back down, wondering if he could fall asleep after such a nightmare. However, the moment he closed his eyes, he began to dream again.

Chapter Eleven

Clara stood at the crest of a mountain pass. Far below, the road wound among the trees and Clara caught a glimpse of sun reflecting off a creek. She studied the valley for whispers of smoke or any other signs of habitation. It had been a day since she left Jarrett and, despite her bravado, her fear of danger had been steadily growing.

Traveling alone had been a lot of fun at first. The feeling of solitude was like a warm bath and she reveled in it. She didn't have to keep defending or explaining her choices. She could just be herself, riding down a road. But, like a bath, it grew cold.

Once, while Emmerich had still been a general, Clara slipped away from her bodyguards to go on a ride by herself. She galloped straight into a band of bandits. If Emmerich hadn't arrived in time, they would have raped her and held her for ransom, something that kept running through her mind now that the joy of solitude had left her.

Emmerich had been so upset that day, more angry than she had ever seen him. Jarrett was going to be in a lot of trouble, possibly losing his rank at best or jailed at worst. And it was her fault.

"It was the best choice," she reminded herself aloud. "Emmerich needs Jarrett."

Something large and dark moved down below in the valley, crossing the creek to vanish back into the forest. She scowled and wondered if a mountain bear newly awakened from his winter sleep wandered the valley. At this time of year, they were hungry and dangerous and more prone to attack people.

On the roadside was a small stone shrine. Inside it stood a white figurine of the Mother and Child. The Mother, the Lady of Sky and Earth, and her Son, the Maker of the world, were worshipped in Lorst. Clara had been raised to have a strong devotion to them.

The shrine's roof was rubbed smooth from sun and rain. Most of the features of the figurine had been worn away. Bright yellow trout-lily grew at the base of the pillar.

She dismounted and walked over to the shrine. Clasping her hands, she bowed her head to recite the familiar prayer of salutation. Cold wind blew and she pulled her cloak tighter. She raised her head. Clouds slipped by overhead and cast long shadows over the surrounding peaks and valley.

She mounted her pony, grimacing at the ache in her legs: riding bareback astride was far more difficult than she had imagined.

From her belt pouch, she drew the folded map she had taken from Jarrett's bags. Clara studied the winding road she knew she was on, tracing it with a finger to Bluebell. She refolded the map, tucked it away, and rode down into the valley.

Soon, large cold drops of rain pelted down. Pulling up her hood, she carried on northward as daylight darkened into a blue and grey wash. A round, orange and red light blossomed in the distance.

For a moment, her heart leapt with hope that there were other travelers or a settlement in the valley close at hand. That is, until she remembered the old folks of her village warning her and the other children about mountain pixies.

The devils appeared whenever it grew dark or stormy. They used their magic to create the illusion of firelight to lead travelers off the road into ravines. Some stories claimed that the pixies then ate the travelers, whether they were still alive or not.

She bent her head and rode onward.

As she passed the flickering light, it grew brighter and stronger. Her heart swelled and she was filled with the desire to pull off the road. She gripped the reins tighter. Trusting the pony to find the right footing in the dim light, she locked her eyes on the mane and ignored the allure of the light. After a few more steps, she dared to look back. The glimmer disappeared.

She squinted against the dark and the rain, trying to find shelter. A steep hill rose to her left. Part of the hill was darker than the rest and could be the mouth of a cave.

She remembered the shadow she saw earlier in the day, what could have been a mountain bear, and worried. However, if she stayed out, she risked illness. And if mountain pixies roamed the area, then Mother only knew what else.

Clara turned left and picked a careful way under dripping branches. The ground began to incline sharply and she wished for magic. Then, she could call up some sort of light to help see the path ahead. Her pony snorted and whinnied as its feet slid. Clara dismounted and began to pull the two mounts behind her, using rocks and trees for leverage.

She struggled up the rocky hill, with tree roots sticking out of the ground, until her lungs burned and legs threatened to cramp. Just as she started to wonder if she imagined the cave, the ground leveled out.

She straightened with a groan. Ahead of her, the dark mouth of the cave loomed. Clara listened. She only heard the patter of rain and the noise of night birds squawking.

After pulling the horse and mule onto the barely level scrap of ground in front of the cave, she took a bundle of torches wrapped in oilcloth from a pack.

She stepped just inside the mouth. Something skittered away. Using flint and tinder from her belt pouch, she lit the torch. Old leaves lay scattered across the stone floor. Above, stalactites hung down like fangs. Drawing Jarret's long dagger, she crept deeper inside.

The splatter of rain outside echoed through the dry cave. Clara strained her ears to hear over it.

A skittering sound passed her left. She jerked around in time to see the tail of a mouse disappear behind a rock. Clara chuckled at herself and started forward again when a bit of red caught her attention.

Holding the torch up high, she stepped closer to the wall. The dancing flames of the torch revealed pictures drawn with red. Stick figures of men with spears chased bears and deer in a wave of color. Hanging above them was a stick figure wearing the outline of a dress.

This image was bigger than the rest and held its arms out, as if hovering over the hunters below.

Perhaps it was made by children a long time ago? Clara rubbed one of the figures but the clay didn't come off.

Leaving the mystery image, she moved further into the cave. The shadows were deep and dark. She thrust her torch toward all the crevices and crannies, trying to banish the dark, until she reached the back of the cave.

From the back of the cave to the mouth, Clara guessed it to be about thirty yards. Something moved to her right and she whirled on it, dagger held high.

A cave cricket, about the size of her hand, crawled under a stone.

She found no other creatures beside the mouse and the cricket (which would probably be the mouse's supper). No scat or chewed bones or remnants of fires to suggest a resident. It would be safe enough to bed down for the night. Protective sigils stamped onto the bags should keep the mouse out of the stores.

Soon, a fire crackled in a ring of rocks near the mouth and the wet gear lay spread out near it on one side to dry. She stirred a small pot of beans and salted pork over the fire.

The solitude felt odd. She'd never been on her own before, not like this. There had always been someone around, even if only servants. She thought, suddenly, of Gavin and wondered how many nights he had spent alone by the fire as Emmerich's spy.

Emmerich.

She wondered what he was doing. She

wondered if Jarrett had found a good place to hole up for the night or perhaps the storm was isolated only to this valley. She wondered if she would find what she sought.

Outside, the blue-grey gloom darkened into true night. The rain storm began to ease and slivers of moonlight slipped through tears in the clouds.

The cave filled with warmth and light and the rank smell of wet wool, leather, and unwashed hair. After supper, Clara moved some of the gear around to even out the drying process.

Sitting back against a rock, she stared out into the dark. Having no one else to keep watch at night made sleep difficult. Several nights of half sleep tugged on her and the warmth of the fire made it hard to resist. Soon, she lapsed into a doze.

What woke her, Clara couldn't say. The fire had burned down to embers and a chill had settled in. The rain had stopped. Water dripped from leaves and stone. She stirred the fire and added more of the dry wood she had found littering the cave floor. The flames ate at the wood and she watched the darkness beyond the cave.

At first, she saw only darkness until her eyes adjusted. Something heavy shifted in the woods below the cave. Her shoulders tensed. She stared into the darkness, trying to make out movement, and heard the gritty roll of rocks under something large. Clara stood. Silence undercut the noise of rain. Something chuffed and growled. She drew the long dagger even as she took a step back.

A roar split the night and something big and black with a humped back hurtled across the level space to the cave's mouth. It burst into the light, as big as a nightmare. Screaming, she slashed upward at its white eyes. A paw half as large as a wagon wheel lashed out to catch her in the shoulder. She fell next to the fire with a cry, the stony ground jarring her.

The creature reared back and roared. Long,

matted brown hair covered a lean body. On its back legs, it stood only slightly taller than a mountain bear, at around eight or more feet. Its head domed in an onion-like shape with bulging eyes and heavy lower jaw.

Clara rolled, grabbed a long, burning branch from the fire, and stood.

The creature came back down on all four legs. Red-tipped spines, like those of a porcupine, ran along its back.

She shoved the burning wood up toward its face.

The creature jerked back and the dome opened into a virulent orange fan. The upper jaw was naked bone. It screeched at her. Clara bellowed in reply and lunged forward, trying to shove the branch into its gaping mouth.

The beast screamed in pain and ran away, kicking up stones as it went.

It smashed through the woods below, the sound growing more distant until the rain swallowed it. Slowly, the night birds and crickets started up again.

Groaning, Clara dropped the wood back into the fire and clutched her left shoulder. Pain throbbed through it but, when she drew her hand away, there was no blood. She was only bruised from meeting the ground.

She dug through the packs with one hand, keeping the bad arm pressed against her side, and found ingredients for a yarrow poultice. She caught rain water in a tin pan and poured in the powder, stirring it into a paste, which she then warmed over the fire.

As she tried to get out of the tunic and shirt, she gasped when a wrong move jarred her shoulder. She swallowed back a whimper as she applied the hot paste to her shoulder and then clumsily wrapped it.

The heat worked into the shoulder and eased the pain to something bearable. As it did, a hysterical giggle bubbled up.

"I just fought off one of Marduk's horrors," she said to herself. "Jarrett and Emmerich would have a fit if they knew." She laughed until tears came to her eyes.

Somewhere in the forest, another roar echoed. The laughter died in her throat. There would be no more sleep that night.

Despite the dull throb in her shoulder, Clara traveled hard the next day. Her body stayed on high alert as she hurried to leave the valley, afraid the thing would follow her. Every crackle of underbrush, every breeze through the limbs of trees, heralded the return of the creature.

She both cursed herself for not listening to Jarrett regarding the dangers of traveling alone and reassured herself that she could do this. According to the map, there was a town in the next valley and, surely, it would be safe there. All she needed to do was keep going.

That night, she camped by a small creek crossing the road as it rose toward the pass. Clara peeled back the dressing. A deep blue and purple bruise blotched her shoulder. Gritting her teeth, she lifted her arm. Pain arched through her and brought tears to her eyes. She made another poultice and spread it on. The muscles were grateful for the warmth of the paste and the security of the bandage.

A pale sickle of a moon rose over the mountains. She felt exhausted from lack of sleep and from pain but Clara didn't collapse into her pallet.

She fed slivers of wood to the fire and listened to the night sounds of the mountain forest rising up in a cacophony of frogs and crickets, with the occasional owl hoot cutting through it. Every now and again, a patch of night sounds would go quiet, only to start up again seconds later. Clouds passed over the moon and stars in speeding skiffs.

After a time, the warm fire and her own fatigue lulled Clara into a doze. She started to give thought to stretching out when the breeze changed direction.

The pony and mule screamed, yanking on

their restraints. Clara sat upright just as a loud crash broke through the night. She stumbled to her feet and faced the forest as the monster lumbered out of the woods.

It hesitated at seeing the fire, as if it remembered last night's fight. Clara drew the long dagger and balanced on the balls of her feet. She wished she had a mace or crossbow. She'd never used either of them but she saw the damage they could wreck on the practice fields.

Wide, wet nostrils flared as it took in her scent. The spikes along its back ended in wicked points. Its oily, brown fur caught the light and the white eyes stared through her from the rounded head. The skin split back to create the bright orange fan framing its slimy, narrow head. Fangs curved over the jaws.

It roared and surged towards her. Clara screamed and met the creature, ducking under its outstretched paw, and slashed at the exposed head.

The knife bit into flesh. A smell like rotten

fruit spilled over her. She gagged. The creature screamed and dropped back a few steps.

Clara lunged again for the chest. It danced out of the way and clawed at her. The claws caught her clothes, ripping them and cutting into her chest. Crying out, she jerked back and then ran forward. The creature, surprised at the move, reared on its hind legs, blotting the stars from the sky.

She buried the sharp knife into its belly and ripped downward in a curve. Ropey, white and pink intestines spilled out.

It screeched and fell to the side. Blood and entrails spilled into the gritty road.

The creature scrambled to get back on its feet. Clara buried the knife into its neck, just behind the fleshy fan. It dropped and she yanked the knife out. Black blood poured from the wound as it jerked and bucked in its death throes. She gagged at the reek of broken bowel. Clara forced herself toward its head and the creature snapped and clawed at her.

She dodged the blows and shoved the long dagger into its eye. The monster went still and Clara, covered in gore, stumbled back and onto her knees.

Gradually, she noticed silence around her. Slowly, like children afraid to be caught at mischief, the crickets and frogs started up again. In moments, it was a noisy, chilly spring night again.

A sense of victory mingled with disgust swept through her. Her skin itched for a bath even while she wanted to do a dance at having won.

"You should have stayed away," she whispered.

With trembling hands, Clara retrieved her dagger.

Thankfully, the pony and mule did not break free in their panic. They didn't like the smell of the monster on her and tried to back away when she came near the bags laid out beside them.

Ignoring them, Clara cleaned her dagger before moving on to the cuts. They were not deep, though they stained her trousers in blood. She cleaned them and pressed powdered peppers and goldenseal into them before binding them as best she could. She had no spare tunic or shirt, so she fetched an undergown. Clara cut the skirt away to make a shirt and slowly pulled that on.

By the time she finished, her mouth felt dry, sweat prickled her brow, and fatigue crushed upon her. She started to reach for a water skin but never made it. The ground rushed up to meet her as darkness spilled over her.

Chapter Twelve

The little aerial watched Emmerich move around his sitting room the next morning, filling him with feelings of curiosity and gratitude.

Emmerich talked to the creature, telling him what he planned to do for the day. He even shared some of his breakfast. Niall ignored the eggs and gobbled the bacon with happy noises of contentment.

When his secretary arrived, the man blanched at the sight of Niall. "Is it safe to have that here, Your Majesty?" he asked.

Emmerich scoffed. "Of course, Wilbur. He's only a nestling, after all. Men killed his mother and injured him. I'm drafting an edict now about the treatment of aerials. Put on the agenda for the Council meeting the proposal for a new law. This edict will only be temporary as I know the Council will want to debate the law to death." He dipped his pen in the inkwell.

"Yes, Your Majesty." Wilbur made the note.

"Also, have the chambers across the hall made ready. Fresh linens on the bed and all that."

The secretary's face lit up. "Is there to be a wedding, sire?"

"What?" He stopped writing. "No. The healer watching over Niall will be staying in those rooms."

"Niall, Your Majesty?"

"Well, I had to name the aerial, now didn't I?" He returned to writing.

"Is it appropriate, having this healer stay there?"

"Don't be daft. Where else is she going to stay? Take the revised agenda to the Council members while I finish this edict."

"Yes, Your Majesty."

Emmerich absorbed himself in the writing. He despised the florid style in vogue at the Court. Reading King Tristan's edicts felt like the vocabulary exercises his grandmother put him through when he was a boy. His read like army camp reports and new assignments. Terse, to the point, and in language so simple, a child could understand it.

Something prodded his leg. Emmerich's eyes met Niall's. The nestling had moved from his makeshift bed by the fire and walked over to Emmerich, his splinted wing bound to his body. Niall chirped at him and bumped his leg with his head.

"You want me to hold you?" he asked.

A warm feeling swept through him. Emmerich bent down and scooped Niall up, cradling him on his lap while he continued writing. Niall sighed and contentment swaddled them both. Emmerich relaxed.

He finished the edict and sprinkled a pinch of sand over it to help the ink dry. Someone knocked at the door.

"Enter," he called.

Healer Paula and Master Amherst entered. They made obeisance.

"How is our patient today, Your Majesty?" asked Healer Paula.

"Awake, hungry, and very interested in the world around him." He stood and pushed the papers aside to set Niall on the table. "Come and see for yourself."

While Paula and Amherst inspected Niall, Emmerich watched from a distance. Fear threaded through Niall, and Emmerich projected soothing thoughts as best he could. It was difficult for him to concentrate, with the rest of the day waiting for him to attend to it, but Niall settled and subjected to the inspection.

"He is not very sore in the sites of bruising," Paula said. "He's healing quickly, like we thought he would."

"Have you spoken to the Master Healer about your change in duties?" Emmerich asked.

"I have and he has deferred to Your Majesty's wishes."

"Good." Another knock on the door. "Enter," Emmerich called.

The Captain of the City Guard, Tarsus, stepped inside. "You wanted me to report if we found the remains, Your Majesty."

"Let us speak outside." Emmerich crossed the room and went into the hall. "I don't want Niall, the nestling, to hear this."

Captain Tarsus gave him a strange look as he closed the door. "Your Majesty?"

"The aerial understands what is happening around him, Captain. Would you discuss the death of a parent in front of the child?"

"Uh, no, sire."

"What have you found?"

"There were reports of a large gathering of aerials in the Low Quarters. It seemed the best place to start. When we arrived, the aerials were gathered around the remains of one of their own that was beaten so badly that if I hadn't known I was searching for an aerial, I wouldn't have known what it was. The aerials allowed us to inspect the remains."

"Any idea who did this?"

"No, sire, we will continue investigating."

"Good. I have an edict I will want posted and

read around the city."

"Yes, sire."

"What became of the remains?"

"That's actually one of the stranger parts, Your Majesty. Two of the aerials carried them away. Perhaps they have their own burial grounds, like from the stories of oliphants."

"Hm."

They re-entered the room and Emmerich went to the table to fetch the edict. The moment he laid his eyes on the aerial, he thought about his dead mother.

Niall's head jerked up and focused on him. Sorrow welled up within Emmerich as Niall threw up his head and keened. The sound filled the room and brought to mind every sorrow and pain Emmerich endured. A sob shuddered through him and he leaned heavily against the table. Paula and Amherst backed away.

When Niall stopped, Emmerich picked him up and held him. "The edict is on the table, Tarsus," he said, his voice thick and rough.

"Yes, sire." Tarsus took the paper and rolled it. "I will report later, sire."

In the silence after Tarsus's departure, Emmerich cradled the nestling and hummed. Paula quietly cried, whispering about the "awful sound". Amherst wrapped an arm around her shoulders.

Finally, Emmerich cleared his throat and said, "I'm having fresh linens and things put in the quarters across the hall, Healer Paula."

She wiped her face with her hands. "Thank you, Your Majesty."

"Is there anything else?"

"There's some discoloration around the broken wing," Master Amherst said, "but I think that's part of the healing process. Lord Bruin will be back this afternoon. I will consult with him then."

"Once you've done that, tell him I wish to see him."

"Yes, Your Majesty."

"You are all dismissed."

They left and Emmerich stroked Niall on the head before walking into his bed chamber and to the window. In the courtyard below, a company of soldiers stood in neat rows in front of a whipping post set into the stone on the far edge of the courtyard.

Two soldiers chained a man to the post. One of them ripped open the back of the man's tunic. The pair retreated and a third man began cracking a whip over the restrained man's back in rhythmic lashes.

He couldn't hear from this distance but Emmerich could easily imagine a lieutenant counting off each lash. The healers would be busy today.

Emmerich left the window for a trunk pushed against a far wall. Scratched and patched, it had served him ever since he first became an officer. He opened it and began sifting through the contents to find something he could use as a sling.

A corner of white caught his eye. He pulled it

out. It was a handkerchief. He felt a hard piece of oval in the folds. Unfolding it revealed an oval medal with the image of a winged angel carrying a sword stamped into it. He brushed a thumb over it.

Worry puckered Clara's forehead as she came to stand close to him, holding her slate. She eyed his armor as if it could bite her. It took only a heartbeat for him to remember that the slavers who held her probably also wore armor.

"I'm told the ladies find this equipage dashing," he said. "What do you think?" He smiled, trying to put her at ease.

She avoided his eyes. Gently, with his spike-encrusted hand, he took her chin and tilted her head back.

"Never fear me," he said. He wanted to kiss the worry from her brow. Carefully, he withdrew his hand and she gave him the medal wrapped in white cloth as a wish for good luck.

Emmerich folded the cloth around the medal as he returned to the present moment. He tucked it into his small belt pouch.

Reaching into the trunk, he found a long piece of red cloth. He would have never purchased such a thing for himself. Perhaps it was meant as a gift for a woman and he moved on before he could bestow it. It would do nicely.

People stared, of course. It wasn't every day that Emmerich, King of Lorst and Hero of the Rebel War, walked around with a small aerial riding in a red sling across his chest.

When he entered the Council Chamber, the members stood from their places around the rectangular table and gawked at the small emerald head poking out.

"My lords," Emmerich said, pretending nothing strange was happening. He fought to keep a smile off his face.

He sat, lifted the sling from around his neck and shoulder, and set it onto the table. Niall, his splinted wing pressed against him, surveyed the members of the table with obvious curiosity. He chirruped and began walking down the center of the table, stopping here and there to sniff at an inkwell or the contents of a goblet. Emmerich picked up a small stack of papers and tapped them into a neat pile.

"I hope all of you received the addendum to our agenda today," he said.

"Yes, Your Majesty," said Lord Barkeley, who watched the aerial as if he expected it to suddenly take a chunk out of someone.

"Very good. We shall discuss that first."

"Your Majesty," said the representative of the Merchant Class, a melancholic fellow by the name of Frederick. For once, a smile lit up his features. He scratched one of Niall's eye ridges. "Does this little one have a name?"

"I call him Niall. He is the reason I suggested today's addendum." Emmerich launched into a description of the previous night's events. Whether or not to include the visions had been something he gave much thought to, but in the end decided they were the crux of the story and proof that these creatures were very intelligent.

Frederick smiled. "Quite extraordinary, sire. And horrible, for someone to deliberately harm such beautiful creatures."

"Not wholly surprising," spoke up another Council member. "They are one of Marduk's creations."

"According to Lady Clara," Emmerich said, watching Niall make his way back to him, "they were born of the only sane thought the elemental spirits had left within them."

The elemental spirits Marduk had used in his experiments had long gone insane from their captivity. The aerials were the only creatures Marduk made that weren't monstrous.

Emmerich continued, "And the assistance they provided at the Battle Outside the Walls should dismiss any doubt about their intentions."

"Sadly, sire," spoke up a thickset woman near him, "many citizens feel that the story is mere propaganda. A story to make them accept these creatures' existence."

"Then we have to fight against that." He patted Niall as he settled into the sling with a sigh. "I've already issued a temporary edict that protects the aerials. I want a permanent law set into place."

Lord Barkeley said, "Sire, it is your royal prerogative to set forth edicts and no one will challenge that, but I feel that you have acted hastily."

Emmerich tensed. "And why do you say that, Lord Barkeley?"

"His Majesty stated that he received images in his mind about what happened to this nestling and things were found just as you saw them. Isn't it possible, then, that the adults could be manipulating us? That they fooled the soldiers at the battle into thinking they saved them as part of a larger plot? Perhaps they murdered the female and conjured this whole thing."

"I did not imagine a group of soldiers abusing a nestling."

"No one suggested that, Your Majesty. Our

concern lies with the events before then."

Several of the Council members, even Frederick, began eyeing the aerial with suspicion. Niall whined and scooted closer to Emmerich, staring at Barkeley. Emmerich held the nestling close and felt it tremble against his fingers.

"We should study the aerials," Barkeley continued, "before issuing laws regarding them. May I make a move to vote on this, Your Majesty?"

Emmerich detested all the voting and discussions. If this was a military campaign and these his captains, he would be in full rights to call Barkeley an idiot and put forth his orders.

And to make matters worse, Barkeley's words carried all the smoothness and comfort of logic and reason, with a dash of fear mixed in.

"I understand your concern," Emmerich said. "However, the aerials have been only kind to us and do not deserve the brutality that has been shown to them. Lord Bruin has felt no need to voice concerns and he is an expert on the aerial situation." *And, of course, he isn't here to defend my view.* "And do you truly believe that General Asher is so easily fooled? Or myself?"

"No, Your Majesty, not normally. These are not normal creatures. And while Lord Bruin is very skilled and wise, if these creatures have the power to manipulate the memory of an entire army, could they not also fool a wizard?"

"You're assuming that they did manipulate an entire army."

He smiled. "I am merely making the suggestion to support my idea that we are moving too quickly to make a law. More time must be given to examine the facts." His eyes flicked to Niall, who shrunk away back to Emmerich. "Your nestling is a charming creature, Your Majesty, but we cannot base an entire species from one example that is not even fully grown."

Emmerich could tell by the expressions of the nine other Council members that some agreed, others didn't, and still others had not made up their minds or were perhaps hiding their positions. "Very well. Let us vote on this. All those in favor of Lord Barkeley's suggestion, raise your hand."

One by one, hands raised into the air. Emmerich's secretary counted them and noted the number.

"All opposed?"

Fewer hands rose. Emmerich felt a sinking sensation in his gut.

"And, undecided."

A couple of hands rose. It was too few. Emmerich didn't even need to check his secretary's notation but he did anyway.

"Very well," he said. "We will wait on this issue. Until further notice, though, my edict stands." An edict that could be challenged legally and could be dismissed upon his death. However, Emmerich had no plans to die just yet. "What is next on the docket for today?"

Niall filtered worried emotions through

Emmerich's mind as he returned to his rooms that afternoon. Not that surprising, since the Council meeting went wrong after losing a vote on merchant taxes. He and Frederick voted against the measure to raise taxes (Emmerich still remembered his father's agony over not being able to enter large cities because of the taxes), as well as a couple of other Guild leaders. They lost in the end. And then the Council tried to broach the subject of his unmarried state.

The Tieran diplomat had renewed his offer of King Precene's daughter's hand. This time, it came with the insinuation that the Tieran government felt offended that Emmerich hadn't at least considered it.

He'd hoped to put off the question of marriage until Clara's return. However, he needed a lasting peace between their two governments. Not for the first time, the Council reminded him that a marriage was potentially the only way.

Niall whined and Emmerich patted him,

opening the door to his chambers. "It's all right, little one. Bruin. About damn time."

Lord Bruin closed the book he was reading and stood. He wore the nondescript clothing of a dock worker: dark grey tunic and black trousers. The tunic was dirty and patched. His boots were scuffed. Dark circles smudged the skin under his eyes. Even looking like this, he was allowed, by Emmerich's order, to enter the chambers at any time of the day or night.

"I see the stories are true, Your Majesty. I did not believe them at first."

Emmerich closed the door. "What stories?"

"That you carried an aerial around as if you were its mother." He came closer to inspect Niall, who chirruped at him in a way Emmerich now recognized as a greeting. "May I, Your Majesty?"

"Go ahead."

Bruin carefully lifted Niall out of his sling, taking care to avoid jarring the broken wing, and cradled him in his arms. "He's beautiful, sire."

"He is." Emmerich pulled the sling off and

tossed it onto a table. At the sideboard, he poured himself a small mug of ale. "Care for something to drink?"

"No, thank you, Your Majesty."

"And what is it that you have been up to in the city?"

"Tracking that foreigner who stirred up trouble that night on the docks."

"Did you find him?"

"No." He scratched under Niall's chin and the aerial's eyes half-closed. "And from what I've learned, he may have already left the city."

"I have the feeling that news isn't as good as I would like for it to be."

"I am afraid not. He may have left because he fulfilled his objective. The Low Quarters is rife with talk about the aerials being a danger and I'm afraid your edict has not helped matters."

Emmerich swore and took a swallow of ale. "Lord Barkeley may have been right that I acted in haste."

"Lord Barkeley will do anything to weaken

you in the Council chamber, Your Majesty. If you had said the aerials were a danger, he may have still swung the Council against you."

"I wish I could get rid of the man but I can't make people think I'll boot out anyone who disagrees with me. I will have to wait out his term and hope a more reasonable replacement is voted in."

"His family has many strong ties, Your Majesty. That seems very unlikely."

Emmerich scowled and set his mug down. He shucked off his crimson royal robe and tossed it over a chair. Underneath, he wore a simple blue tunic with dark blue trousers. Sitting in the nearest chair, he scrubbed his face. "What have you learned of the aerials?"

Bruin went to return to his seat on the couch. "Only that they are very intelligent and possess strong magic, which we already knew. I've found some people, when the aerials try to communicate with them, can hear words and there are those who only perceive images and emotions."

"I only receive the latter from Niall."

"Whether the level of communication is dependent on the aerial or the person or the situation in which they meet, I cannot say, sire."

"Aerials aren't a threat."

"Not as far as I can find."

"Is there a way to prove that?"

Bruin shook his head. "I can point to evidence but there are those who say that the aerials are biding their time."

"Barkeley suggests the aerials used magic to fool the army in the Battle Outside the Walls into believing they were attacked and the aerials rescued them."

"It's amazing what people find easier to believe. People would rather believe a disaster is imminent than that they're being protected by magical guardians. And Marduk's time here was very dark. It will be a long time before those memories dull."

"And no matter how beautiful the aerials are,

they are a reminder of Marduk."

"It is as you say, sire."

They lapsed into silence, each to their own thoughts. Bruin dangled his sleeve in front of Niall, who batted at it in the same way a cat would.

"Any new word on the creatures in the woods?" Emmerich asked.

"I have not had a chance to read the reports, Your Majesty."

"Do you think any of them did go north?"

"I am not sure. People are traveling through the passes by now. No doubt we will hear soon."

Emmerich rubbed his jaw. "The giant seems to have disappeared, for the lack of reports. I wonder what it all means."

"Nothing good, Your Majesty."

"Are you going to return to the Low Quarters?"

"After some rest. I still have some contacts to ferret out."

"Good. The sooner we put all this behind us,

the better."

"Yes, sire." He tilted his head slightly. "It would go the more quickly if Lady Clara were here."

Emmerich's heart clenched at the mention of her. "She'll return when she wants and not before."

"You could order her return."

"How long do you think it will take for Niall's wing to heal?"

"I'm not sure. I suppose you could check in a fortnight."

Emmerich stood. "I'll do that. If you have nothing else?"

"Yes, sire." Bruin set Niall down on the floor and bowed to the King.

After the wizard left, Niall attacked a ball of yarn one of the serving maids had left for him. Emmerich watched him but his thoughts were far away, resting on a stubborn girl with hazel eyes.

Paula dropped her pack onto the bed. The

few things she fetched last night had allowed her a change of clothes in the morning, but she needed to be prepared for an extended stay.

In their first years, new healers were expected to travel before settling into one place, partially for experience and partially to pick up new techniques. Her pack showed the wear of those years, with patches along the bottom and threadbare straps that would need replacing soon. And she would replace the straps, rather than get a whole new pack. Her fellow healers called her sentimental. Paula didn't care.

She looked around the bedroom. The bed itself, with a canopy, was a masterpiece carved from rosewood. Delicate vines trailing roses decorated the poles of the canopy. The foot and head boards were covered in a pomegranate and star motif.

Paula sat on the bed and felt the feather mattress give beneath her. The coverlet was scarlet, with ivy embroidered in gold.

She stood and wiped her hands on her dark

robe. The robe was linen and cotton. No embroidery decorated it and she had sewed it herself.

A large rosewood wardrobe sat against a wall. Like the bed, it was carved with a pomegranate and star motif. Curious, Paula crossed the room and opened the wardrobe.

Gowns of every hue imaginable hung in the wardrobe. Silks and velvets dyed varying shades of blue, green, and red hung beside chemises of muslin so fine, they felt as if made out of air.

Paula closed the wardrobe. Those clothes had to have been made for someone. Someone other than her. She'd stayed in a lot of different places during her time of travel but the sense of not belonging in that room was nearly overpowering.

She snatched up her pack and returned to the sitting room. The couch would be her bed and to hell with what the King thought.

Chapter Thirteen

"Bran!"

The young page sat upright, his heart lurching into a gallop. Late afternoon sunlight poured through the windows and he rubbed at the crusty sleep in his eyes. The Pagemaster, Thom, loomed over him. He held out a rolled and sealed message.

"Take this to the King. Immediately. He will be in his wing, seeing private audiences."

"Master?" Bran took it and stared at the missive.

"Wake up, boy." The Pagemaster bumped Bran's shoulder. "There is no one other than you. Blast it, I can't find Xavier, who is the page on duty." He waved a hand. "Just hurry."

Bran kicked off his covers and dropped the message onto the bed so he could yank on his clothes. His training wouldn't allow him to ask about the message. That didn't keep his curiosity quiet, however. Master Thom left the boy running hands through his hair to pull it into order.

Scooping up the sealed missive, he ran out of the dormitory, the path to the King's chambers a now familiar section of halls he could probably run blind. The sound of his boots on the slick floor echoed around him and the back of his neck prickled. Hadn't he dreamt this?

Movement at a corner. A black blur. Instinct took over and he danced out of the way, street reflexes snapping his arm out and grabbing the person. The would-be assailant overbalanced and he spilled to the floor. His head smacked the wood with a sharp crack. Bran stared, horrified, into the wide-eyed gaze of Xavier. Slowly, as blood pooled from the back of the boy's head, Xavier's eyes lost focus.

Bran took a step back. Then another. He bolted down the hall faster than was safe, his lungs gasping for air the entire way. He ran as if Death's hounds nipped at his heels.

He skidded to a halt at the doors to the Royal

Wing. A small crowd of supplicants stood in the hall, waiting their turns, and a few watched with curiosity the panting page with trembling legs. Trying to ignore them, he went on and the guards opened the doors for him.

His Majesty had a private study on the second floor, where he received audiences too sensitive for open court. Bran took the stairs two at a time. His legs screamed but he ignored the pain.

A man in blue and grey, the symbol of the Merchants' Guild embroidered on his tunic, was leaving the study when Bran arrived. Bran ducked around him.

King Emmerich stood behind his large oak desk, flipping through a heavy book. A tiny aerial with a splinted wing and mangling a bone lay beside the desk on a cushion.

"Your Majesty," Bran panted, holding out the scroll. "Master Thom said this was urgent."

"It must be. Shouldn't you still be in bed?" He took the scroll. "Is there something wrong, Bran?"

The trembling in Bran's legs crawled up to shake his entire body as tears welled in his eyes. The aerial dropped his chew toy and mewed.

With a gasp, he said, "I killed Xavier."

Emmerich dropped the message and book onto the desk and knelt in front of Bran. He laid his hands on the page's shoulders. "Tell me what happened."

Through stuttering gasps and tears, it all tumbled out: the bullying, Xavier's distaste for him, and his own fateful dash down the hall. "I didn't mean to do it, sire. I didn't mean to."

"I'm sure you didn't."

Something bumped against his ankle. Bran gazed down into the eyes of the small aerial. It rubbed its head against his leg.

"That's Niall," the King said. "I think he wants to make you feel better. Why don't you sit down with him while I speak to the guard outside the door?"

"Yes, sire." Bran sat and let Niall crawl into his lap. The splinted wing draped over his leg. He scratched Niall on the neck as the King walked out of the room.

A few minutes later, he returned. "They've gone to find Xavier's body." Emmerich knelt on one knee next to Bran. "You know, lad, Xavier may not be dead. You might have just knocked him asleep."

"I've seen dead people in the Quarters before."

"Ah."

"And what makes it worse is I knew it was going to happen." He wiped his running nose on his sleeve.

"What do you mean?"

"I dreamed about it, sire. It was because of the dream that I slowed down before he grabbed me because I remembered the dream and what happened if-if he did get me. I died in the dream, sire."

Emmerich settled down onto the floor. "Let me see if I understand this. You had a dream of the future?"

"Yes, sire."

"Is this the first time or have there been others?"

"The first time, sire."

"Does anyone else in your family have this gift?"

"No, sire." As far as he knew, no one other than Lady Clara could do such a thing. The word 'gift' brought to mind the aerial in the garden and he gasped. "I think it was the aerial, sire."

"The aerial?"

"Yes, sire." Bran told him about that day, about Xavier and his friend teasing him and Master Thom's reprimand. He described his encounter with the aerial that blew into his face and told him to no longer be sad. "I heard the aerials are all magic. Do you think he gave me some of his magic?"

"I don't know, Bran. I will try to find out." The King patted him on the shoulder. "I have to read that message now. You stay right there."

"Yes, sire."

Bran reached out and picked up the bone Niall had dropped. He held it over Niall, who swiped at it. It reminded him of kittens he used to play with in the street. A small smile formed on his face as he dangled the bone, pulling it out of reach whenever Niall went for it.

"Shit," Emmerich spat.

Bran's head jerked up. "Sire?"

"Nothing to concern yourself with." He dropped the parchment onto the desk. His grey eyes, usually serious, became cold and calculating. It rather reminded Bran of some men coming out of taverns, shoulders hunched against a wind that wasn't blowing and the lump of weapons beneath their cloaks.

"Should I run an errand for you?" Bran asked. There had to be something he could do to help.

"No. You need to stay here." He left the room again.

Bran lowered his arm but Niall didn't go for the bone. Like him, the aerial stared after the King. Bran said, "I think something really bad has happened."

Niall chirped, as if to agree.

Chapter Fourteen

Clara awoke next to cold ashes. She stared at them and struggled to remember why she wouldn't bank a fire before going to bed. For that matter, why wasn't she on her pallet?

A rank scent and the caws of crows invaded her senses. Wrinkling her nose, she lifted her head. A large, rotting bulk lay across from her. Two crows pecked at it, one at the head and the other on the innards.

She shifted. Hot pain coursed through her body. The large black birds took off, scolding her.

The sight of the corpse brought the taste of remembered fear, sharp and coppery. With her good arm, she pushed herself onto her feet. Her joints ached and felt stiff. The sun hung toward the west, putting the day in the afternoon. How long had she slept?

She stumbled to the creek and pulled off her makeshift shirt. Clara craned her head until she could just make out the wound. The skin around it was mottled purple and green from bruising. Dried, red-black blood crusted the cuts themselves.

She didn't smell any infection or decay. She splashed cold water onto the wound and winced. A snort drew her attention to the side. Her pony and mule stood huddled under the tree to which she'd tethered them however long ago.

Using slow, deliberate movements, she ventured to the packs for her herb kit and a pot. It took time to gather water and start the fire again. The reek of the carcass was an ever-present background to her actions. The crows returned to their meal. She tried her best to ignore them.

After warming the water, Clara cleaned the wound and packed it with herbs. She bound it with the last of the clean bandages. Her body wanted to remain by the fire and recover. It was her nose that couldn't stand another moment so near the decaying corpse.

It took all her strength to pack up the

campsite. The pony didn't want to walk past the dead creature but she kicked him in the ribs. After that, he gave her no more trouble.

Chapter Fifteen

Master Thom swelled with rage.

Emmerich and the Pagemaster stood in Emmerich's study. He had left the boy in his sitting room with Niall and Asher. Emmerich needed to talk to Asher and have someone keep an eye on Bran in case the boy decided to run from what he had done.

For a brief moment, Asher had seemed slightly panicked at being left alone with a distraught child, but then Bran settled down to play with Niall. Emmerich left his general watching the boy with an almost tender expression.

Emmerich studied Master Thom with what he hoped was a blank face while he waited for the older man to master his emotions.

The missive Bran had carried to him sat on the desk. Its presence burned a hole into Emmerich's mind. He needed to deal with that but he forced himself to focus on the present situation.

"I demand that Bran be turned over to me this instant, Your Majesty," Thom said in a tone of forced calm. "This is the second page to die under my supervision and this time, I have a culprit. I cannot let this go unpunished."

"From Bran's account, Xavier tried to harm him and Bran, being a child of the streets, reacted in a defensive move. He did not mean to kill him."

"I have to inform Xavier's father, who is on the Council if I may so bold to remind His Majesty, that Xavier is dead. What shall I tell him about his killer?"

"There is no killer. It was an accident. That is what you will tell him."

"Your Majesty—"

"Master Thom." Emmerich hardened his voice into something quietly dangerous. He tired of people second guessing and arguing with him. "This was an accident. You will stand by that. You will also say that Bran has been expelled from the page program and you will find a replacement for him. If anyone asks you what became of Bran, you will tell them that after the punishment, he was no longer your concern. Do you understand?"

Thom was a veteran of the Court and had ridden out the usurper's reign. From his expression, Emmerich could tell the older man knew there was something to this. The question was, would he be willing to let it go?

"Yes, Your Majesty," Thom replied.

"Do you know where to find Bran's mother?"

"Yes, Your Majesty."

"Tell a guard so that she can be brought here immediately. Have her taken to the Academy. Now, you may go and inform Xavier's father."

"Yes, Your Majesty." He bowed and began to walk away.

"And Master Thom?"

Thom stopped. "Yes, Your Majesty."

"Which Council member is the father of Xavier?"

"Lord Barkeley, Your Majesty."

Dammit all to Hell. It would be him. He nodded. As soon as Master Thom closed the door behind him, Emmerich picked up the missive. Unrolling it, he read it for the eighth time.

Giant sighted in foothills. Believed to be going to Candor City.

City being evacuated. Am organizing local wizards and soldiers for a defense.

Man seen with giant. Possible wizard.

They may be going to Bertrand.

Malcolm, General of the Northern Armies

"Dammit all to Hell," Emmerich muttered. He left the study and returned to his sitting room just in time to see Lord Bruin take a seat beside Asher on the couch. Bran sat on the floor with Niall.

The three stood. Bran cradled Niall in his arms and the aerial wiggled, head stretching toward Emmerich.

"Bruin, two questions," he snapped. "Can an aerial give a human the power to see the future and can a wizard control a giant? Those two questions are not related."

Back in his customary robes and with a freshly washed face, Lord Bruin appeared ready for any challenge. However, the King's questions did provoke a puzzled crinkle in his brow. "For the aerial, Your Majesty, yes. It is very possible. Humans with magic must obey certain rules. That doesn't necessarily hold for creatures made of magic, like the aerials. Nearly anything is possible. As for the other question, the Academy refused to even acknowledge the existence of giants until recently. We only have folklore to go on. According to folklore, a giant can be summoned like any other being but not controlled. May I ask why these questions, sire?"

"If giants are real, Bruin, then I wonder how many other creatures of folklore are real."

"That's one of many questions, sire, that keep me from sleeping well at night."

Emmerich handed him General Malcom's missive. Asher read over Bruin's shoulder.

Leaving them to it, Emmerich knelt on one knee beside Niall and Bran.

He scratched the top of Niall's head and said, "Bran. I know you're frightened right now. Everything will be fine."

Bran's gaze dropped to the aerial in his arms. Emmerich felt the urge to hug the boy. Instead, he squeezed Bran's shoulder and stood.

"General Malcolm is a capable soldier," Asher said. "And not given to panic or wild assumptions. I'm sure he will clear Candor as much as he can before the giant arrives and be able to defend it. And if he believes, for whatever reason, that it's coming here, then we should take that seriously. I am curious as to where he got such an assumption. He must have been too busy for a fuller report."

Emmerich grunted. "Bruin, are all of your wizards accounted for? Do you have any idea who this could be?"

"I have men scattered through the kingdom, sire," Bruin replied, "and have received regular reports from everyone. I have no idea who this could possibly be."

Emmerich rolled that around in his mind for a moment. "Could it be an unknown wizard? One that's escaped notice?"

"It's possible." Bruin clasped his hands. "Wizards come into their power during childhood and it's easy to spot: objects moving on their own, items breaking during bouts of great emotion, that sort of thing. Originally, children like that were either apprenticed to a known wizard, taught by a family member of the same power, or, in worst cases, driven out of their villages. Marduk, during his reign, used enchanted suncatchers to discover both children and adults to have them brought here, either as students, teachers, or researchers. It's possible he missed one, though not likely."

"When I took over the Palace, a great many wanted all of the wizards exiled." Emmerich put his hands on his hips. "Only your vouching for the remaining wizards kept that from happening.

You said Marduk controlled you all because most of you are academics and scholars who wouldn't be willing or capable of hurting another person."

"I remember saying that, Your Majesty."

"There will be very grave consequences if this isn't a stranger after all or some pet pupil of Marduk's that went into hiding. People are frightened enough of magic as it is."

"I understand, sire."

Emmerich ran a hand through his hair. "Very well. Enough of that. We've a new development."

"One to do with aerials and this lad, I take it?"

He told the two men what had occurred in the last two candlemarks.

"I think," said Emmerich, "that an aerial gave him the gift of seeing the future. Bruin, I want you to train him."

"I will do my best, sire, Lady Clara is better equipped for that."

"We will make do."

Asher asked, "Sire, should I send someone to find her?" He took Malcolm's missive from Bruin.

"No. We will need everyone here to defend the city. Lord Bruin, take Bran and give him a suitable room in the Academy. His mother will be arriving at the Academy shortly. I want her told what has happened with her son. Also, gather the masters to formulate a defense of the city. I expect a report tomorrow morning. Asher, call a War Council." He gathered Niall into his arms. Bran, his eyes wide and afraid, stared up at him.

Bruin smiled and held out a hand to the boy. "Come. Let's get you settled."

Bran didn't take Bruin's hand. His face was still pale but he straightened his shoulders before saying, "I'm ready, my lord." He bowed to Emmerich. "Thank you, Your Majesty, for, um, everything."

"You're very welcome, Bran," Emmerich replied and watched the pair leave.

"Your Majesty," Asher said, "I was coming here anyway to report that the creatures are beginning to gather in one place just west of here."

"Do you think it's connected with the giant?"

"I think it's a distinct possibility, sire."

In that case, he didn't want Clara in Bertrand. The wizards hadn't been able to scry her, but perhaps she was safe. At least Jarrett guarded her. "Go and gather the Council. I want the meeting to begin within the candlemark."

"Yes, Your Majesty." He returned the missive and bowed.

Emmerich stood there for a short while, cradling Niall and musing over the latest developments. Where in all of this did the traitor fit? What if he didn't?

"I hate politics," he muttered. He rubbed the aerial's neck. "You can't come with me, Niall."

He left his room and knocked on the door across the hall. After a moment, Paula answered the door and curtsied. Behind her, a few new books were stacked on a table and a cloak had been tossed over a chair. It was nice to see this room finally used, even if it wasn't as he had hoped.

"I have business to attend to," he said. "I need you to watch Niall."

"Yes, Your Majesty." She took him from his arms. "Has he shown signs of pain, sire?"

"No, thankfully."

"I heard Your Majesty took him around in a sling."

"You heard correctly. But, where I go now, he cannot come."

An awkward pause stretched between them. Finally, Emmerich walked away. At the entrance to the Royal Wing he dismissed the crowd of supplicants before going to the War Council Chamber.

The War Council met in the regular Council Chamber. Servants had set a scale model of Bertrand on a table beside the round one where the War Council members would sit. While all of the regular Council members sat on the War Council, it held the additions of the Captain of the City Guard, the Captain of the Palace Guard, and General Asher, the head of Emmerich's army.

Emmerich arrived first. He walked over to the model. He'd had it commissioned when he took the throne, employing the best artisans. No matter how often he saw it, he still marveled at the craftsmanship and detail. He could even make out the figures on the lintels of the Cathedral's doors and see the twisting willow tree in the center of the Weaver's Market.

A scuff at the door drew his attention. Lord Barkeley, a silky blue cloak tossed over his shoulders, strode in. He glared at the world with red-rimmed eyes and he held himself with a stiffness that would have made a general proud.

Barkeley swept a bow to Emmerich and came to stand across from him on the other side of the model.

"My condolences for your loss, my lord," Emmerich said.

"His Majesty is too kind." His jaw flexed. "I am told the boy responsible has been expelled from the program?"

"He has." In Emmerich's mind, Xavier was the 'boy responsible'. If Bran hadn't had forewarning, Emmerich would be offering condolences to a poor woman from the Low Quarters.

"That is very good, Your Majesty. How else will he be punished?"

"That is still being decided."

"May I offer His Majesty a suggestion?"

"You may." Emmerich fought to keep his face straight.

"A good, long lashing and a fine, Your Majesty, and that is the least possibility."

"If the family had anything they could be fined. And if he was anyone other than a boy barely out of childhood, a lashing would be considered. However, with the situation as it is, neither is feasible. I think a severe depletion in income is punishment enough."

Fury and sorrow were barely concealed under Barkeley's expression. The moment balanced on a knife's edge as Emmerich watched him consider his next words. Finally, Barkeley bowed.

"My lord," Emmerich said, "perhaps you should be with your family during this time."

"Duty obliges me to be here, Your Majesty."

"I understand. However, I insist that you take time away from the Council, at least for a month."

Barkeley's face whitened. "Is that an order?"

"It is. When you return, you'll be able to focus better on Council matters."

More Council members entered, saving Emmerich from one tense situation and delivering him into another.

Once everyone had arrived, save for Bruin, and were seated, Emmerich informed them of what he had learned. He wasn't worried about Bruin's absence. The wizard would arrive soon and be able to slip into the conversation as if he'd been there all along. It was an odd talent Emmerich kept meaning to ask him about.

"I am open to suggestions," Emmerich said.

The Captain of the City Guard leaned forward. "We should evacuate."

"To where?" spat Lord Barkeley. "The North is no longer safe and there are no fortified cities further to the South."

"Candor is evacuating and that is supposed to be a city that cannot be breached."

"I breached it," Emmerich said, forcing a small smile. "We do have one advantage over Candor. We have the plains where the giant can be challenged."

"The plains? That is madness!"

Arguments broke out among them. Emmerich's eyes met Asher's and the two men shared a look. It was going to be a long night.

Lord Bruin took Bran to the Academy. To the young boy, the school's dark and mysterious buildings loomed out of the dark. Their footsteps echoed in the hallways and the shadows were thick enough for monsters to hide in.

He'd heard the King say he would be trained at the Academy. Did that mean he was no longer a page? And what about his mother? Would she be all right without his pay? He worried at his bottom lip with his teeth.

Lord Bruin took Bran to a small, empty parlor on the second floor. Two chairs faced each other across a table in front of a fireplace, and a couch with two other chairs stood grouped together in the center. Flickering lamps lit the room.

"Wait here," said the tall wizard. "Your mother will be here soon."

Bran sat in a nearby chair. Bruin closed the door behind him as he left.

How had this happened? If the aerial had given him this ability, what was it for? So far, it only seemed to cause trouble.

Bran wondered about the other students. Would he be bullied? When the Lady Seer everyone spoke of returned, would she teach him? Was she a nice person? He had never met her but he'd heard enough stories to know she was only person in the whole kingdom who could see the future.

No, that wasn't right. He could see the future

now, too. That thought made Bran gulp.

Despite how distressing all these questions were, they were better than the memory of Xavier's dead eyes.

He hadn't meant to kill the boy. He just reacted. But why would Xavier do something so stupid? The floor was hard and slick. All the new apprentices, Bran and Xavier included, spent an entire day, once, practicing running along the floors to keep them from hurting themselves. They knew how dangerous it was. Maybe if Bran had slowed down more when he reached the turn, things would have ended differently.

Miserable thoughts joined the questions buzzing in Bran's mind, despite trying to think of other things.

The door opened and he sat up. Instead of his mother, his friend Robert entered.

"Rob!" Bran cried, slipping out of the chair. "What are you doing here?"

"I saw you come in." Rob wore a new uniform and someone had taken a comb to his red hair.

"What are you doing here? Did they reassign you?"

Bran felt his face grow cold. "I did something bad, Rob."

"What did you do?"

Bran didn't want to tell his friend but he also knew that gossip flew fast and thick in the Palace. If he didn't tell his friend now, he was going to learn, eventually. So, Bran told the whole story from the aerial on to the present moment.

"Wow," Robert whispered. "That is bad."

Bran shrugged, feeling miserable and tired.

"But, hey!" His friend gestured around him. "At least you're here and not in the dungeon. You and I can see each other again."

"The King says I need training and you have your duties."

"Yes, but we'll still see each other." Robert thrust a thumb over his shoulder, pointing behind him. "Bran, I have to go. They've got a matron that minds us and she's going to notice soon that I'm not in bed now that my shift is up. We'll talk later."

"All right."

Bran watched his friend leave and tried to feel happy that he would see Robert again. It didn't feel right to be happy.

The door opened again and his mother, in her stained, pale blue dress, rushed inside.

"Ma!" he cried, holding out his arms.

She held him tight. "Oh, my sweet boy. Are you all right?" She pulled away. "Did you get hurt?"

"No."

"They told me what happened. Is the family going to claim Blood?"

Bran's eyes widened. Claiming Blood came from when feuds were more common. If someone killed another person, the victim's family could claim Blood. That meant they could kill the guilty person. The family of the guilty person couldn't do anything and could be punished if they tried. That way, an all-out feud could be avoided. That hadn't even occurred to Bran.

"No, Mistress Mandy," said a voice behind her. Lord Bruin entered the room. "Claiming Blood is not allowed among the nobility. Bran has been expelled from the pages and that will be the extent of his punishment."

Bran's mother curtsied. "My lord. Why is he here?"

"Young Bran has a gift. He is here for training."

"I don't understand, my lord."

"He can see the future, Mistress Mandy."

Her eyes widened in surprise. "My Bran?"

Bran slid off the chair and stood. "I knew Xavier was going to hurt me before it happened. I just didn't remember until it almost did. My lord, I swear it wasn't on purpose."

Bruin smiled and the expression brought kindness into his eyes. "Accidents happen, Bran. Nearly every student here has some similar story."

"Is he to be a wizard, then?" asked his mother.

"No. As far as I can tell, he has no talent for magic. We will put him in academic classes with the other students but his training will be separate from them. We've never taught a Seer before."

Bran's mother rubbed his shoulders, her expression pensive. "He'll be all right?"

"He will be safe and well-treated here. He'll even be able to go home every rest day, a privilege we extend all our students that come out of the city. Would you like for me to show you the classrooms and dormitory?"

"Yes, my lord."

They followed Lord Bruin. Upstairs, he showed them the laboratories where the natural sciences were taught and then led them downstairs. He took them to the library and introduced Bran to the librarian on duty, as well as to the masters at work there. Students in their grey apprentice robes peered curiously over their books at the newcomer. Bran glanced over them before fixing his eyes on the toes of his boots.

Next, they went outside and along a cloister walk to an adjoining building. He showed them the refectory, a large room furnished with long tables with one table on a dais at the head of the room. No paintings hung on the walls and dark wood reflected the glow of lamps. To Bran, it was the exact opposite of the noisy, warmly furnished servants' dining hall where the pages took their meals.

Their final stop was the boys' dormitory on the bottom floor.

"The girls' dormitory is a floor above," Bruin explained.

Narrow beds ran down the length of the dormitory. An aisle split the beds into two columns. At the foot of each bed rested a trunk for the boy's belongings.

"How much will all this cost?" blurted Bran's mother.

"The children from nobility do pay a tuition," Bruin explained. "However, non-noble children pay their way by doing chores. All of them are expected to furnish their own clothes and supplies."

Bran stared up at his mother. All of his wages, except what he needed for his own upkeep, were sent home. Did she have enough laid by?

"Lord Bruin," she said, "I am honored by this offer for my son. I can't afford to buy him new sets of clothes or any supplies. I'm sorry. I'll take him home now."

"The King is very insistent that your son remain here. I'm sure he will pay for Bran's needs from his own coffers."

Her mouth dropped open in surprise. "I will never be able to repay him."

"Repayment will be in Bran's service to the kingdom." Footsteps approached. "Ah. Mistress Olivia."

A tall woman in long, black wizard's robes whose skirts billowed as she moved and belted a blue and white cord, entered the dormitory. She curtsied to Lord Bruin. "I apologize for not being here sooner, my lord. There was an emergency in the greenhouse."

"Quite all right, Olivia. Bran, this is the house mother, Mistress Olivia. She will finish your tour. I have an important meeting to attend."

Once Bruin left, Mistress Olivia said, "Well, Bran, would you like to see which bed is yours?"

He nodded, his throat feeling too thick for speaking. The buildings felt too big and the people too strange. Everything was changing so quickly, Bran expected to be knocked off his feet at any moment.

Chapter Sixteen

Emmerich waded through corpses toward Clara, who shouted for his help. Something grabbed him by the shoulders. Terror and adrenaline surged, breaking the dream, and he seized his assailant.

Twisting, he yanked him onto the bed and pinned him with a forearm to the throat. In his other hand he grasped the dagger he kept under his mattress.

"Your Majesty," croaked the person beneath him.

Shock washed over him as he felt the soft, familiar contours of a woman beneath him. His eyes adjusted to the dim light spilling through his window and he made out the features of Healer Paula.

He rolled off of her and stood. The night air, not as cool as it had been before, chilled the sweat on his skin. Emmerich realized he was naked and snatched up a blanket that had fallen to the floor. He draped it around himself.

"Healer, my apologies," he said.

Paula pushed herself off the bed. She wore only a chemise that fell to mid-shin. "No, Your Majesty. I'm sorry. I should know better than to awake a warrior in mid-nightmare like that."

"Why did you come here? Is something wrong?"

"Your aerial, Niall, woke me. He came into the Queen's chambers, I don't know how, and woke me. He was terrified. When I came in here, you were struggling in a nightmare."

Emmerich frowned. His nightmare must have awoken the creature.

"I can make you a tonic," she continued, "that might help with the nightmares."

"No." That came out harsher than he meant it. He repeated his refusal more gently. "No, thank you, Healer. I know of that tonic and I have no interest in its side effects." Emmerich had heard stories ranging from strange-colored urine to losing any desire for sex.

The thought of love making reminded him that it had been a long time since he'd had a woman in his bedroom, let alone waking him from a nightmare. His body warmed to the thought. He shoved it to the back of his mind.

"Thank you, Healer Paula," he said before the pause in their exchange grew more awkward. "You can return to your bed. I'm fine."

"Your Majesty—"

"Really, Healer. You can go back to bed."

After she was gone, Emmerich leaned against the wall. A small squeak drew his attention to the doorway. Niall, barely discernable in the dimness, stared up at him with eerily glinting eyes.

"You're going to get me into trouble," Emmerich admonished him.

Niall only chirped.

Paula leaned against the door. Her face felt hot and she knew she was blushing.

King Emmerich was a handsome man and still young by most standards. His achievements as a soldier only added to his desirability. Most of the women in Court, as well as a few men, would have given their left hand to wake the King from a nightmare.

"That aerial is going to get me into trouble," she muttered. "Mother Above help me."

She rubbed her face and returned to the couch, on which were piled pillows from the bed and a blanket. It did trouble her, Emmerich's nightmare. Warriors sometimes were haunted by the past and those bad dreams could bleed into the waking day.

Hopefully, that wasn't the case.

Jarrett stepped off the boat onto the dock. Around him, ships were loaded and unloaded while City Guards and guild officials watched. Ahead of him, the Low Quarters rose. Beyond them, out of sight from where he stood, would be the Palace on its hill. He considered briefly stepping onto the next barge to the great southern plains, if only to avoid Emmerich's wrath.

The familiar smells of fish, rotted vegetables, offal, and wood smoke wrapped around him. The muddled voices of people talking, crying orders, or trying to sell wares filled his ears and overrode the quieter sounds of water lapping against the docks and boats.

Ah, Bertrand, he thought. He walked down to where the horses were being unloaded. Heartsblood nickered as he approached, and he patted the gelding's neck.

After saddling his horse and accounting for all of his luggage and the pack mule, Jarrett mounted and rode to the Palace. He rehearsed his speech every step of the way. He carefully planned what to say but, the closer he drew to the Palace, the more feeble his explanation became.

When he first received his commission as a Palace Guard, Jarrett's father called him into his study. Decades past his prime and Captain Kendrick still cut an imposing figure. Perhaps that was only in the eyes of his children, who still remembered their father's punishments. Jarrett, uncomfortable in his scratchy, new uniform, stood at attention in front of his father's desk.

"No need to do that," Kendrick said. He gestured for his son to follow him to the window. It wasn't the view that drew him. Kendrick settled his sharp gaze on Jarrett. "You're about to carry on the tradition of our family. We've spilled our blood for this country since its founding. My father gave me one piece of advice when I received my commission. He claimed he received it from his father before him. Now, I give it to you." He laid a hand on his son's shoulder. "Make your death count. You only have one. When do you report to Captain Emmerich?"

"This afternoon, Father."

Kendrick squeezed Jarrett's shoulder. "You'll do us proud, son."

His father didn't explain what he meant about "making your death count" but there wasn't a need. Ever since, Jarrett tried to be honorable and loyal in all he did. That way, when he died, it would matter.

As he traveled through the city to the Palace, turning his hollow words over in his mind, he realized that if the King ordered his death, it wouldn't matter. It wouldn't count. No matter what he thought to say, it didn't make up for losing a woman prized by the King and leaving her to travel alone through mountains haunted by giants, even if it seemed like the only thing he could do.

To add salt to the wound, it would be King Emmerich he would be speaking to, the same Emmerich Jarrett had reported to that day all those years ago. The same Emmerich who trained him, lectured him, and helped form him into the man he was.

"I'm a fool," Jarrett muttered.

When he arrived at the Palace gates, smiles flashed on the Palace Guards' faces before they hid them. They saluted.

"Good to have you back, Captain," one of the

said. "Where is Lady Clara?"

"She's not with me." He held up a hand at the guards' alarmed expressions. "She's fine. It's a long story. How has Valiance handled things while I've been gone?"

The two guards glanced at each other.

"Enough said, then. Well, carry on." He saluted them and rode through the gates.

Everything was more or less as he had left it. Everything made of stone and brick, anyway. The guards he encountered seemed vastly relieved to see him and nobles tensed at the sight of him. They gazed beyond him, as if expecting to see Lady Clara a step behind.

After leaving the animals with a stable boy, Jarrett inquired with a page as to the whereabouts of the King.

"At this time? He is in the Council Chamber, sir," the boy replied.

Oh, wonderful. He'll be in a fantastic mood. Jarrett thanked the boy and moved on.

Though several people wanted to converse

with him as he approached the Hall of Justice, Jarrett didn't let his stride slow. He approached just as the Council Chamber doors opened and the lords and ladies strolled out. Lord Barkeley swept past him without greeting Jarrett while the rest of the nobles were in too deep discussion to notice him. Jarrett stopped at the threshold.

Emmerich, flipping through papers, stood by his chair. A small aerial with a bound wing nosed at food on a plate. Jarrett watched the creature for a moment, wondering about its presence, and cleared his throat.

The King looked up. Surprise flashed over his face, followed by a hopeful expression so intense, it embarrassed Jarrett.

Jarrett bowed. "Your Majesty. I hope I'm not intruding? I see you have a visitor."

Emmerich smiled at the aerial. "That is Niall. I rescued him. Come in. Is Clara with you?"

"No, she isn't, Your Majesty." He crossed the room and stopped a few feet from the large table.

The hope faded from Emmerich's face, followed closely by suspicion. "Where is she?"

"Still in the mountains, sire."

"What is she doing there?" He tossed down his papers.

"Going to Bluebell. She's traveling disguised as a boy."

Emmerich's face went still and fury filled his grey eyes. The aerial, Niall, squawked, spreading his good wing. Emmerich reached out to run a hand down its back without taking his eyes off of Jarrett. "You let her go alone? I put her in your care. I thought you were a man of honor, Jarrett."

"Clara feared for your safety, Your Majesty. She expressly wished for me to return to Bertrand to assist you in the coming crisis."

"Then why isn't she with you?"

"I intended on persuading her to return with me. Before I could, she slipped away during the night. I tried to follow but I lost her in the mountains. She took my long knife and spare clothes."

Emmerich walked around the table. The way he moved, walking on the balls of his feet, reminded Jarrett that Emmerich started his life as a fighter. He fought the urge to drop his hand to his sword hilt.

Emmerich stopped on the other side of the table, less than a foot from Jarrett. Niall mewled and walked across the table. He bumped his head against Emmerich's arm. The King ignored him.

"You couldn't track her?" he asked, his voice as smooth as oil.

Jarrett straightened his shoulders. "No, Your Majesty."

"Why not?"

The excuse of simply being unfamiliar with mountains and tracking people felt feeble in his mouth, so he spoke the truth, no matter how badly it hurt. "Lady Clara took a mountain road I could not follow on because of my horse. She had advised me to change mounts in Hernesferry. Like a fool, I dismissed her advice. She used my own stubbornness against me. And even if I could have changed mounts right then, she would have had too much of a lead on me. I chose, then, to return to your side."

"And if she should die out there in the mountains?"

"Then I humbly submit myself to the executioner's sword."

"I wouldn't let you get that far."

Jarrett laid the hair on the table. "She left this behind. This is why I believe she's traveling as a boy."

Emmerich ignored the braid of hair. "Why should I allow you to continue in your position after this failure?"

"Because, sire, I am still loyal to you despite my mistake."

For a moment, Jarrett thought the King would refuse and have him thrown in the dungeons. The air felt heavy with that possibility.

"You may go debrief Lieutenant Valiance," Emmerich replied. "There's been a murder on Palace grounds, Captain Jarrett. I hope you have a better time tracking the killer than you did the Lady Seer."

Jarrett bowed and walked out. He wasn't sure if it was the weight of his sovereign's gaze on his back or his own conscience that he felt. Either way, he did not let his shoulders bow.

Acting Captain Valiance had taken up temporary residence in Jarrett's office and that was where he found him, poring over scrolls.

Jarrett entered without knocking. "Reading up on how to hold a sword?"

Valiance jerked upright and snatched up a dagger. On seeing Jarrett, he relaxed. "Captain. I didn't know you were back."

Jarrett raised a brow at the weapon. He very carefully kept his hands in sight and away from his sword. "I was coming here to inform you. Are you going to put that down?"

"Hm? Oh." He dropped it. "Apologies." Valiance stood. "I trust you and Lady Clara didn't have any problems on the road?"

Jarrett's instincts clamored in his ears. He took in the dark smudges under his lieutenant's eyes and the way one hand fidgeted with the edge of his surcoat. "I had no problems. Unfortunately, I've returned without the lady."

"Is she···that is···Is she all right?"

"I hope so. I'd rather not talk about it, if it's all the same to you, Valiance."

"Yes, Captain."

"Is everything all right?"

Valiance rolled up the scrolls. "Everything is fine, Captain."

"Is it your family? You know I'm more than happy to loan some money if you need it."

"No." The word came out sharp and loud. "I mean. No, thank you. We're fine."

"Really?"

"I managed to pay it all up."

That was a surprise. If Jarrett had understood rightly, it had been a large sum owed to several gambling establishments, a legacy from a squandering grandfather. "Well, that's good.

Congratulations. The King told me there had been a murder?"

"Yes. A page named Matteo Havens was killed outside the barracks. I think it was a rendezvous gone badly. From what I've learned, Matteo dallied with married maidservants."

"That would do it. Do you know if he carried a message?"

"No, Captain. Our witness was another page named Bran Weston. He saw Matteo Havens leave but said he wasn't carrying anything."

"Do you know who he went to see in the barracks?"

"No, Captain."

Valiance gathered his scrolls in his arms. Despite the casual nature of their conversation, he moved quickly as if he wanted nothing more than to be out of the office. He stilled, as if a sudden thought struck him.

"There is another matter, Captain," Valiance said.

"Oh?"

"It's more like gossip, really."

"I'm a soldier, Val. I've never said no to gossip."

For the first time since Jarrett had entered, Valiance smiled. Calling him by a seldom-used nickname probably helped him to relax. "It's about the King. Palace rumor is that he's taken up with a woman."

Jarrett felt a quiet sort of anger curl in his gut. "Taken up with a woman?"

"A healer. She's moved into the Queen's quarters across from him. There's been no news of marriage. It might have to do with that aerial orphan he's adopted. No one knows for sure but the rumor is that there's more happening than healing."

Men did have urges and men of power often took mistresses. Jarrett had even played a time or two in houses of pleasure, back before he became a captain. He just never thought Emmerich was the type to take a mistress. It clashed with the rage Jarrett only just escaped.

He tried not to think about how hurt Clara would be if she found out. And to have the mistress staying in the Queen's quarters?

"Is that all, Captain?" Valiance asked, breaking Jarrett's train of thought.

"No." He stepped aside to let Valiance leave when a sudden thought brought a hand up. "Wait. General Asher wrote to me over the winter to tell me someone tried to poison the King?"

"I believe it's linked to a faction in the Court. We were never able to come up with substantial evidence, unfortunately."

Jarrett grunted. "Well, at least we know to watch that faction."

"I wrote a report. It's in a packet on your desk." He gestured at a bundle on the desk, tied with twine. "I've added important items to it as they happen."

"Good. Good. Well, I suppose you're Lieutenant Valiance again. I hope that's not too much of a letdown?"

"It's fine, Captain."

"You're dismissed, then, I suppose."

Valiance bowed and strode out. Jarrett closed the door behind him. There was something wrong with Valiance. And how did the man finally manage to pay off all that debt?

It worried Jarrett but he couldn't think of anything to do about it. He sat at his desk, pulled the bundle of reports to himself, and untied them. He would much rather have gone to his quarters for a bath. Yet Emmerich's dressing-down still rung in his ears, as well as Valiance's disturbing bit of gossip. Work would distract him.

Chapter Seventeen

Asher slapped his gloves against his thigh in a rhythmic pattern as he waited. Night soaked the surrounding city in darkness. Men stumbled out of a nearby tavern, talking and laughing at the tops of their voices. Asher shrank deeper into the shadows as they stumbled past. Across the street, stray dogs pawed through garbage.

Boots scraped against dirty pavement and Bruin materialized out of the blackness of an alley. He wore the dirty, torn clothes of a dock worker. "Asher, my friend, you stick out like a dove among crows."

Asher considered his clothes. In his eyes, he was dressed like any sell-sword. Perhaps a bit too clean, however. "Well, I didn't exactly have time to go shopping."

Bruin smiled and walked down the street. Asher fell in step beside him.

"Why did you oust me from my warm bed?" the general asked.

"I've heard a rumor that some men will move against an aerial nest soon."

"What? Why didn't you say so, man? I would have roused the City Guard."

"If we went in with swords slashing, the men would scatter. Besides, what's a group of men versus a wizard and the King's right hand?"

Asher shook his head, his blond curls bouncing against the tops of his ears. "I think you're enjoying this cloak and shadow life too much."

Bruin let out a rare laugh. "It is a nice change of pace from lecture halls and laboratories."

"What's wrong with scattering them? Perhaps they'll think twice before causing mischief again."

"We need to know who is behind these thugs, if it's the same person responsible for the riot down on the docks."

"What do you mean?"

"Someone would need to organize this. This isn't like going after a gang whose hideout is well-known. It's more like hunting wolves. And trouble with aerials will only cause more trouble for the King. It's too calculated and too coincidental."

Asher thought about that. "Very true. I'm not even sure myself where aerials nest."

"It took a great deal of research and time to gain their trust before I learned. Most favor the attics of temples. I think a few are starting to use the abandoned buildings along the river. If that's the case, then the fiends will be going there."

"If it took that much work for you to learn, then how did our troublemakers?"

"Exactly. The person behind all this would need the same resources as myself and it confirms our fears that this is a known wizard."

"Do you realize what this will do to Emmerich's confidence in you, if it turns out the traitor was a wizard lurking in your Academy?"

"He may never trust me or another magic worker again."

"Dammit, man, it may mean the dissolution of the Academy."

"I will accept that risk and the consequences. There is so much at stake."

Asher stared off into the night. "I hate politics." He focused back on Bruin. "Where are we going?"

"It's only a few blocks away. What do you think of that boy, Bran?"

Asher frowned at Bruin. "Why do you ask?"

"Mistress Olivia says he's very quiet and withdrawn. She's worried about him. I wondered if there was anything you could tell me that might help her in getting him adjusted to Academy life."

"Bran caused the death of a fellow page and he's been thrown into a new routine. That's enough reason for him to be withdrawn." Asher still remembered how it felt, after a skirmish with Tieran soldiers, to clean blood from his blade. He threw up and couldn't eat his breakfast. Killing someone was never simple or easy. He couldn't imagine what it would be like for someone as young as Bran. "Why are you asking me?"

"You were alone with him for a time after the murder. I hoped you had a rapport with him."

"He'd expressed interest in the military to me before but we didn't speak that evening." Asher thought about the haunted look on Bran's face and felt a wave of concern. "If you're worried about him, let him come to the practice yards during his free time. I think it will do him good."

"I'll see to that."

They didn't speak again as they walked. Bruin seemed unaffected by their conversation regarding the traitor. It was rare for him to be anything other than affable and in control.

Asher tucked the problem of Bran away in favor of brooding over what it could mean if a magic worker they initially trusted stood as the source of so many problems of late. Emmerich wanted people to see that wizards were natural philosophers, that their work dealt with the contents of books, and that those who brought nightmares out of the shadows were scarce and few.

If Emmerich was proved wrong, it would give the people yet another reason not to have confidence in their sovereign. And a people without confidence in their King was an uprising waiting to happen.

Bruin's hand on his arm brought him out of his thoughts.

They had turned onto a narrow, crooked street that dead-ended in a cul-de-sac. In the center of the cul-de-sac stood a broken fountain. Old wooden and brick buildings leaned over the street. Broken and boarded windows looked down on them.

Several boys clustered on the stoop of a building, taking turns tossing rocks at bottles lined up in the streets. Their shouts of triumph and disappointment, mixed with the tinkling of glass, ricocheted off the drab, drooping buildings. A scattering of windows glowed and street lamps cast dubious yellow light over the scene.

"Which house is it?" he asked.

"The one where the boys are sitting."

"Coincidence?"

"Doubtful."

Asher pushed back his cloak to reveal the sword strapped to his side. "Well, let's get this over with."

"My good friend, wait." Bruin held up a hand and it glowed purple. The world shimmered around them, dulling to shades of grey and white.

"Mother's milk," he swore softly. "What is this?"

"A cloaking spell. Those boys will no longer pay us any attention."

"How are you doing this?" Asher twirled in a slow circle to take in this new view of the world.

"It would take a diagram and a few equations to explain."

"I've never been much for schooling, Bruin. I think I'll take your word for it. Where to, now?"

"An alley on the other side."

They walked past the boys, who didn't pause in their game. Asher noticed that while one focused on trying to smash a bottle with a rock, two others watched the street. The way they were seated, someone wanting to enter the building would have to push them aside, and these were boys past their twelfth year. Street kids who no doubt had handmade daggers tucked into their shoddy shoes or hidden in their dirty tunics. Asher thought about Bran, the young page who caused the death of another page, and he had only been defending himself.

Bruin dropped their cloak after they entered the alley, the world coming into sharp focus again. Dirt crunched under their boots as they walked to a makeshift wall of broken crates and boards. Asher couldn't see details in the dim light but it wouldn't surprise him if there were rusty nails in the mix somewhere.

"Huh," the wizard said.

"You sound surprised."

"I always scout ahead. I don't remember seeing this earlier today."

"Can you get us through?"

"Without making a lot of noise?"

Asher unclipped his thick wool cloak and tossed it over the boards to cover sharp edges and any nails. With careful hands and feet, he climbed the wall. Wood groaned and shifted underneath him and he paused near the top, his heart hammering his throat. The pile went still and he finished the climb. He jumped down from the top, hit the ground at an awkward angle, and pitched into a roll to keep from spraining an ankle. Pushing to his feet, he surveyed the small yard.

A high wooden fence lined the back end of the dirt yard and faced the parallel street. From a window in a neighboring building, a young woman with her shoulders bare watched them. When her and Asher's eyes met, she stepped back and pulled a tattered curtain into place.

In one corner of the yard, a shed with a collapsed roof stood under the shade of a twisted apple tree. An overweight dog chained to the tree watched Asher. An empty, bent pan lay near the dog, as did a water trough. A clump of daffodils grew by the back stoop of the building.

The dog's tail *thunked* the ground, sending up a small cloud of dust, but he made no move to bark or lunge.

A thud followed by a muffled curse announced Bruin's arrival. Asher turned to see his friend getting up.

"Didn't hurt yourself, I hope," Asher whispered.

"Only my pride."

"You should come to the practice grounds more often."

"I'll put it on my daily agenda."

They approached the back door of the house. Asher held up a hand to make Bruin wait and tried to see through a sooty window. He could make out a dim hallway with light spilling into it from another room further down. He tried the latch and the door opened easily. Laying a hand on the hilt of his long dagger, he entered the hallway.

It smelled like dust, grease, and mildew. He pressed his nose to the bend of his elbow to suppress a sneeze before edging deeper into the house. The sounds of men talking floated to them from the lit room ahead.

Bruin came up behind him and closed the door. Asher pointed to the side of the hall, against the wall on the side of the lit room, and used his fingers to mime walking. Bruin nodded. They began to creep down the hall near the wall and away from loose boards.

They passed darkened rooms and Asher's shoulders tensed with the fear of someone rushing them from out of the darkness. No one came. Soon, he could make out the words of the speaker.

"It's as simple as layin' with a whore, lads," the speaker said. "We come in through the back there and herd 'em into the main room. Do some damage and then set the place ablaze."

Asher met Bruin's eyes, which mirrored his own shock and fear. Wooden buildings composed most of the Low Quarters, with the exceptions of one or two stone temples. If these men succeeded in their plan, they could burn down half or all of the Quarters.

"Have to stop them," whispered Asher and he drew his dagger. "We go in on three. One, two—" He burst into the room, long dagger in hand, bellowing, "Stop, in the name of the King!"

The room was empty.

Asher stared, as if waiting for men to materialize out of the dirty furniture and the web-swathed rafters. The source of the room's light came from a glowing ball of flame which hovered in front of the fireplace. The man's voice emanated from it.

"Any questions?" asked the ball.

Another man's voice came in, asking about escape plans and how the aerials could fight back. It was such a lucidly put question that Asher knew these couldn't be disgruntled dock workers or frightened laborers.

"What in the nine hells is going on, Bruin?"

Asher demanded.

Bruin stepped forward and examined the flame. "It's a recording spell. Very advanced."

"What is that?"

"It's a spell that records sounds, like a conversation."

"How did they know we were going to be here?"

The wizard didn't answer, only stared at the globe.

Asher grabbed him by the shoulder and spun him around. "Answer me! How did they know!"

His eyes were dark with fear and pain. "I was deceived. All those weeks working on this and I was deceived. Whoever did this knew how I would react, Asher. They made sure I received a false meeting time. This is a decoy. They are already hitting the nest."

The general stared at his friend and recognized the defeat and disappointment in his voice. He'd heard it in his own voice more than once.

Bruin ended the spell with a wave of his hand. On the floor below where the ball of fire had floated lay a scrap of parchment on which runes and diagrams had been drawn. A bloody thumb print marked the center. He picked it up. "This was written up before the fact. All the speaker needed to do was put some of his blood on it to activate the spell, then they held their meeting and left. The spell kept repeating the meeting over and over until we arrived."

"You know this spell, then?"

"I invented it."

Asher swore, inventively and at great length. "Emmerich is going to have us thrown in the dungeons. Do we still have time to stop this?"

"Perhaps."

He strode out of the room and down the hall to the front door. As he shoved the door open, the boys scattered, shouting in surprise.

They took off, leaving the bottles and rocks behind, their task as pretend watchmen now over. That's not what made Asher stop. The acrid scent of wood smoke, heavier than normal in the city, tickled his nose.

"Mother's milk," he muttered and took off down the street, back the way they came. Bruin's running steps pursued.

They ran until they came to a temple and Asher burst in. The presbyter, in the middle of the nightly prayer, stopped in the middle of his chant to stare as the two men rushed down the aisle to the sacristy. Every temple's floor plan was the same, mimicking that of the Great Temple. Asher found the stairs of the bell tower in the sacristy with ease and ran up the spiral staircase, taking the steps two at a time.

Reaching the top, he flung himself to the side facing the river. The ruddy glow of firelight lit the sky and it took a second for him to find the building in flames. As he watched, another building beside it caught fire.

"Sweet Child," Bruin said, watching.

"Can you stop the flames? From here?"

Bruin held up his hands, closing his eyes in

concentration, and muttered. His hands lit a dull blue and Asher watched the clear sky. No clouds formed. Not even a breeze stirred into being. Bruin lowered his hands.

"The air is too dry," he said. "I cannot make it rain. And there's no spell to just make the flames go away. I have to defeat them with their opposing element."

As they watched, another building went up into flames.

Soot and ash swam in the air. People in dirty, charred clothes, faces smudged black, stood in the smoke-choked streets with lost expressions on their faces. They had so little and now flame and men's hate took even that much away.

Emmerich rode his horse down the center of the street, guards trailing behind him with Jarrett at their lead. The blaze had consumed about a third of the Low Quarters before guardsmen and other locals could put it out after a night-long battle.

He stopped his mount to watch men lay bodies out in the street while a presbyter chanted prayers. A few had cloths draped over the faces. Most didn't. Some were surprisingly intact with serene expressions, others were twisted, charred shapes of agony. A breeze came up, sweeping the gagging tang of burned flesh and hair over him.

Another presbyter, an elderly man with soot streaked across his sweaty face, approached Emmerich, pausing a respectful distance away. Emmerich dismounted and gestured for the man to come closer. He did, bowing when he stopped.

"Thank you, Your Majesty," the man said, "for coming here."

Emmerich nodded, unable to speak for a moment. When he had traveled in his father's caravan, fire had been both friend and enemy. It cooked their food and warmed them in winter.

It also threatened their very lives. Wagons, after all, were made mostly of wood. He felt these people's pain. He cleared his throat. "How many bodies have been found so far, do you know?"

"Rough estimates have put the death toll at four hundred, Your Majesty."

He winced. The figure would no doubt go up. "There is a woman I wished to inquire about." It occurred to him that he didn't know Bran's mother's name. "She's the mother of one of my pages. Or, he was a page until he entered the Academy. His name is Bran Weston. I can only assume her surname is the same."

If the presbyter was surprised at the King requesting information about a Low Quarters woman, he did a good job of hiding it. "I will ask my brother presbyters, Your Majesty." He bowed and walked away to a knot of fellow priests.

Low Quarters people were beginning to gather nearby, in front of a blackened skeleton of a building. The presbyter might have been grateful he came out but these people did not seem to have the same appreciation. They regarded their King with sad and angry eyes. One of them held a rock as if he intended to throw it.

The guards edged closer to Emmerich. He waved them back.

The presbyter returned and led Emmerich over to the far end of the ever-growing column of corpses. A middle-aged woman with silver in her hair lay on the cobblestone. Her wide eyes were frozen in a mask of fear and her mouth gaped open as if she still cried for help. Her hands curled against her chest.

"She was well-known," the presbyter said. "She was a washer woman for some merchants and very kind. Had many friends. It's sad. From what I've been told, she died trying to rescue a child trapped in one of the buildings."

"Mother above," Emmerich swore softly. He shook his head. "I will pay for her funeral."

"And the rest?"

The question caught him off-guard and he stared with a vacant expression at the presbyter.

"Your Majesty, with all due respect, most of these people will be interred in a mass grave. Only trouble is, we don't have any single cemetery in this city even remotely large enough. The catacombs under the temples are reserved for merchants and nobles. And then there are the orphans to consider. The lame. The wounded who could recover fully under proper treatment. We need money and help."

"I will call an emergency meeting of the Council and see to it you receive all the help you need." Even if he had to invoke all his power to do it, and anger half the guilds, he would make sure these people were seen to.

"It is most appreciated, Your Majesty." His tone was dry, as if he didn't expect Emmerich to keep his word.

Emmerich took a small pouch of coin from under his tunic and gave it to the presbyter. "See to this woman's interment in a catacomb. Let me know which temple you select so I can tell her son."

He accepted the money with a bow and Emmerich started toward his horse.

"What of the rest of us!"

The shout brought him to a stop. It was from the crowd, much larger now.

"We need food!" another person yelled.

"An' clothes!"

"My babies are dead!"

The last shout ended in a screech. Dozens of voices raised in protestations of pain and anger.

Guards surged forward to disperse the crowd. Several men didn't care for that and struck at the guards with boards and crude cudgels. Emmerich stepped forward, his first instinct to help, but Jarrett's hand on his arm stopped him, reminding him that he was King. Backing away, he returned to his horse, where several guards still waited. He left the Low Quarters at a trot.

Asher didn't like that the King went down to the Low Quarters again. He was wise enough not to say anything.

He felt as if he carried most of the blame for what had happened. He shouldn't have let Bruin coax him out with just himself, as if this was the sort of game nobles liked to play in the taverns by the docks, pretending to be lower than they were. He should have brought with him some men. He should have run faster for help. There were dozens of things he should have done.

He kept that to himself as he stood in Emmerich's chambers, with the stink of ash and smoke on his clothes, and watched Emmerich pour himself his third cup of wine. It appeared his King, his commander, his friend, was steadily working on becoming drunk. Jarrett stood by the door and their eyes met briefly. He, too, seemed concerned for their sovereign but bore deeper disgrace than Asher. He did not dare speak.

"There was nothing you could have done, Your Majesty," Asher finally said.

"The nest was destroyed." Emmerich took a swig of his wine. "Once the remains of the building cooled, Bruin's men managed to clear enough away to find where the nest had been. Twenty aerials and about thirty eggs, all destroyed. One of the wizards thought that a clutch was in the middle of cracking open when the fire was lit." He swallowed more wine.

"Your Majesty—"

"And now the death toll is reaching nearly five hundred. Will be a thousand by the time they're done counting and it probably will still not be all of them. They'll probably be pulling corpses out of there for months to come. I've ordered supplies and the army to help the City Guard. The Council wasn't entirely happy. They can go to the ninth level of Hell for all I care." He drank again. "And I've ordered the purchase of a large tract of land outside the city. That will be the cemetery. Maybe we can erect a monument once all the corpses are in mass graves." Emmerich poured more wine. "And I had to tell Bran his mother died. You can imagine how that went."

Asher felt his guts squirm with guilt. If he had done something different, then Bran wouldn't be an orphan. What would become of the boy? Would he be raised solely by the dormitory matron and the wizards? That didn't seem like much of a home to Asher.

He brushed aside those worries to focus on the matter at hand. "Sire, where is Niall?"

Maybe the aerial's presence could calm Emmerich. Jarrett had told him about their confrontation when he arrived in Bertrand and mentioned Niall being in the room. It was Asher's opinion that it was what kept the King from losing his temper and putting Jarrett in chains. Asher wanted Emmerich to be kept from saying or doing something he would later regret.

"With Healer Paula," Emmerich replied. "Niall wouldn't stop crying when I came back." He ran a hand through his hair and then sniffed his fingers. "I've bathed thrice now and I still smell like smoke and burnt flesh."

"There was nothing you could have done."

Emmerich threw the goblet. It broke against the wall by Jarrett, scattering fragments and wine everywhere. To his credit, Jarrett didn't flinch.

"That. Doesn't. Matter," Emmerich replied. "Those are my people. It is my duty to care for them."

Asher spoke slowly, choosing his words with care. "This is not an army, Your Majesty. Or a caravan. Or a squad of men. You cannot account for everything that might happen. What happened was a tragedy but we were outwitted—"

"I want no excuses!"

He winced at the shout. Asher watched as the old Rebel General, the warlord on his quest for revenge, took over in every taut line of Emmerich's body.

"I want no excuses," Emmerich repeated more softly. "The traitor must be behind all of this."

"It's a safe assumption, sire. This was too well-planned and executed to be anything else. For some reason, he wants to excite fear regarding the aerials and encourage people to take action against them."

"You find the son of a bitch, Asher. I want him

hung, drawn, and quartered in the city's center, outside the Great Temple. I want all the people of the Low Quarter in the front of the crowd so they can watch justice—*my* justice—being enacted. And until further notice, the Council is disbanded. I am in charge. This is my kingdom, and I will no longer waste time arguing with bureaucrats! Do you understand me?"

"Yes, Your Majesty."

"And what members of the army are not helping in the Low Quarters, send them to fortify the city walls. Tell the City Guard that a curfew is in effect. No one is to be out after dark save on official business. This is until further notice."

"It will be done, sire."

"Jarrett, if you think you can manage it, have the Palace Guards double up on their patrols and drills."

"Yes, Your Majesty," Jarrett replied.

"You both may go."

They bowed and began to leave.

Just as they reached the door, Emmerich

called out, "And cut the stipend of the courtiers. Their money will go toward the relief of the people who lost life, home, and income in the Low Quarters. If they protest, tell them they should do some useful work if they want money."

The general bowed ascent to Emmerich before leaving. It was going to be a bad night for the King. He knew Emmerich well enough to know that he blamed himself for the fire.

He and Jarrett walked side by side until they left the Royal Wing.

"I heard what happened," Asher said. "With Lady Clara."

"Are you going to give me a talking to as well? A good reprimand?"

"No. Jarrett." He stopped the younger man with a hand on the shoulder. "You aren't the first person to lose Lady Clara."

"What do you mean?"

"When King Emmerich was still General Emmerich and in the North, he took the castle of a baroness. It happened before I arrived from taking a sea fortress, so I wasn't there. The other captains couldn't wait to tell me. It was the talk of the barracks for a month.

"Apparently, during a ride in the countryside, Lady Clara gave the slip to three guards and was nearly killed by a group of bandits. None of them were on mountain ponies but their horses were bred for the terrain. Now if she managed to give them the slip, how could you have hoped to keep track of her?"

"Are you calling King a hypocrite?"

"No. I'm saying you shouldn't be too hard on yourself."

"They found her, didn't they?"

"The King led a squad of men out immediately and found her defending herself against the bandits."

"I didn't find her, General Asher. She's still out there and if anything happens to her, it is my fault."

Asher couldn't think of a reply to that. An awkward silence passed between them before he asked, "Have you made any headway in finding the murderer of that page, Matteo?"

"Lieutenant Valiance believes a jealous husband is the culprit. Apparently, Master Thom's nephew dallied with married servants. I did want to ask: do you know who the page saw that night?"

"I've asked my captains. No one has admitted it."

"That's very strange."

"Now that you're here, you won't mind me looking into it?"

Jarrett frowned. "Of course not. Did Valiance mind?"

"He minded very much. I wanted to take command of the investigation as it took place outside the barracks. Valiance argued that it should be him since it happened to a Palace servant."

"He didn't offer to work with you since it might involve one of the soldiers?"

"No."

"None of this was mentioned in the reports he wrote. According to him, you gladly gave him jurisdiction over the investigation." He stiffened.

"There's another matter, as well."

"Oh, I can't wait to hear this."

Asher cocked a brow. "I'm not sure you do. During the Mid-Winter Festival, King Emmerich was nearly poisoned."

"I'm aware."

"Valiance couldn't be found anywhere. Later, he claimed a family emergency. His family vouched for him. It was still odd that he couldn't be located for two candlemarks."

"I didn't know he was gone for so long."

"I've been considering bringing charges of possible treason against him, so that I can investigate more fully.

Jarrett glared at the General. "Lieutenant Valiance has always performed admirably. I have never had reason to suspect he could be a traitor."

"Captain—"

"If that's all you have to say, General, I need to go speak with my lieutenant."

Before Asher could stop him, Jarrett strode away.

Chapter Eighteen

Paula waited until she heard the arguing men leave the hall, presumably to exit the Royal Wing. Cradling Niall in her arms, she left the Queen's quarters and knocked on Emmerich's door.

"Leave me be," came the muffled shout.

Niall whined, his head stretching toward the door. Paula swung it open and entered.

"Isn't it early for wine, Your Majesty?" she asked, watching him finish off a goblet.

"I said I wanted to be left alone." He slammed the goblet down.

Niall crooned. Emmerich went still. Paula crossed the room to him and held out the nestling.

He took Niall with trembling hands. The aerial pressed against his chest, cooing and crooning. With Emmerich distracted, Paula began collected the flagons of wine.

"What are you doing?" Emmerich asked, his voice low and hoarse.

"Your Majesty, as a healer it is my duty to make sure you remain in good health. You won't if you make a habit of early morning drinking."

"My people suffer."

She set down her armful of flagons and looked at him. Emmerich looked tired and thin, as if he had just struggled through a bout of illness.

"This wine," she said softly, "won't help that." Paula hesitated, then laid a hand on his shoulder. "Your people need you clear-headed. And I know that you are doing all you can."

"How can you know that?"

"If you weren't, you wouldn't be so deeply troubled."

He didn't reply. The deep, soothing sounds rising from Niall's throat filled the room like a lullaby.

"Thank you, Healer Paula," he said. "Leave the wine. I won't touch any more today."

"I'm glad to hear that."

"I suppose you've treated many old warriors."

"I wouldn't use your name and 'old' in the same sentence, Your Majesty."

He laughed, low and husky. "You know what I mean."

"I have. My older brothers fought in the last Tieran war. I saw what it was like for them when they came home." Her eldest brother had killed himself not long after returning and the memory of finding him hanging in the barn flashed through her mind. "Believe me, Your Majesty, wine is not where you will find comfort. Your values and that aerial, those are the places you should look." She cleared her throat. "If it pleases Your Majesty, I'll leave you to your day."

"Very well. And thank you, Healer Paula."

"Only doing my duty, sire."

Lieutenant Valiance's room was on the second floor of the barracks, beside Jarrett's quarters. In the early hours of morning, with the floor below noisy with men preparing for the day, Jarrett knew Valiance had to be doing the same.

The whole way to the lieutenant's room, Jarrett fumed and considered demoting Valiance or altogether kicking him out of the Palace Guard. However, standing in front of the door, he couldn't bring himself to do something so drastic.

On the one hand, Valiance had long been a friend. On the other, if he had taken a bribe or sold secrets, it would best to keep him close so as to watch him.

He pounded a fist on the door. "Val? I need to speak to you."

Bedsprings creaked, followed by footsteps. The door opened wide enough for Valiance to lean out. His dark brown hair was tousled and stubble peppered his chin.

"Is something wrong, Captain?" he asked.

"Get dressed and meet me in my quarters."

"Yes, Captain." The door closed.

Jarrett went into his quarters, which included a private bath and a bedchamber. He started to unbuckle his sword belt but changed his mind.

He didn't suspect—didn't want to suspect—Valiance of treachery. He wasn't stupid, however.

It wasn't long before Valiance joined him, knocking politely before entering. The golden double-headed eagle on his chest caught the light spilling in through the window.

"Have a seat, Valiance," Jarrett said, gesturing at the wooden chairs in front of the fireplace.

Valiance didn't appear worried as he sat in a chair. Jarrett took the other chair without speaking right away. He stared at Val, waiting for his expression to change. It didn't.

"I read your reports," Jarrett said, finally. "I have a few questions."

"Yes, Captain."

"Where were you when the King was nearly poisoned?"

"I had a family emergency just before it happened. I was in the city taking care of it. I wrote that in my report."

"You did. What you failed to note was that you were missing for two candlemarks and no one knew where you were. Do you mind telling me what that emergency was?"

"It's a very personal matter, Captain."

"When the King is nearly murdered, there's no such thing as personal matters."

The chair creaked as Valiance shifted in it. "It was my sister, sir. She had been accosted."

"Accosted?"

"She works as a tavern maid in one of the cleaner places older nobles enjoy attending. As she was returning home, a man tried to force himself on her."

"Did you notify the City Guard?"

"No, sir."

"Why not?"

"I taught my sister to fight, Captain. She managed to get away from the man. My mother asked me to come home, find who did it, and persuade him to never do it again. I didn't see a reason to bring the City Guard into it."

"For all you know, this man may make a habit of accosting tavern maids."

"I only thought of my sister, sir."

Jarrett rubbed his jaw. He had met Valiance's sister, Abelia, and found it hard to believe that a slip of a girl could get away from any man. However, if she knew how to make a man hurt in his private places, then that was another matter altogether. And most men don't expect a woman to fight back.

"What about the murder of Matteo Havens?" he continued.

"What about it, sir?"

"You said General Asher gladly gave you control over the investigation. General Asher tells me that you insisted."

Valiance reddened. "That is true, sir."

"You didn't mention that. Why did you insist you take on the investigation?"

Valiance looked down.

"Lieutenant?"

After a handful of heartbeats, he answered, "I wanted to prove myself, sir. I wanted to show that I could handle the job of Captain. I also didn't want to seem weak in front of the General. I thought if I held my own, he would respect me for it."

"Who did Matteo see that night?"

"I don't know."

"Did you try to question the captains under General Asher's command?"

"I did." He shifted from one foot to another.

"Were they forthcoming?"

"Not all of them. I think some were with women."

"Did you think to ask for General Asher's help?"

"I didn't want to bother him with it. I already suspected that it was a love affair gone askew."

"Was the page seeing any particular person on the side?"

"I said so in my report."

Jarrett smiled and it didn't feel like a nice one. "Tell me again."

"Mara Hawkins. She's married to one of the stablehands."

"And you talked to her?"

"Yes, Captain." He cleared his throat. "Why the questions, Captain?"

"I'm just checking facts, Lieutenant. I have one more question."

"Yes, sir?"

"How did you pay off that gambling debt?"

Valiance shifted in his chair again and cleared his throat. "I'm getting married."

That was not the answer he suspected. "Pardon?"

"You know the town of Spiderweb?"

"With an odd name like that, it's hard to forget once you've seen it on a map. It's near the coast."

"My mother arranged a match through a family friend and the dowry paid the debts."

"That's a bad use of a dowry, man. It's meant to help you set up house."

"I know, Captain. We were running low on options. I didn't want to admit it to you when you asked the other day."

Jarrett considered this. It sounded like Valiance had made some stupid decisions, the sort anyone new to a high-pressure position would make. And he'd known him for years. So, why didn't he feel better about it all? Was it because he was still questioning himself after leaving Clara behind in the Larkspur Mountains?

Valiance asked, "You don't believe me, do you, Captain?"

"It's not that, Val. Really. Some hard questions are being asked. I need to show I made due diligence."

He sighed. "Yes, sir. Am I to be put on leave?"

"No. I still need you."

"Yes, Captain. Thank you."

"You may go."

Valiance stood and saluted. Just as he reached the door, Jarrett called out, "Val?"

"Sir?"

"You didn't tell me your bride's name."

"Oh. Uh. Cassandra. Her name is Cassandra."

"It's a lovely name. I'm sure she'll make a

good wife."

"Thank you, Captain. Good day."

"Good day."

Jarrett didn't move to go downstairs and see to the day's roster. He sat in his chair, considering the likelihood of a traitor sleeping mere feet away.

The Palace kitchens were going at a full run to prepare for lunch, full of chatter, clatter, and steam, when Jarrett arrived. He snagged a passing maid holding a platter of steaming mushrooms and onions.

"Can you tell me where your mistress is?" he asked.

"She's outside checking the garden, Captain."

He released her and threaded through the crowd of cooks, helpers, and servers. The outdoors nearly startled him in their sudden quiet. An older woman with her grey hair pulled into a bun was inspecting a bed of herbs.

"Mistress Catriona?" he called as he walked

down the path.

She beamed at him. "Captain Jarrett, home from his travels. We missed you."

"It's good to be missed. How are you today?"

"As well as you can expect at my age."

"And your army?"

She laughed. Jarrett liked to tease her that she would never need to raise an army as she already had hundreds of loyal servants at her command.

"They're well, Captain. What brings you to my side of the Palace?"

"I wanted to speak to one of your maids, a Mara Hawkins."

"Mara? She's not in trouble, is she?"

"Not at all. I'd like to talk to her."

"That'd be very difficult, Captain. She left service over a fortnight ago."

He frowned, planting his hands on his hips. "Really?"

"Oh, yes. She had to hurry home to take care of her ailing father."

"Do you know if she had an admirer?"

"I try to stay out of the servants' lives unless I hear their work is being affected. I did hear that she was having a dalliance with one of the older pages."

"And where's home for Mara?"

"A hamlet downriver, called Patience."

"Can she read and write? Would she respond to a letter?"

Catriona raised her chin. "I expect all my servants to know their letters. If you write her, she'll reply."

"Good. And what of her husband?"

"He was a stablehand. He left service as well to go with her. I'm not sure he ever knew his wife was sneaking out on him. He never was a quick fellow."

"Did he have a temper?"

She shook her head. "He didn't have enough cleverness to have a temper. It was an arranged marriage and Mara never was happy with it."

"Was Mara seeing someone else, too?

Someone else who would have objected to her having another lover?"

Catriona stared off into distance while she thought about that. "No. I don't think so. Like I said, I don't pay much attention to my workers' private lives."

"I see. Thank you, Mistress."

"You're very welcome. She isn't in any trouble, I hope?"

"Not at all."

"Very good. Help yourself to a sticky bun on your way out."

"I have one more question."

"Oh?"

"Did Lieutenant Valiance, when he was Acting Captain, come down to talk to Mara?"

"He did. And it was a good thing, too, as her father fell ill not long after."

"Is that so?"

"Yes."

He smiled. "Thank you again. And thanks for the sticky bun."

She chuckled. "Men need to eat."

He gave her a salute and she laughed, shooing him away.

Jarrett's smile vanished as he considered her words. The fact that Mara left so soon after questioning struck him as suspicious. In fact, it rankled him so much that he left the kitchens without getting his treat.

Asher brought his shield up in time to block the soldier's cudgel. The blow reverberated through the steel and down his arm.

"Good," he shouted, side-stepping so that the western sun was in the soldier's eyes. "Again!"

The soldier swung again, coming in at an angle that threatened to knock the shield up and away, despite the light in his eyes. Asher stepped back, laughing.

"Ho!" He lowered the shield. "Excellent, soldier! Very good! You may rejoin your squad."

The soldier saluted and walked away. Asher enjoyed visiting the practice yards behind the barracks and working with the men. It kept him from being only "the general" and helped him to know where some of his men were in their training. And exercise helped him work out tension, especially after last night's fire.

He walked over to the low fence surrounding the yard and saw a small figure in grey robes standing by a rack of spears. A bit of surprised pleasure ran through Asher when recognized the person.

"Bran," he said, leaning the shield against the fence, "I'm glad you were able to come to the practice yard after all." His smile slipped away as he took in the boy's somber face, and the guilt he had been trying to ignore awoke in his heart. Not for the first time, he wondered how things would have been different, of the lives saved, if he had stopped Bruin and called for the City Guard. "I'm sorry about your mother."

Bran's eyes were red and swollen from crying but his voice was steady. "Thank you, General. Mistress Olivia said I was still allowed to come here. I have the afternoon to myself."

"I'm glad to hear it. Let me see if I can find someone to help you." He looked around for a captain or lieutenant to call over but saw no one in earshot. He started to tell Bran to go back to the barracks when he caught the lonely, longing expression in the boy's eyes. Pity welled up in him to nearly smother the self-incrimination. "Bran, would you like for me to teach you how to use a short sword?"

Bran brightened. "I would like that very much, sir."

"Hop over the fence, then, and we'll get started." Asher could not give back to Bran his mother or home, but he could at least give him some of his time. It wouldn't make up for his actions that led to Bran's mother's death, but it was something.

Chapter Nineteen
Two Weeks Later

Clara trembled as she neared the curve in the road.

The branches of the sycamores cast dappled sunlight. Their trunks were thicker and taller than she remembered.

Her pony responded to the tension in her legs, whinnying and prancing a small two-step. She loosened her grip on the reins and forced her legs to relax. Rolling her shoulders, Clara tried to beat back her sudden case of nerves.

The injured shoulder had mostly healed but still felt stiff. She rubbed it. Her chest was better, as well, and she thanked the Mother the cuts weren't deeper.

The pony flicked an ear at her but didn't try to dance around again. The mule nipped at Clara's pant leg and she smacked him on the nose.

They rounded the bend and stopped. The

tension roared back with a rush. Her pony snorted and sidled to the side.

Sheep grazed around the remains of a house. A stone chimney jutted upward and the lines of where walls once stood could be discerned in the sod. A shepherd boy sat on a stump of a tree Clara remembered her father cutting down for firewood on one of his rare sober days. The boy watched her with bored eyes.

Clara called out, "You live around here, boy?"

"All my life," the shepherd replied. He couldn't have been more than nine summers.

"Do you know when this house burned down?"

"No. It happened a long time ago. Story is, the man living here did it on purpose, because his wife killed and cooked their little girl."

She'd forgotten how tales could grow in small villages. "What happened to the man and his wife?"

"The wife ran away. Took up with some fellow a valley over. The old man still lives here.

He carves toys and things for Sal. He's the dry goods merchant. The old man—he was sittin' by the fountain when I drove the sheep out at dawn. He's probably still there. If he ain't, then Sal knows where he is."

Clara thanked the boy and left the sad ruin behind. As she approached the village, she had the disconcerting feeling of being present both in the now and in the past.

A field of burgeoning corn grew to the left and, in her memory, she saw children playing in it. As if it was that day all over again, the baker's girl stopped and waved at her. The wind shifted and, for a brief moment, Clara thought she heard the sounds of the spring festival. The smoke from the smithy rose in the air, in the same place it always did. She caught a glimpse of the shape of the first buildings of the village and realized nothing had changed.

The lump in her throat felt so large, she feared it would choke her.

In the village, people walked along the dirt

street. A man drove a wagon toward her and she edged to the side to let him by. Children ran from an alley, crossed the road, and on into another alley. A peddler set up his cart beside the apothecary, calling out to everyone who passed by that he had the best ribbons this side of Candor. Up ahead, the fountain gurgled water. Women were crowded around it, filling buckets as they chatted. A wizened old man sat in a slat chair beside the fountain, whittling.

Her mouth went dry and her heart thundered in her ears. Clara stopped her pony.

Even though his shoulders were slumped and his hands were bent from arthritis, she recognized Da in the way he propped his elbows on his knees and in the scuffed boots he wore.

Da didn't react as she approached. His attention centered on the narrow block of wood in his hands. He paused in his whittling to turn it over in his hands. "Listening to it", he used to say.

On evenings when he wasn't drunk or the

weather was too bad to go to the tavern, he would talk to her while he whittled. He used to tell her that the wood would only be what it was and if the carver, tried to push it elsewhere, then it wouldn't take. The result wouldn't work or would be ugly. So, he stopped and listened every now and again.

Clara dismounted. Opened her mouth but nothing came out. She swallowed. "Da," she said.

Watery hazel eyes—her eyes—gazed up at her. "Do I know ye, boy?" he asked, taking in her clothes and short hair.

"I'm Clara, Da. It's me."

Disbelief mingled with hope on his face as he pushed himself out of the chair, leaving the knife and wood in the seat. He was slightly stooped and at Clara's height. He took a step forward. "Clara? You ain't dead?"

Tears clouded her eyes. She wiped them away. "No, Da."

He started to reach toward her throat. His hand dropped away. "I don't see a collar on ye."

"I'm not a slave. Not anymore."

His mouth worked. "I tried to get to ye. It took so damn long for the drink to clear from my head and by the time I got there, it was too late."

A brief smile burst onto Clara's face as a fear she didn't know she had, that Da hadn't really cared after all, faded. "I kept thinking, for the longest time, that you would find me."

"I tried. When I got back—half mad with grief I was. Burned the house down. The old lord, he nearly had me killed for that. The presbyter stopped him. Your mother, she ran off and I haven't seen her since." Da straightened as best he could. "I haven't tasted a drop of ale or beer since, either." His eyes searched her face. "Will ye ever forgive me?"

She swallowed. "I was angry at you for a long time." Tears slipped down her cheeks. "And then I was angry at Mother. And then I was angry at my master. And then I was angry at the usurper. Then there wasn't anyone to be angry at anymore except myself."

Da laid a hand on her arm.

"I knew, Da." More tears fell. "That day she sold me. I knew what was going to happen. I didn't understand, so I didn't run. I didn't try to wake you until—" She sucked down a ragged gasp and it came out a sob. Da drew her into a hug and she rested her head on his shoulder.

She cried for all the years lost. She cried for the mistake of a child. She cried for the childhood she could have had.

He rubbed her back in soothing circles. "You were a wee girl. I was s'posed to've protected you. An' I didn't. I was a worthless drunk. I am so sorry, Clarie."

It wasn't until that moment that Clara remembered the nickname he had for her. And once he said it, she wondered how she could have ever forgotten it. Pulling back, she wiped her face with her sleeve and sniffled. "I forgive you, Da."

He squeezed her hand. "I don't deserve it. Thank ye. How did you come to be free? And why are you in man's clothes with your hair chopped off?"

"It's a long story."

"We have the time. Let us go into the tavern and you can tell me."

Clara and her father, hand in hand, slowly crossed the square to the tavern.

The small tavern stunk of pipe tobacco, ale, and fried grease. A few patrons mulled over bowls of porridge. Clara's father waved at the tavern keep.

"Bring some eggs and ham, Ivan," he said. "And some milk. You still drink milk, Clarie?"

"I do." She pulled out a chair for him at a table.

Ivan replied, "That calls for quite the coin, Egbert."

"I'm good for it. Today's a special day. My daughter's home."

Ivan's eyes widened in surprise and gave Clara a curious glance before slipping off to the back. In no time, he brought out steaming platters of fried ham and scrambled eggs, with thick slices of brown rye bread. Egbert tossed a coin at him. The tavern keeper bit the round piece as he walked away.

"I live over the dry good merchant's place," Egbert explained, "an' he gives me a decent cut of whatever he sells that I've made. Good man, he is." He layered ham and eggs on one of the slices. Clara picked up a slice of bread and shoved egg onto it. She wasn't sure how much of the story to tell.

"Go on," her father said. "I know it isn't all 'appy."

So, she told him, skipping over some of the uglier parts of her tenure on the slave market. She made special note of the cook, Relly, who more or less raised her. Clara told him about Lord and Lady Dwervin and the handmaiden Lily, as well as Gavin and how she helped in the taking of the castle. Then came Emmerich and the campaign. Finally, Marduk and her time at his Court. When Clara finished her tale, Egbert held his half-eaten bread and meat in one hand while he stared off into the air.

After a long pause, he swallowed and set his food down. "You always was stubborn. I suppose I shouldn' be surprised that ye would slip off from your protector like ye did, to come here. Yer mother—she knew you'd be special."

Clara laughed, surprised. "Da."

"Naw, naw. Not my thrice-cursed wife. Naw. Yer mother, yer *real* mother. She should've raised you. She saw in you wha' no one else did 'round here." He smiled. "Aside from me."

Clara thought her heart might burst from her chest from surprise. "So, my real mother didn't sell me? Was my real mother Tieran?"

"Aye. She said she was from Aphos, the capital of Tier."

"Was?"

"Well, is. I s'pose. I 'aven't seen her in many years."

"Why didn't she stay? What happened?"

He cleared his throat. "I was a soldier, in the first Tieran War. Men took up wi' all sorts of loose women on the other side. We on the border like to say that a lot of our children have the Tieran look. Well, on t'other side, on their border, I'm sure people say a lot of the children have the Lorstian look. Anyway, I met yer mother on the return trip, when we was done on that venture. I wanted to bring her back to be my wife." He paused, his face taking on a thoughtful expression.

When he spoke again, his voice was sad and wistful. "Her name was Thalia. My mother 'ad arranged my marriage, as was proper. I thought that if I showed up with a pregnant Tieran wife, it would end that mess." Egbert cleared his throat again. "As I'm sure you know, armies move slow. Ours 'ad alotta wounded so we was slower than most. We got trapped in the mountains over t' winter. Thalia gave birth t' you up there. Ah, the wind was howlin', snow was flyin' and lightnin' split the air."

Egbert sat back in his chair, his eyes grew distant. He shook himself. "I'll never forget. There is Thalia, holdin' you, feedin' you, and she gets this funny expression on her face. She says, 'Egbert, I can't come wi' you. I gotta stay here. You need to take this 'un to Bluebell and raise her. Say she's an orphan you picked up so's that woman your ma picked out will marry you'. I tried to get her t' tell me why but she wouldn't. The next mornin', she was gone. Luckily, one of the captains' women had a babe, so she acted as a wet nurse. When I got back t' Bluebell, I did as Thalia said. Tol' everyone you was an orphan I picked up an' wanted t' raise you as my own. Lorna wasn't 'appy. She married me all t' same because she had less choice than me at the time."

"Do you think Thalia could see the future, like me?" Clara pushed aside her barely touched platter.

"Now that, I dunno. Closed-mouth, Thalia was. Always proper-like. I was suspicious, y'know? I've always thought she was runnin' from somethin'. Tierans, they can be a funny people. More superstitious than a lot of folk around here and they do believe in their Seers. I guess it's possible she had the gift."

"A Tieran diplomat once told me that an empty seat is kept beside their throne, in honor of a Seer that once saved their kingdom."

"Hmph. Speakin' of a throne, why aren't you in Bertrand with the King? You got a gift, Clarie. Y'ought to use it."

"I would if I could, Da." She felt her face heat up. "I haven't had visions since the end of the war."

Egbert patted her hand and held it.

After a brief silence, she said, "I'll stay here with you."

"Why would ye do a thing like that?"

"You're my Da. I should take care of you."

"You belong with the King."

"I don't have visions anymore."

"They'll come back one day. Bluebell ain't a place for you. Thalia thought ye was special. You need to go where your specialness can be seen an' appreciated."

"Da, no."

"If I say I want t'go meet the King, will ye go with me?" A mischievous light glinted in his eye.

"What?"

"Bluebell ain't the place for you and you are gonna be stubborn about wanting to take care of me. So, let's get a wagon and go to Bertrand. Mayhap the King will let us stay a time."

"Da!" Clara suddenly had an image of Emmerich formally asking for her hand and it flustered her beyond words.

He laughed. "Where did you think you got your stubbornness from?" He shifted in his chair. "Ivan! Know anybody sellin' a wagon? And we'll need new and proper clothes for my daughter."

Chapter Twenty

A scream ripped from Bran's throat. He jerked upright in his bed. Gasping and shaking, he covered his eyes with his hands, as if that could keep the images from replaying in his mind. Mutters and questions filled the dormitory as the other boys sat up and wanted to know what just happened. The door opened and Bran heard the solid steps of Mistress Olivia, the dormitory matron, as she approached his bed. The mattress dipped. A soft hand lay on his shoulder.

"Bran?" Olivia asked. "What happened?"

There had been flames and screaming. Not just human voices but also aerials, their cries both in his mind and in his ears. The charred scent of burned flesh caked the back of his throat. He still felt the heat of the fires against his skin. A sob bubbled up and the tears weren't far behind. The matron drew him to her and he cried into her soft shoulder. She rocked him, rubbing his back until the tears eventually stopped.

She pulled away slightly. "Would you like some warm milk and honey?"

"Yes, please."

Together, they left the dormitory and Bran tried to ignore the stares. He tried to not think about what the other boys might have been thinking, that the poor orphan boy who could see the future was getting special treatment again.

In the small kitchen that served the dormitories, the matron heated some milk at the hearth and stirred honey into it. She didn't say a word until Bran had the warm mug in his hands and they sat across from each other at the table. She clasped her hands on the worn table.

"Bran," Mistress Olivia said, "was the nightmare about your mother?"

He sipped the milk, his shoulders relaxing as the warmth seeped through him. "I don't think so. There was fire but not the one that hurt her."

"Is that the only reason why you think it wasn't about her?"

"There was a giant and a man was riding him." Bran still could feel the way the ground rattled beneath his feet, jarring his bones.

While the matron kept her face neutral, he could see the sudden tension in her clasped hands. "Are you certain?"

"Yes, matron."

"What else did you see?"

"Fire. And I heard aerials screaming."

"I'll be right back, Bran. Don't go anywhere." She stood and left him alone in the kitchen.

Where would I go? He kept the question to himself. Slipping down from his chair, he went to sit cross-legged in front of the hearth with the mug of milk.

He wondered if Robert was awake somewhere in the building. Despite their first encounter when Bran came to the Academy, he'd hardly seen the other boy. Class and chores filled up Bran's days, and the wizards kept Robert busy. Other than saying hello in the halls, they hardly ever spoke.

And what would good would seeing Robert do? He wouldn't understand. Rob belonged to a huge family near the docks. His father was a shipwright and his mother a baker. When the fires hit, Rob's family was able to escape but they still lost their home.

Bran wished he could see the King.

King Emmerich was a nice man and perhaps he would have good advice for him, about how you're supposed to live without a family.

And there was Niall, the beautiful aerial fledgling. If Bran held Niall, maybe Niall would know that Bran's two biggest wishes were to have his mother back and to not be able to see the future anymore and Niall would use his magic to grant those wishes.

No, it probably didn't work that way. The aerial had given him the ability but maybe couldn't take it away.

Bran never wanted to know the future. Well, no, that wasn't quite right, either. As he thought about it, Bran realized that he had wanted to know when the bullies were going to come after him so he could avoid it. He hadn't known how to understand the dream, not until it was too late.

The image of the boy's dead eyes filled his mind.

Bran winced away from the memory and focused on the glowing embers in the fireplace. The fire had been banked before everyone went to bed and it only threw enough heat to warm. His meditation teacher, Xander, used a candle when teaching them how to focus and clear the mind. Ember-glow would have to do. Straightening, he held the mug loosely in his hands as he focused on the red lines snaking through the black char.

He breathed in and out in slow, measured breaths. Just like Master Xander explained, Bran paid attention to the way he sat, the feel of his clothes and the stone beneath him, and then began to forget them. There was only the flame and his breath. In and out. In and out. There was only the warmth of the fire and throb of Bran's heart as he breathed—in and out. In and out.

Fire leapt from the wood and engulfed Bran, dragging him headfirst into its heart. He opened his mouth to shout for help. Nothing came.

Grass replaced stone. A cold clearing replaced the warm dormitory kitchen. Bran stood just outside the light of a campfire. One person slept beside it while another slept in a wagon. In the near distance, he could see moonlight gracing the tops of mountains.

Wrapping his arms around himself, he walked into the light of fire. How did he even get here?

One of the people stirred and sat up. It was a pretty woman, her short curly brown hair tousled from sleep. Her Tieran-tilted eyes widened at seeing him.

She stood, her blanket falling from her. Dressed in a woolen dress with an overgown, she could have been one of those sprites his mother used to say lived in the woods. The lady was certainly small enough, with a delicate face. She walked over and knelt in front of him.

"How did you get here?" she asked.

Bran opened his mouth. Again, no sound came. His eyes widened in fear.

The woman reached out to touch his shoulder. Her fingers passed through it. Understanding lit up her hazel eyes. "Oh. I see. Don't worry. It's normal to not be able to talk. My name is Clara."

The Lady Seer! Bran grinned.

"You've heard of me, then?" Something rustled in the bushes. It sounded like someone moving through the woods. Clara gestured at him in a shooing motion. "You need to go back."

Bran widened his eyes and shook his head. He didn't know how.

"You can do it. Picture where you were. How you were sitting. What the room was like." The noise drew closer. "Close your eyes and concentrate. Go on. I'll try to find you if I can."

He did as she told him, remembering how the stone felt underneath him and the warm mug in his hands. The cold eased away, the chirp of crickets and night birds faded, and the light of the fire blossomed before him. The kitchen materialized around him, like an image coming into focus. Mistress Olivia and Lord Bruin knelt on either side of him.

Bruin cocked his head. "I thought you were told not to go anywhere."

"I saw Lady Clara," Bran replied.

"You did? Where was she?"

"On a mountain, I think."

"Did she say anything?"

"She said she was going to try to find me and help me. She told me how to come back."

"Anything else?"

"There was something coming in the woods."

The matron explained, "Probably just a deer."

"Probably," Lord Bruin agreed. "All right, young Bran, let's get you up and to the table. You can tell me all about the nightmare you had. Mistress, you can return to your duties. I'll take care of the youngster."

Mistress Olivia left them and Bruin took Bran,

wobbling on legs gone to sleep, back to the table. Only a thin level of cold milk remained in the mug. Bran sucked it down. He knew better than to be wasteful.

Bruin clasped his hands on the table. "So, Mistress Olivia tells me you had a dream about a giant?"

"Yes, sir, but I don't know why."

"Has anyone mentioned a giant to you?"

"When I was a page, I heard some things."

Nothing in Bruin's face betrayed his reaction to that. He only asked, "And what happened in this dream? Mistress Olivia said you saw fire and heard aerials."

"The giant was destroying the city and everything was on fire."

"Like the fire that killed your mother?"

"I guess."

"Did it feel like a vision to you?"

Bran considered this. "It seemed really real."

"Nightmares can feel that way."

He hung his head, feeling miserable for some

reason he couldn't quite explain. It felt like the older wizard brushed off his bad dream, like it somehow didn't matter. Why should it matter, anyway? Feelings tangled in Bran's chest and he couldn't make head nor tail of the snarl. "Is the King all right?" Bran blurted.

"Why do you ask?"

"Just wondering."

"King Emmerich is fine," Bruin replied. "He's worried about what's happened in the city and he has a lot on his mind."

"Will you tell him I said hello when you see him again?"

"I will do that. Are you ready to try to go to bed again?"

"Yes, sir."

Bruin led the way back to the boys' dormitory. Bran came to a halt just up the hall from the door.

"I'd like to go in alone," he told Lord Bruin.

If the request puzzled the wizard, he didn't show it. "Goodnight then, Bran. I'll see you tomorrow afternoon in our alchemy class."

"Yes, sir." He entered the dorm and ignored the whispered conversations that came to a halt.

Bruin walked slowly back to his quarters, his mind full of what the matron had told him about Bran's dream. Cool night wind caught his hair as he left the students' residence and crossed the courtyard to the staff quarters. He stopped in the center, searching out constellations in the sky. There was the Water Jar and the Goose Girl directly above. To the south, he found the Phoenix and the tail of the Unicorn.

"Fire and a giant," he muttered. *And aerials screaming.*

Had Bran been dreaming about the night his mother died and his mind threw in the giant because of something he overheard? Or had it been a hint of the future? And Bran seeing Lady Clara, was that like Emmerich seeing her? Was there something special about the lady or was it a common trait among those who saw the future?

Second Sight was so rare in Lorst that very little had been written about it. He asked the Tieran diplomat about such appearances, in a theoretical fashion. He had only replied vaguely that anything in this world could happen. Bruin wasn't sure if it was because he didn't know either, or because Tier was angry at Emmerich for ignoring their offers of marriage to a Tieran princess.

Earlier that day, Bruin sought out some of the aerials, to see how they fared. They conveyed to him their intention to leave Bertrand. By noon tomorrow, the only rainbow-feathered creature in all the city would be in Emmerich's red sling. So, didn't that mean Bran's dream was only that—a dream?

An owl hooted from somewhere. Bruin began to walk toward the staff quarters.

Clara should have reached Bluebell by now, so what was she doing in a clearing? And who was the other person with her?

At that moment, he decided not to speak of this to King Emmerich. He was under enough stress and Bruin did not want to bring him more unsettling news.

Chapter Twenty-One

Clara watched as the boy faded from sight. The rustling behind her grew closer. She stood and faced the woods. Egbert still hadn't stirred, which seemed unusual. Perhaps old age made sleep deeper? Nevertheless, a bad feeling stirred in her gut.

The head of a giant wolf, as if formed from shadow and forest, loomed at the edge of the clearing. It stared at her with eyes that glowed with a dull, blue flame.

From its head to the ground, it stood as tall as a horse. That thought made Clara acutely aware that the ponies they got for the wagon were each blissfully asleep despite the predator's appearance.

She stared back at it, afraid to move or shout. If the creature decided to charge, then it would. Movement or noise would only speed that decision.

After a taut moment, the wolf faded back into

the woods. She heard the slithering susurration of paws over leaves, the crackling of twigs underfoot, and then silence again.

She considered her next step. A sense of intuition that had lain silent and dormant for months now clamored for attention and urged her to chase after the wolf.

If she had learned anything over the last year, it was caution. Sometimes, it was good to charge ahead with reckless abandon. Her sense of self-preservation warned against that this time.

Walking over to her father, she shook him. The old man made no move. She laid a hand on his chest and felt his heartbeat. Its soft rhythm was steady and strong.

Da had been in good spirits all day. As they left Bluebell, he told stories and made jokes. When they bedded down, he didn't make any complaints. Furthermore, it was still too cold at night for snakes to be about. Even if it wasn't, he didn't appear in pain or dying, so it wasn't venom.

She thought about the wolf's appearance and lack of response from their ponies. Going over to where they were tied, Clara examined them and found them to be more deeply asleep than she thought an animal could manage. It all pointed to one thing: magic.

Could this be connected to the giant? To Marduk's creatures?

The pull became more insistent, to follow the giant wolf.

Moving to her bed roll, Clara buckled on her long knife and tossed her heavy cloak over her shoulders. She'd discarded it earlier as the fire had been enough for her. She would need it now for her climb. From their bags, she fetched a small pouch containing flint and tinder, as well as a dry torch and a water skin. The water skin she slung over her shoulder, and stuffed the fire making pouch into the larger one that hung from her waist. The torch she stuffed behind her belt.

Clara couldn't imagine what else to take. She doubted she would need more provisions beyond water.

"Nothing else to do," she muttered to herself and strode over to the camp's edge. A small game trail snaked into the dark forest from the edge of the clearing.

Plunging into mountain woods at night was an invitation for death-by-sudden-drop. She plunged forward anyway. She hadn't gone more than a few feet into the woods, batting at unseen branches and vines that snatched at her skirts, when a blue glow, unlike anything she had seen before, appeared.

Coming to a halt, she watched as the glow strengthened into a light that cut a path through the woods. She could make out the rise and fall of the ground, the way around holes that could break her ankle. Somehow, this made her feel threatened rather than comforted. Her intuition tugged her forward. She began to follow the blue-lit path.

As she walked, the forest outside of the path

faded away. Clara got a sense of movement, things shifting all around her. When she tried to see, her eyes couldn't focus on anything and nausea rolled over her. She focused on the path at her feet and hoped her father would be all right while she was gone.

The grassy, root-strewn ground rippled, though it felt solid beneath the soles of her boots. Her stomach did another flip and she raised her head. The blue light ahead shone like a star.

Was she still on the mountain? How far had she come? What if the light ended and she came out on the other side of Tier, at the foot of the legendary Sawtooth Alps? What if the light ended and she plummeted into the Bell Sea? She dared not stop. Clara pressed on until the light dimmed and the world solidified around her again.

She stood on an uneven mountain road. To her left, a wall of rock towered. To her right, the light of stars revealed an outline of the familiar, smooth shoulders of the Larkspurs.

She pulled the torch from her belt and lit it. The crackling, orange tongue of flame revealed a curve in the path ahead. Somewhere before her, a large animal chuffed and shifted. She laid a hand on the hilt of her knife and slowly walked forward.

At the bend in the road Clara halted.

A dozen yards ahead, tall torches lined the road that snaked up the mountainside to the crumbling fortress. More torches and balls of white witchlight lit the old stone walls. What arrested her attention, however, were the creatures.

They lay or sat scattered along the road. Panthers and bears three times normal size with scales glittering along their shoulders and spine. Six-legged lizards the size of ponies with horns twisting from their heads lounged beside dog-like animals with long fangs and spines on whip-like tails.

The creatures watched her.

Clara's hands clutched torch and hilt as she began to move forward. Fear burned in her gut and veins. Her shoulders ached with tension as she passed each of the living nightmares. Their eyes reflected fire and starlight.

When Clara reached the steps leading to the open portcullis, a new rush of fear left her light-headed.

Flanking either side stood a pair of man-like creatures. They had mottled gray and brown skin and stooped backs, their knuckles dragging the ground. Each of them stood a full foot taller than the tallest man she knew. Jarrett's war horse, Heartsblood, would be like a stringy foal next to them.

She'd seen a picture of these things once in a book in the Palace library. The book called them ogres.

Neither of them reacted to her presence. Staring dully ahead, they could have been mistaken for statues. However, they stunk too much to be stone.

She reminded herself that Emmerich wouldn't turn back at this moment. Also, she'd been brought here for a reason. She rather doubted she would be allowed to flee now.

Clara ascended the steps and passed under the portcullis into the keep. She found it empty.

She flexed the hand on her knife's hilt, grimacing at the ache in her knuckles. The wrappings on the hilt and the steel ball of the pommel left impressions in her palm. She moved forward.

Halfway across the keep, the doors to the Great Hall opened. Clara jerked her knife from her scabbard and settled into a fighting crouch, hoping her skirts wouldn't hinder her.

A woman stepped out onto the wide stone porch before the doors. She wore a bronze-colored gown that Clara recognized as Tieran: low-cut, tight bodice whose skirt flared around her. Her gray-streaked hair was caught up in a bun with a cascade of curls framing her face.

The woman held her hands out. "Welcome,

Clara. It's so good to see you." Her voice had the curious, lilting accent of all Tierans.

"Who are you?" Clara replied, not bothering to move from her defensive posture.

"I am your mother." The woman came down the steps and stopped. The train of her gown spread behind her.

"That," remarked Clara, "is incredibly convenient."

"Not as convenient as you think. Please. We don't have much time. Put your blade down."

It occurred to her that, if this woman had control of the creatures outside, with who knows how many inside the fortress, then there wasn't much she could do with a long knife. Clara lowered her arm and straightened.

"What do you mean," she asked, "that this isn't as convenient as I think?"

The woman stepped closer. Clara could see a hungry, desperate expression in her eyes.

"My son," she said, "your half-brother, brought you here. You and I are both his prisoners now."

Clara frowned. Both his prisoners? How could she be the prisoner of anyone with the portcullis open?

Dread shot through her as she realized she'd walked into a trap. Turning on her heel, she bolted for the exit, only for the portcullis to slam closed just as she reached it. She skidded to a halt and cried out in frustration. She kicked the iron grille.

"There has to be another way out," she declared, turning to face the woman. "There's always another way out."

"Trust me. I've tried."

Clara strode across the keep. "How about the sewer?"

"Tried that, too." The woman's lips curled wryly. "I ruined a perfectly good gown in the process."

On closer inspection, Clara could see the woman was of an age to be her mother, with lines and crow's feet, and they certainly shared the same nose and shape of the eyes. But while Clara's eyes were hazel, hers were brown. "What's your name?"

"Thalia."

That was the name Da had given but what if this was a trick and the woman knew that? "Why would my half-brother trap us here?"

"Because he doesn't want either of us to stop him." She pointed at the torch. "That's burning low."

Clara cast it aside on the stones. "Stop him?"

"He's the wizard preparing to attack Bertrand."

There were so many questions she didn't know where to start. She pinched her nose and forced her mind to take this in. She had every right to doubt this woman. The same intuition that prodded her earlier whispered that Thalia spoke truth.

Clara wanted to ask about the wizard, yet the desire to learn if this was really her mother burned hotter. Dropping her hand and falling back to habits born of a mute, she remained silent, scowling at Thalia.

Thalia smiled. "Please, come in. I have some mulled wine." She started back up the steps.

After hesitating a moment, Clara sheathed her long knife and followed. It wasn't as if she could do something else, and staying out in the cold seemed too petulant.

A few balls of pale mage light lit the dusty Great Hall. The vague shapes of banners hung from the walls. The remains of a long table lay in the center of the room. As they passed it, Clara could make out ax and claw marks.

Thalia led the way into a room that might have once been a gathering area but which she had turned into her room.

A couch sat before the fireplace. A makeshift kitchen had been set up on the hearth with old, dented copper pots and pans. A cot piled with furs stood to one side beside a scratched wardrobe with a warped door.

Thalia knelt at the hearth and drew mulled

wine from a small pot to fill two cups. "Let's sit," she said.

Clara took a seat on the couch. Thalia handed her the drink and sat on the other end. Beyond the crackling of the fire, the rest of the castle was silent. By now, Clara had finally selected a question.

"Why did you leave?" she asked. "After my birth, you just handed me over to Da and left. Why?" Perhaps the answer could help her decide whether to believe her.

"I had a vision while I held you. I saw that my family would find me and force me to return. They would take you away. I feared you would be left out to die. However, if I walked away at that moment, there was a chance that you would grow up and I would see you again. Not only that, I knew you would serve a greater purpose."

"Where did you go afterward?"

"I returned to my family and they married me off. I had two more children. One of them is Remus and he's the one who trapped us here."

"Remus?" Clara thought about the young man she met in Bluebell, who she assumed was the unnamed wizard Jarrett had met. "Is he my height, blue eyes, and with a small scar on his lower lip?"

"That's him! Have you met him?"

"He approached me in Hernesferry. I just thought he was some wizard Emmerich had sent to check on me. Why would he do that?"

Thalia smiled grimly. "He was always fascinated by you. When he was growing up, he felt isolated by his powers because there was no one else in the family quite like him. None of them had his quick-thinking or brilliance. To make him feel less lonely, I told him about you, his elder sister living in a faraway land who would one day grow up to be a woman of great talent. It was his favorite bedtime story."

"I've been reduced to a bedtime story. Lovely."

"I was trying to comfort him. I fear it did more damage than good."

Clara felt as if all this information was going to split her head open. "I don't know whether to believe you."

"Please do. I have the Sight, same as you, though it comes to me only rarely now. It saved Egbert's life more than once." Thalia chuckled. "He didn't recognize my gift. He just thought I was lucky."

"Let me see if I understand this. You ran away from home, met my father, had me and left. Now, one of your sons from your other marriage has trapped us in this castle."

"Missing some pieces of information, isn't it?"

"I should say so." Clara sipped the wine without thinking and raised her brows. "This is really good."

"It's an old family recipe." She sipped her own before setting it down on a crate serving as a table. "I come from nobility. For me, it was a cage. All I wanted was my own life. That caused a disagreement with my father and I ran away to punish him. The war with Lorst broke out soon after and I joined a camp of soldiers on their way to the front. As you can imagine, there are very few jobs for women in a camp.

"I'm not proud of that. I didn't know what else to do. After a battle where we Tierans lost, the Lorstian soldiers came to raid the camp. A group of them took an interest in me. They tried to rape me. Your father intervened." Thalia smiled. "He was quite handsome and courageous, your father. He offered to make sure I returned to safe territory in Tier. I didn't want to go back. I offered myself as his paramour if he swore to protect me. He agreed but it wasn't long before he asked for more."

It was all so detailed. Clara wanted to believe her. "Did you know his mother had arranged a marriage for him here?"

"I did. He didn't try to hide that fact, or the fact that he didn't really love me. He only wanted to do what I had done: shake off parental control for his own desires. I agreed to marry him, if only to get out of Tier. After the wedding, I set about trying to get pregnant as soon as possible so he wouldn't abandon me once we were in Lorst and he'd shown his family what he was willing to do to be his own man."

Clara wondered if Thalia had been happy when she discovered her pregnancy or only resigned to her fate. However, she kept her curiosity to herself and waited for her mother to continue.

Thalia said, "When I had you, and received my vision, I realized I had brought a child of importance into the world. I also realized that I love you very much and wanted a chance at seeing you again, rather than have you taken away forever."

"Are you sure about that? Are you sure you wouldn't have seen me again?"

"Do you ever doubt your own visions?"

That caught Clara up short and silence drew out between them as she considered that. Finally, she said, "Maybe I would have done the same."

"It wasn't easy to walk away. And into a

snowstorm, no less! I have minor magic and it wasn't enough to guarantee I would survive."

"So, you went home and let yourself be married off."

"I married a minor member of nobility." She made a rolling gesture with her hand. "The closest Lorstian term is 'baron'. I had two children, both sons. They aren't much younger than you. The very youngest, Remus, whom you've met, displayed magic. We had him trained by the best magicians but he disappeared after he reached his majority."

"Why is he attacking Bertrand?"

"Like many young men of station in Tier, Remus hates Lorst. They claim it's because of a loyalty to Tier. I think they hate their own lives, so they turn that anger elsewhere. When I received a letter that he had joined the Academy in Bertrand, I was surprised and hopeful. I thought maybe he had let go of his hate. After a time, he offered to bring me to the Court to meet the new King Emmerich. However, the men he sent brought me here and I quickly learned I was a prisoner. It seemed he feared my intervention. What he feared exactly, I don't know."

"So, he's just doing this because he doesn't like Lorst?" Clara shook her head. "There has to be more to it than that."

"I'm sure there is. Unfortunately, I don't know it. When he came here and declared his intentions, I tried to talk sense into him. All he would say is that you would be coming here soon. That he saw to it the moment he discovered you."

"Discovered me? At Court?"

"He claims he recognized you the moment he saw you."

The idea of a half-brother in eye line without her knowing sent a shiver down Clara's spine. "You said he was the youngest. What about the other?"

"His name is Alexander and he's only a year or year and a half younger than yourself. He has a commission in the Tieran military, where he serves in the cavalry."

I have a family. Clara's mind spun with the possibilities. "This could all be a trap or-or something. You could be lying."

"Child, what have you been through in life to make you so slow to trust?"

"I'm going to find a way out." Clara set her cup down with a clack and stood. "You can come if you wish." Turning on her heel, she strode out of the room and into the Great Hall.

Chapter Twenty-Two

Emmerich woke sweating and shaking.

Another nightmare.

Another trip to that damn underground ritual room.

Another replay of Gavin dying while Emmerich watched.

He sat up and scrubbed his face with both hands. He half-expected to see Clara in the room, watching him with worried eyes. Of late, he'd been seeing her everywhere. It happened so often that a part of him whispered that it couldn't really be her reaching out to him. He had to be going insane.

He got out of bed and tugged on a robe, belting it tightly around his waist, and went into the sitting room. From his nest of blankets in front of the fire, Niall lifted his head to watch Emmerich go to the sideboard.

He wrestled out of the twists of cloth he wound around himself and fluttered over to the sideboard. Now with the splint off and fully recovered, Niall loved to land on the furniture. His landing and taking off left marks that the maids were constantly trying to buff out.

Emmerich poured himself some water and scratched Niall on his eye ridges. Niall sniffed at Emmerich's cup.

"Oh, no." He lifted it slightly out of reach. "This is for me."

Niall chirped. Emmerich felt the creature's mind brush against his, sending feelings of worry and fear with snatches of a dream about darkness, earth, and blood.

"Are my dreams invading your sleep?" he asked. "I'm sorry, young one."

Scooping up the aerial, Emmerich carried him to the couch, where he sat and arranged Niall on his lap. Petting him, he sipped his water. Ever since Healer Paula had warned him about relying over much on wine, he'd been careful to scale it back. But thinking about it brought a wistful longing. He just wanted the dreams to stop, if only for a short while. The wine helped.

Healer Paula had returned to her normal duties after Niall made a full recovery. Emmerich suddenly wished her back, if only to have someone to talk to.

Sometimes, it felt as if the self-doubt and the fear ate away at him. How could anyone expect a former general, with hands drenched in the blood of his friends, to be a good king? He couldn't even prevent the slaughter of aerials or people from rioting. It didn't matter that this all appeared to be a scheme long in the making. Emmerich was a failure. Perhaps he should trade the water for wine, if only to forget for a while.

Niall made a soft crooning sound and rose up on his back legs to rub his cheek against Emmerich's. Unfolding a wing, the aerial draped it over Emmerich's shoulder. The arm holding the cup of water froze.

An aerial is giving me a hug, he thought.

Niall lifted his head and cocked it so that one bright emerald eye stared into one of

Emmerich's. A feeling of calm, joy, peace, and serenity washed over Emmerich. Unbidden, thoughts of how good of a person he was, how kind he was, floated up in his mind. Tears welled in his eyes. Leaning forward slowly, he set the cup on the table and with a now-freed hand, he caressed Niall's back.

"Thank you, little one."

Running footsteps broke the moment and Emmerich surged to his feet as a guard burst into the room. The guard stumbled to a halt at seeing his king standing there and saluted.

"Your Majesty," he said, "the creatures are attacking. And the giant—with a wizard. They're destroying the Low Quarters at this moment."

Excitement, dread, and anticipation, all of the old feelings he once felt before battle, snapped through Emmerich like lightning through a tree.

"Go fetch Healer Paula from the Healer Hall," he instructed. Emmerich couldn't leave Niall alone while he faced danger. Over the past few weeks, a deep bond had developed between the pair. Niall had become more than simply a pet or an amusing creature. And he knew Niall would go half-mad with what he was feeling. Emmerich would do his best to block it but there were no guarantees. Someone needed to remain to soothe him.

"After you speak to her," Emmerich continued, "find me a squire."

Valiance felt sick. The bells of the temples rang, their rolling tolls filling the night air and tumbling through the open window by his bed. Unlike the measured tones of bells telling the time, these were ongoing peals of panic.

He studied the letter in his hands. His sister's handwriting was fine and spidery in the lamplight. The seams showed the wear of repeated opening and closing.

It was short, unlike Abelia's usually long and flowery letters. Dated from three weeks ago, it only read,

Mother and Father are doing well. We're

leaving on the morning barge to the coast, and from there to Mauvia. Father understands how you need to stay behind. Mother and I think it's awful! Please be at the docks and come with us.

All my love, Abbey.

By now, if nothing had gone wrong and if the winds had favored them, then Abelia and his parents were just arriving to the port city of Mauvia in Arvent. They had all the money left over from his mysterious employer's payment. It was blood money: a wage earned through treachery.

When they landed, hopefully they could begin again beyond the shadows of the mad wizard Remus, Marduk's creatures, and Valiance's betrayal of his vows.

Boots pounded down the halls in the floor below. One set followed by another and another in a crescendo of shouts and the jangling of gear. Someone raced up the stairs and pounded on his door.

Valiance folded the letter. "Yes?"

The door opened and a Guardsman, his bright red hair sticking up where he ran his hands through, stepped inside. "Lieutenant, we're under attack. Captain Jarrett needs you right away."

"I'll be right there."

The Guard bowed and left, slamming the door shut behind him. Valiance started to put the letter into a chest. He hesitated.

Whether he lived or died, it didn't matter to him. Valiance felt the need to leave behind some sort of explanation if···if one was needed. Abelia's letter was the closest thing he had.

He laid it on his pillow and tugged on the scarlet surcoat of a Royal Guard.

Remus rode on the shoulder of his creation, the height of his alchemical talent, as the creature crashed through the Low Quarters.

"This is for you, sister!" he shouted into the wind. "This is for both of us!"

With a sweep of his hand and word, he set a nearby building aflame.

When I'm done, he thought, *Lorst will weep that it ever fought against Tier and the Court will weep that it ever ignored Sister and me.*

Chapter Twenty-Three

Clara hadn't made it halfway across the Great Hall when the swish of cloth brought her to a halt. Thalia trotted up to her.

"I will help," the older woman said, "though it's a waste of time."

Clara considered refusing but couldn't see a reason to do so. They started across the hall again.

"How did Remus even know to find me in that clearing?" Clara asked.

"He has agents everywhere. He's worked on this for years, you know. That is plenty of time to acquire allies and lay careful magics."

Clara swore.

They entered a small hallway and began walking toward where Clara hoped they would find stairs. Was her father still sleeping? Would she be able to return to him? She couldn't bear the thought of disappearing and Egbert never knowing what happened.

Thalia said, "I had heard the new king had a Seer in his Court. I suppose that was you?"

"I'm not much of a Seer anymore."

"Oh?"

Clara didn't want to say more, so she stopped to pull back a tapestry, as if she expected to find a door there.

"Clara, speak to me. What did you mean by that?"

With a sigh, she dropped the dusty, moth-chewed cloth. "I haven't had a vision since Marduk's death."

"Marduk? Wasn't he the king before King Emmerich?"

"He was the usurper and a king-killer, if that's what you mean."

"Of course. You haven't had a vision since then?"

"No." She walked on into the deeper portions of the hall.

Thalia called up a mage light, its cold blaze throwing hard shadows around them. "That's not uncommon, you know."

That made Clara stop again. "What?"

"It's not uncommon for Seers to suddenly not have visions for a time. Usually, it's caused by an emotional block or overuse. Tell me about your gift. Perhaps I could help."

Clara could have told Thalia her story from the very beginning. She could have talked about the horror of Gavin's death and the pain of leaving Emmerich. Telling her about her gift or life felt too difficult, too personal. In the white light, Thalia's eyes were darker and the planes of her face sharper. If anything, it made her more mysterious and more strange. The old feeling of a wall between herself and the other person welled up in her heart.

"Maybe some other time." She started down the hall again.

Clara explored the fortress, ignoring Thalia whenever she said things like, "I've already looked there" or, "Don't bother with that door; it's locked." Parts of the crumbling ruin were too treacherous to enter. One whole wing was inaccessible because of a collapsed roof.

Eventually, they entered the dungeons. It stunk of mold and old blood. Thalia's mage light cast harsh shadows over chains and instruments stained black with gore. The stench of the place—rotting blood, mold, and other things—coated the back of her throat and her gut heaved as last night's grilled oat cakes surged upward. She stumbled to a corner and vomited.

A cool hand brushed strands of her hair back and pressed against her forehead. After the last bit of vomit cleared her throat, Clara spat for good measure and straightened. She side-stepped away from Thalia, uncertainty at how to feel about the woman's touch roiling her stomach almost as badly as the smell.

"Thank you," she muttered, finally.

"You're welcome." Thalia smiled softly.

Clara hunched her shoulders and continued

to search.

It didn't take long to realize that there was nothing. No drafts to suggest hidden doors. Even the air shafts were grated and a blue sheen covered them. She didn't need Thalia to tell her those were wards. With a growl of frustration, she kicked a wall and trudged back upstairs. Since there was nowhere else to go, the pair returned to Thalia's room.

Fatigue nibbled at the back of Clara's mind. Flopping down into a couch, she groaned and buried her face in her hands. The cushion beside her gave with the weight of Thalia settling beside her. A soft hand settled onto her shoulder.

Clara stood. "Stop doing that!"

Thalia's eyes widened in surprise. "Stop doing what?"

"That!" She gestured vaguely at her. "Being motherly."

"I am a mother. I'm your mother."

"Well, you're late."

"I would disagree."

"You would?"

"Yes. I would."

"I raised myself just fine without any assistance. What makes you think you can just swoop in now?"

"You never stop needing a mother, Clara, no matter how old you are!"

"Really?" Clara snorted.

Thalia shot to her feet. "Yes, really. You need someone to talk to, someone to care about you, in a way only a mother can provide."

"When has that ever helped me?"

"Can you honestly tell me that no one has ever cared for you? And that caring didn't help you?"

Emmerich's face flashed through her mind and Clara looked away, unable to answer.

Thalia said softly, "And I'm sure that caring helped you more than once."

"I was just a tool to him," she said bitterly. "And now I am not even that much."

"No one can be in your presence for long and

see you only as a tool."

Clara froze. Memories washed over her: Gavin spending long evenings with her, telling tales and singing songs; Relly the cook giving her an extra portion of food when she was sick. Finally, she remembered Emmerich discovering her hiding behind a tapestry and inviting her to take a place at his War Council.

Thalia took one of her hands in both of hers. "Let me be a mother to you."

It was irrational and stupid. Heartbeats ticked by and with each one, Remus drew closer to Bertrand. He was probably already there, laying waste to the city. That didn't stop the tears from welling up and spilling over or the sob that crawled out of Clara's throat. Thalia drew her close and let her weep onto her shoulder.

Clara didn't know how long she cried. By the time she finished, her head and eyes ached and mucus clogged her nose. She pulled back and Thalia drew a handkerchief from her sleeve. She pressed it into Clara's hand. "Let's sit and try to work this out."

It was tempting not to listen, but Clara allowed Thalia to draw her to the couch. "Work what out? My lack of visions or our imprisonment?"

"Both." Thalia smiled. "It really probably is an emotional block on your part. Your visions will return in time."

"That is what Da says. Well, I certainly don't miss the fits I used to have whenever Emmerich went into battle."

"Fits?"

"Whenever Emmerich went into battle, I would fall into a fit where I was with him. I would see every possible end to the battle."

"Are there any other times you see him? Outside of a vision of the future, that is."

"Sometimes, when I dream, I go to visit him. And I think he sees me. I've warned him a few times about danger he didn't see." She scowled. "Why? Why are you looking at me like that?"

Thalia stared at Clara like she suddenly

sprouted a third eye. "Dear heart, I haven't heard of a Seer having those gifts since the Great Seer centuries ago."

"Great Seer? Is that the one that helped to save Tier?"

"Yes. An empty throne is left by the monarch's throne, in her honor."

"What does it mean?"

"It means you are very powerful." She smiled. "It means you can help Emmerich without even having to leave this fortress."

Headache and stuffy nose forgotten, Clara sat up. "How?"

Chapter Twenty-Four

Smoke and screams stifled the air. Emmerich braced himself against the stone of the rampart. Jarrett wouldn't hear of Emmerich riding into the Low Quarters to face the horde and, despite his anger at his disgraced Captain, Emmerich saw the wisdom in his words. So, he stood on the walkway running along the top of the wall that surrounded the Palace, giving orders and overseeing preparations.

Down below on the Palace grounds, soldiers, guards, and squires saw to various tasks. Captain Jarrett oversaw the evacuation of nobles and courtiers from their quarters to the older parts of the Palace built of stone, whose doors were heavy oak and iron. Under the new Lieutenant Valiance's watch, others prepared barrels of water to douse flames and oil to cause flames.

Squires and junior guardsmen assembled weaponry in neat piles while, off to one side, Bruin spoke to a knot of wizards. They were preparing to go down into the city itself with some staying behind to help guard the Palace. It made for an orderly chaos and Emmerich felt peace all the way down into his marrow.

This was his storm. Just as a sailor belonged on the heaving, rocking deck of a ship, Emmerich belonged in the fire and violence of battle. As he watched the burning city, he realized that.

He also realized a king had no right feeling this way. What choice did he have? He needed to find a balance, an anchor. If Clara refused to return to him, who or what could it be?

"Your Majesty?"

Asher's voice cut through his thoughts and Emmerich straightened. "What is our status?"

"Most of the nobility are as safe as we can make them. We have a few stragglers who insist they can fight. Wearing ceremonial armor and jeweled scabbards isn't helping their case." A smile warmed his voice. "We'll get them out."

"Good. And Lord Bruin?"

"He's remaining behind with some of his best

pupils."

"Any sign of the aerials? We may need their assistance."

"The only one anyone has seen is Niall, Your Majesty."

Emmerich faced Asher. "We could use their help."

"I know, Your Majesty." Guilt, dark and ugly, filled his face.

"The last position of the creatures and that giant?"

Lord Bruin approached from his other side. "It's not a giant, Your Majesty."

"It's not?"

"No. One of my arcane wizards says it's a golem."

"What's the difference?"

"Golems are created from magic. That means they are impervious to it."

"Captain Jarrett did report finding glass at the area where he believed the creature had appeared. The wizard must have created it there."

"It is very possible, Your Majesty. I suggest your men use the ballistas when the golem draws close."

"Asher."

The general bowed. "I'll relay the order, sire." He strode off.

In the distance, at the wall that separated the Low Quarters from the marketplaces, an explosion brightened the night. A plume of flame shot into the sky like a lance.

"Mother Above," Emmerich said. "How powerful is this wizard?"

"It may not have been magic, Your Majesty," Bruin said. "There are some powders from the East that can cause such explosions."

"How in the hell is that supposed to make me feel better?"

"It wasn't, sire. I was simply making an observation."

Emmerich shot Bruin a withering glare before going toward the stairs. "Do you have any idea what this enemy of ours could want?"

"No, Your Majesty. We think we know who he is, however."

Emmerich stopped halfway down the stairs. "And I'm just finding out about this now?"

"I only learned about it a candlemark ago, Your Majesty. I was going over the rosters again. One of the wizards, a fellow by the name of Remus, is unaccounted for and has been for the past fortnight."

"Could it be possible he died on one of your missions?"

If the barb stung, it didn't show on Bruin's face. "No, Your Majesty. Remus was strictly a researcher and alchemist."

"Could he be one of Marduk's minions?"

"It's not possible. We all took an oath of loyalty. We swore upon our magic and such an oath cannot be broken without great consequences."

"Well, obviously you've missed something." He continued down the stairs. "Again."

"This way, children!" Mistress Olivia stood by the door to the cellar beneath the Academy. "All the way down."

"It smells," complained a young girl.

"Yes, but it's safe."

Bran looked over his shoulder. When the bells in the city began to clamor, Mistress Olivia began gathering up all the students too young to help. He didn't need to ask what was happening. He knew, in a gut-deep way that made his legs shake, that it was his vision from earlier come true.

The line moved forward but Bran remained rooted to the spot. Something urged him not to go forward but to remain where he was.

Mistress Olivia had her back to him as she calmed one of the children who'd started to cry. He didn't let himself think about it. He slipped through an open doorway into a darkened classroom. Hunkering into a corner, he waited until the sounds of students faded and the cellar door closed with a groan.

Bran held his breath, half expecting to hear the matron to return in search of him. He waited until his chest burned. Slowly exhaling, he stood and walked out into the hall.

The sense burning in the back of his mind didn't tell him to go forward and it didn't tell him to go to the cellar. Frowning, he tried to hear what it said.

No one had told him, yet, how to listen to his new gift. Everyone seemed to think he should only receive visions. But Bran sometimes felt like his gift was this tiny spirit living in his head that sometimes showed him things and sometimes gave him feelings, like when it showed him Xavier attacking him and then reminded him later with a feeling, just in time to avoid the attack.

And kill Xavier. He shook off that thought and focused back on the feeling.

The itch-voice-feeling whispered, or seemed to whisper, that Bran should stay put. Why, though?

No answer came.

"What would General Asher do?" he asked aloud. The general had been very nice when he taught him the right away to hold the wooden short sword. To become a general meant he was very smart, and Bran wanted to be like him and like King Emmerich.

Was he supposed to stand watch, like the Guards at King Emmerich's door? The idea went through him like lightning. Bran had long admired any soldier in uniform and had often wondered what it would be like to protect someone as important as a king or serve under someone like General Asher.

The children downstairs in the cellar weren't kings but they still needed protection. Bran searched for something to use as a weapon but the hallway was bare.

He stepped back into the dark classroom, lit only by thin streams of moonlight from outside. Book-shaped lumps sat on the desks but something long leaned in a corner. Bran grabbed it, dragging it back into the light.

It was a halberd. One end was capped with a wickedly curved blade while a knob on the other end made a cudgel. On a man, it wouldn't have been that very long. But it stood almost as tall as Bran.

What was a halberd doing in one of the classrooms? Maybe it was one of the advanced defense classes he'd heard something about, where the students learned how to defend against weapons.

It wasn't at all like the short sword the general had him practice with, but he picked it up. The weight made his arms tremble as he went to stand in front of the cellar door. Bran moved his feet slightly apart, like how General Asher showed him, and gripped the unwieldy weapon with both hands.

No person or thing was going to get past him.

Thalia cleared the makeshift kitchen from the

hearth and laid down furs and pillows. She directed Clara to sit there while she rummaged around in a trunk that sat beside the cot.

"I didn't bring many of my supplies," she said. "I thought I would have access to whatever your wizard's academy had on hand. I did bring something that should help." She returned with a small pouch in her hand. Thalia sat beside her daughter.

"What is it?" Clara asked.

"A powder that will help you fall into a deeper trance than what you can obtain during sleep or normal exercises. It will allow you to interact with the physical world on your spirit walk."

"Spirit walk?"

"In Tier that is what it's called when you visit someone in your dreams or in trances. A few wizards and witches can do it, but not in the same way you have described. They see things as if from a distance and only another magic worker can sense their presence."

"Lord Bruin said he never heard of anyone

being able to do what I can do."

"I doubt Lord Bruin knows much of anything about Tieran magic. Ever since the last war, information in all its forms has been guarded." She opened the pouch. Clara caught sight of something glittery and grey-green. "Are you ready?"

"What do I need to do?"

"Just relax and stare into flames. Do what you normally do to fall into a trance. At the right moment, I will blow the powder into your face. Once you've inhaled it, you will be able to go on your spirit walk. While you're gone, I'll protect your body here."

Clara bit her bottom lip, considering this.

Thalia might very well be her mother. This could still be some sort of trap. However, she needed to trust someone and, so far, Thalia had not given her any reason to not trust her. And Emmerich needed her.

What would Emmerich do in this situation? Explore all of his options before trusting. Hadn't she done that? Clara had explored every bit of the castle that she could reach. Nowhere was there a way out.

Her mind suddenly went to Gavin. Gavin, who had been a friend to her long before anyone else. Gavin, who died at the hands of a monster. What would he say?

He would ask me what my gift told me, Clara thought.

Closing her eyes, she listened to her bone-deep intuition. She shut out the musty smell of the room and the crackle of the fire. She shut out the presence of the other woman. She listened and heard⋯peace.

Clara opened her eyes. As far as she could see, there were no other options and her gift wasn't trying to warn her.

She settled more comfortably onto the furs. "All right."

She gazed into the dancing flames of the fire and focused on her breathing. Muscle by muscle, she relaxed, starting from her legs and working her way up. With each exhale, she became more aware of the quiet burn of her gift in the back of her mind. It was the first time in months since she had felt it and, at first, she only basked in the sensation.

She couldn't remain like that. After fully relaxing, Clara reached into her gift. It shied away from her, worming more deeply into her mind. Faint lines of distress pulled at her mouth.

"Don't fight it," Thalia said softly. "You can do this. Let it come to you. Your gift is still there. It's never truly left you."

Clara wanted to say that she felt it. To talk, however, would break the beginnings of the trance that was starting to steal over her. The bright glow of her gift drew closer to her and Clara let it grow larger in her mind with every exhalation.

Thalia blew something into her face, something that smelled like cedar and frankincense with a bitter aftertaste, like myrrh. Something within Clara tore loose. It felt as if she held a bird that suddenly sprung from her hands.

She drifted up and away, catching only a brief glimpse of herself and Thalia sitting in front of the fire. Wind caught her, blowing her over a wide space with stars above and below, and, then suddenly—fire.

A city burned beneath her.

Men, women, and children died in the streets underneath claws and teeth reddened from blood and the glow of flames. Soldiers and wizards poured into what she now recognized as the Low Quarters.

They were too late and far too few. A hole blown into a wall disgorged creatures in a tide of fur and scales, fang and claws. Focusing, Clara flew further ahead, toward the giant figure lumbering toward the Palace.

Focusing hard, she shot forward and stopped just in front of the giant and the wizard that rode on its shoulder. The giant stopped.

Now that Clara could see him clearly, she could make out blue eyes that didn't come from

Thalia. She did recognize the nose and hair. She recognized the pinched look of hate and anger on his face. It was the same expression she sometimes caught herself wearing if she happened to pass a mirror.

The man—Remus—smiled. "I see Mother managed to help you join me. Are you enjoying the book I bought you?"

"I am. I wish you had told me who you were in Hernesferry."

"I couldn't, sister. I had to do things according to plan."

"Were you afraid I would stop you?"

"Of course I was. Why do you think I arranged for you to be locked away with Mother?"

Clara couldn't imagine how she was supposed to stop Remus, or what to say next, so she said, "Nice giant you have there."

"This isn't a giant. He's a golem."

"I have no idea how that's different."

"Giants are born. Golems are created. A giant

can be summoned but not controlled. A golem can be."

"And Marduk's creatures, how are you controlling them?"

"Like golems, they are creations, even if they began as humans once. Anything created may be controlled, Clara. It's one of the fundamental rules of magic."

"This is wrong, Remus. You're hurting innocent people."

Hate and anger darkened his face. "Innocent? *Innocent?* Every one of these people would see all Tierans dead. Not a single one of them is innocent. Marduk was no better. And neither is that low-born bastard that calls himself a king." He made a slashing motion with his hand. "I can't let this stand, Clara. I have to punish them. All of them."

"Emmerich wants peace. He doesn't want war anymore and neither do the people you're harming."

Remus's anger faded long enough for her to

read pity in his eyes. "Clara, you should be able to see more clearly than anyone. I heard at Court that you were enslaved. How can you help the people that put you in chains?"

"I can't condemn an entire nation because of the actions of a few." It was the hardest lesson she had ever learned and it cost the life of a good friend for her to learn it. "And is it really only because of the war between Tier and Lorst that you're doing this?"

Sorrow, dark and deep, flashed over his face. "You wouldn't understand. They all have to pay, for what they did to our country, to you, and for all that happened to me."

"Remus, brother, you're not making sense."

"I'm sorry that this is necessary. Maybe one day, we can be a family." He waved his hand and a bright flash of blue exploded before her.

Magic slammed into Clara's chest, a thousand thorns pricking her, and she fell back, sky and burning city spinning around her. For a moment, she flew in a place of infinite stars. The world rippled around her and she stood in a shadowy corner by the stairs leading to the main doors of the Palace.

Emmerich, in a utilitarian set of chain mail armor, spoke with Lord Bruin a few feet away as they studied a map. Joy and relief rose up in her like a shout. She stepped forward.

Her movement drew his attention and he stared. "Bruin," he said.

Lord Bruin raised his head at his king's tone. "Your Majesty?"

"I think I've gone mad."

The wizard looked in the direction his King stared. Surprise covered his face. "No, Your Majesty. I see her, too."

Clara strode forward and stopped within arm's reach. "I'm not really here."

Emmerich reached out and laid a hand on her shoulder. "You feel as if you're here." Moving slowly, he drew close to her and bent down just enough to plant a soft kiss on her mouth. "I would say you're here." He gazed at her with hungry eyes, as if he had been starved for the sight of her. "I rather like your hair so short."

She frowned, seeing the dark circles under his eyes. "Emmerich, are you all right?"

He drew back, dropping his hand away. "Aside from the city being under attack, everything is glorious."

She raised a brow.

"Excuse my interruption," Bruin said. "What did you mean about not being really here, my lady?"

Clara gave a brief explanation, beginning with finding her mother, being put into a trance, and ending with, "She didn't say how long I would be here, though."

"I can't even hazard a guess," Bruin broke in. "I counsel caution, my lady."

"I will keep that in mind. What's being done to stop the wizard, Remus, and the golem?" Clara decided it would be too complicated to mention her relationship to him.

"So, it is Remus," Bruin said. "I hoped I was

wrong."

"Mother told me he's been planning this for years. He feared her intervention, so had her imprisoned near Bluebell. He lured me to her. I suppose he wasn't expecting I would be able to come here like this."

"It's very possible that he's arranged for the protesters and the chaos in the streets, Your Majesty. Perhaps even the page's death."

Emmerich asked, "To what purpose?"

Clara raised her hands, as if to stem the flood of new information. "I only know he's angry."

"He's chosen a destructive way to display it."

Bruin said, "Your Majesty, I strongly suggest you evacuate. It is clear Remus has carefully planned all of this. He could have allies; we don't know who to trust."

"I will remain here." Emmerich cast a glance out toward the ruddy glow in the distance. When he turned back at them, his eyes were dark and dangerous. "I would rather be out there in the city."

"No," Bruin and Clara said together.

Emmerich snorted. "Clara, you said you came here to stop Remus?"

"I did," she replied. "He cast me aside with magic."

"Take Bruin, then, and his wizards. Meet Remus on his way."

"She'll need more than that," Bruin said. "Remember, this is a golem. We'll need archers at the least. I would prefer to have a wheeled ballista." He gestured at one such device being wheeled outside for the defense of the Palace. It was a giant crossbow on a cart with a bolt as large as a battering ram.

"Take archers. They will help buy time for a ballista to get to you."

"I think I should leave at least one of my staff here to protect you, sire."

"Do that. I want your best to go with her, as well as Jarrett's lieutenant."

Bruin bowed. "I'll make the arrangements." He jogged off, the sleeves of his black robe flapping like the wings of a very large crow.

Clara stared up at Emmerich, concerned about the determined, almost manic, expression on his face. He caught her staring. "What is it?"

"You're up to something," she said.

"Of course I am. I can't keep the city from burning to ash by doing nothing."

"You know that's not what I meant."

"I don't think this is the time for an argument."

She laid a hand on his chest. "Don't be rash, Emmerich. Lorst needs her King."

"Is that the only reason?" he asked, covering her hand with his.

If she had an actual mouth to go dry, it would have. "No," she replied.

His eyes lit up. "We'll talk more about that later, then."

"You're not all right, are you?"

He patted her hand and drew back. "Bad dreams. All warriors my age have them."

Clara opened her mouth to say more but a

shout drew their attention to the walls. Emmerich ran to the nearest stairs. With a thought and a step forward, Clara appeared atop the walls. The soldiers there jerked back with cries at her sudden appearance. She ignored them.

In the distance, an arrow's shot from the base of the hill on which the Palace sat, the golem lumbered toward them. Its size didn't cease to make the pit of her gut turn cold. Tall enough for its shoulders to brush third-story windows, it was the color of earth. She could make out the black speck that was Remus. It passed a mansion, which burst into flame from Remus's magic.

Asher called out, "Archers! I need archers on the walls! Why aren't the ballistas manned?"

Bruin's voice cut over the noise of boots on stone: "Lady Clara! We are ready!"

She moved with her mind and came to stand beside him. Bruin still faced the walls. On noticing her, he flinched. She smiled at being able to unsettle him.

Behind him clustered five wizards, three

Guardsmen, and several archers. One of them had the gold knot of a lieutenant on his shoulder. It took her a moment to remember his name was Valiance.

The wizards seemed as if they were better off in a library or some lonely, crumbling tower, poring over dusty manuscripts. Clara had seen white linens that were a darker shade than their faces. This was their best, for good or ill.

"Who is being left with Emmerich?" Clara asked.

"Harold Raines, my lady," Bruin replied. "He's a good magic worker. He'll guard the king well."

"Do you have a plan?"

"I hoped you did."

"We'll have to figure it out, then." At that moment, the archers assigned to the group arrived. They saluted and bowed. Clara ignored the trembling fear in her guts. "Let's go."

Chapter Twenty-Five

Wind heavy with screams and the scents of ash and burnt flesh swept through the streets. Clara was glad she didn't have a stomach to heave.

"I'll be the bait," she said in a low voice as they left the Palace behind, keeping to shadows. "I'll distract him while archers get to the rooftops. They will take care of the golem. Lord Bruin, you and your wizards will fight Remus. I'll help where I can."

Bruin scowled. "His Majesty won't like you being the bait."

"It's a good thing he isn't here to argue, then."

"Hm. Lieutenant Valiance, you and your men will remain with the lady to guard her."

"Yes, my lord," replied Valiance.

It wasn't hard to select a location. The golem's footsteps rumbled like the thunder of an approaching storm, steadily coming closer. Clara stood in the wide street while archers broke into the buildings to reach the rooftops. Bruin and his men hid using shadows and magic. Soon, she felt like a lit torch in a cave.

The ground beneath her feet trembled. The golem lumbered around the corner. Black panthers the size of horses spilled around its feet like a living stream. They ran past Clara as if she was a stone in their path, coming so close that she felt their fur brush her arms. It made her think of the furs she sat on in the fortress and, for a moment, her grasp on the time and place wavered. She felt herself start to slip away.

"Stay with it!" she heard her mother cry.

Gritting her teeth, Clara clamped down on her surroundings and tasks. Her thoughts drew her to float in the air at Remus's eye level. The golem came to a stop. It huffed and bathed her in its hot, rank breath.

"Trying to stop me again, sister?" Remus asked. "That didn't work last time."

"Remus, we're family," she said. "I've never had a brother before. I don't want us to fight. I want to help."

He straightened. "You agree with me now? What brought about that change of heart?"

She gestured behind her, toward the Palace. "The King is talking about killing you. He wanted me to help him. When he asked, I realized I didn't have it in me to murder my own brother."

"You've had no problem murdering before. Don't think I haven't heard the tale of what you did to Marduk."

"That was different. Emmerich was all but paying me to do that—and I wanted my freedom. You grew up in nobility. You grew up with every freedom. You don't know what it's like to be a slave. It makes you desperate and angry."

"How do I know I can trust you?"

"Who can you trust if not your own flesh and blood?"

Remus hesitated. Movement caught the corner of her eye and an arrow slammed into the golem's temple. It screamed, a high-pitched and terrible sound, and twisted. Remus fell to the ground, breaking his fall with a flash of his magic.

Clara thought herself from the air to the ground just in time to see Remus pick himself up. Just as Jarrett had taught her, she swung her fist and caught him with an uppercut.

Stumbling back, his boot caught a broken cobblestone and he dropped onto his back. Clara kicked him hard in the ribs. Above her, the golem roared and slammed into one of the buildings. Its hands scrabbled into it to get at the men firing at him. She dodged falling masonry. Remus clambered to his feet, flinging himself to the other side of the street. His right hand glowed blue.

Bruin with his wizards materialized from their hiding places. From their open hands, balls of fire and streams of bright light flung toward Remus. The enemy wizard threw up his hands. The fire and light spilled over him like water. Bruin shouted an order and his men spread out in a loose circle around Remus.

"Lieutenant Valiance," Clara said, "can you—what are you doing?"

Valiance, his sword drawn, advanced on her.

"I'm sorry, my lady," Valiance replied. "I have a job to do, for the sake of my family."

He lunged at her. Clara danced out of the way. The nearest Guardsmen rushed to her, catching Valiance's sword against his own. The two men began trading blows.

Growls drew Clara's attention back to the main battle at hand.

From behind the golem, more of Marduk's creatures—the unnatural boars and bears and things for which Clara had no name—charged down the street toward them. Clara thought she heard the winding sound of a horn. Soldiers were on their way.

A shout split the air. Valiance, his chest opened and red, dropped to the ground.

Screeches brought Clara's attention up. Three aerials, their feathers catching the flickering light of flames like bits of gold in the wind, dived at the golem's head. It backed from the building and swatted at the dragon-like birds.

They turned neatly out of his way, red-orange fire gushing down from their open maws and scorching over the golem. It roared in pain and struck out, knocking an aerial out of the sky. It fluttered to the ground like crumbled paper.

Aerials screamed and wheeled more tightly around the golem. With massive hands, it caught one and shoved the creature into its mouth. Blood spurted from its mouth as it chewed.

Horror flowed over Clara as she watched the last aerial, screaming even higher, soar away. In the distance, she heard more high-pitched keening that signaled mourning among the aerials.

She wondered how they knew to come back and if they would continue to fight.

The golem stumbled in her direction. Clara retreated behind the soldiers, who formed a phalanx in front of her. A grating sound from behind called her attention. Oxen, their heads low from the effort, pulled a ballista but they were too far away.

She thought herself to the golem's shoulder as it surged toward the ballista, knocking the wizards every which way. Clara latched onto some wiry hair and hung on as it ran. Her hand fell to her waist only for her to remember: no weapon. Now what?

Down below, Marduk's creatures met the soldiers. Their swords sang in the ash-ridden air to bite into unnatural flesh. They were too busy to try to attack the golem's ankles and the wizards were still fighting Remus. All the archers in the damaged building had to be dead. Clara was on her own.

An idea struck her. Before she could doubt herself, she squeezed her eyes shut.

Will this even work? she wondered. She thought herself into the golem's skull.

Everything became tight and hot and there was no air and she was going to *die*—

Clara swung her arms outward, tearing at soft

tissue. She clawed, fought, kicked. The world convulsed. She felt the gut-dropping sensation of falling. She felt weightless and as if she floated in the gel and flesh around her.

Everything jarred, slamming her forward. There came a distant boom just as her hands found a bony shelf and thick strands of flesh. Latching on, she yanked and dragged herself. Fluid washed over her as she scrabbled for purchase. A soft wall before her gave way and sweet air flowed over her.

Clara dragged herself onto the ground, gasping for air. She flipped onto her back and stared up into the sky.

Two soldiers came running up.

"Is it dead?" she asked.

One of the men made a noise that sounded like a giggle. The other said, "Yes, my lady. You just crawled out of his eye."

She pushed herself onto her elbows. In front of her, the golem's right eye was a red ruin. A trail of gore led from it to her. Clara was covered in blood, soft tissue, and clear liquid. Everything smelled like raw, spoiled meat. The two soldiers helped her to her feet.

Beyond the golem, she saw Remus fall to his knees. Sweat coated his face and he panted. Clara took a few steps forward. Bruin and his men began to close in on Remus.

Remus smiled at her, sweet and sad. Something stirred in Clara and she wasn't sure if it was pity or compassion or something else entirely.

He screamed a word, arching his back, and erupted in brilliant yellow. She threw a hand up to shield her eyes. When she lowered it and blinked away the black spots in her eyes, he was gone.

Fear rose in her throat as she ran around the golem's corpse to where Remus had stood. In his place was a smear of ash.

"Where is he?" she asked. "Bruin, did he get away?"

Bruin, his face sweaty and with a burn across

his cheek, came to stand beside her. "He is incinerated, my lady." He gestured at the sooty mark on the ground. "The bastard took his own life rather than be captured. What happened to you?"

"I decided I wanted to see what the inside of a golem was like."

A slow smile split across his face and he laughed. It struck Clara how odd of a figure she probably cut but she couldn't laugh. Not while she stood over the ashes of a brother she could have known. And, in knowing, might have saved from himself.

The world tilted sickeningly as a rush of tingles tumbled down her spine—

Emmerich strolled along the walls, yelling encouragement at his men as they dealt with the monsters attacking the Palace walls. Harold, the wizard left behind to protect Emmerich, followed him, only to suddenly stop. He leaned over the wall as if something below caught his attention.

One of the captains ordering the archers

whirled around and slashed a knife at Emmerich's throat.

"No!" Clara twisted and thought herself to the parapet lining the wall of the Palace.

Ahead of her, the wizard came to a stop and turned to look over the edge of the wall.

She screamed, "Emmerich, behind you!"

Emmerich twisted around in time to stop the captain's arm with his forearm. Grabbing the would-be assassin's throat, he slammed him against the wall, then lifted and shoved him over the edge. The captain fell screaming.

The wizard Harold raised his hand, blazing with blue fire, and slashed outward toward Emmerich.

Clara flung herself forward.

The air lit up, blinding her, and the stench of lightning scorched her nose.

Her hands found the man and she yanked, shoving him off his feet and to the ground far below on the Palace side.

The light faded.

Her eyes slowly adjusted.

Emmerich lay unmoving on the stone walkway lining the parapet.

Clara ran to him and dropped to her knees. "Emmerich," she gasped.

His grey eyes stared up into nothing. She pressed her hands against his throat. No pulse fluttered against her hand.

This can't be right, she thought. *This can't happen again.*

Clara felt the world wobble around her. For a heartbeat, she knelt beside Emmerich and beside the fire at once.

A captain—she didn't know who—came forward, tried to pull her away, and Clara jerked from his hands. "No!" she screamed. "Stay back! Stay back!"

The stones beneath her solidified. The ghost of the fire faded away. Emmerich's corpse was as solid as ever.

Niall keened, arching his back into it. Paula

shushed, running her hand down his neck. But the aerial ignored her. The high-pitched, heart-rending sound filled the room.

She blinked back tears. "It's all right!" she cried, though the noise drowned her out. She held the aerial against her chest and prayed it would be all right.

There must be something I can do.

Squeezing her eyes shut, Clara focused with all her strength on Emmerich. On his touch. On his scent. On the way he tasted when he kissed her. She focused on how she felt about him, calling up every ember of feeling she had buried deep inside. She fanned them into flame.

The world shifted again and she opened her eyes.

Clara stood, suspended, in the air. Stars were strewn above and below in an endless indigo. Ahead of her, a woman in blue and silver robes sat on a throne. Stars, as bright as miniature suns, crowned her head. At her feet, a boy dressed in a linen shift played with blocks. Beside them stood a figure shrouded in grey.

Something about this felt eerily familiar. Had she dreamed of this place before?

She approached the throne and the boy, stopping a respectful distance away. On closer inspection, the woman was far more beautiful than anything human. Her lips were the color of pink coral and her eyes the endless blue of a summer sky.

"Are you the Mother? Our Lady?" Clara asked.

The woman smiled softly and gestured at the boy playing at her feet.

The boy had hair the color of autumn wheat and on his shift were embroidered green leaves. He patiently stacked and arranged his blocks. Clara knelt.

"Are you The Child?" she asked. "The Blessed One?"

The boy looked up. He had his mother's blue eyes. "Would you like to play?" He held out a red block.

Clara shook her head. What did the presbyters say? The Child built the world and the Lady, with threads made from the souls of humanity, wove fate's tapestry. However, the only person doing anything was the Boy and he played a game. "I'm searching for someone. It's very important."

"He hasn't been judged yet." The Child began to carefully build a tower.

Clara studied the grey figure. Could that be Emmerich?

"I don't want him judged," she pleaded. "I want him brought back to life."

"Why?"

"I love him."

The Boy considered that and went back to building. Clara turned to the Mother.

"My Lady," she said, "please help me."

The Mother reached into her robes and drew out a drop spindle. "All lives must end. Death cannot be put on hold simply because of a loved one's attachment. If that were so, no one would die."

"Maybe no one should die!"

"You would deny him the next phase of his journey? Death is not an ending, after all. Not for someone such as your Emmerich."

"I would not deny him anything. I would only have you delay it a while. Please."

"Because you love him?"

"Aye. I know I left him before but I had to."

"Of course you did. How else would you know who you were? You cannot love someone if you do not know yourself."

Reaching out with delicate fingers, the Lady plucked at the grey figure, drawing out a long piece like it was carded wool. She fastened it to the tip of the spindle and began to spin.

The world of stars dissolved around Clara. Thick clouds of white and grey surrounded her.

Beneath her feet, ground formed. The clouds parted. She stood again on the parapet. Emmerich, gasping for air, struggled to get up. Clara, joy blazing in her like the noon sun, tried to reach for him. The clouds overtook her.

From far away, she heard Thalia's voice calling out for her.

"Mother!" Clara cried and threw herself toward the sound.

Standing guard was boring. And holding the halberd hurt his arms. It didn't take long before Bran leaned the weapon against the cellar door and sat next to it. After a while, he slipped into a doze, his chin against his chest.

Time ticked by slowly. No sounds came from below, in the cellar, and no sounds seemed to come from outside. When Bran first came to the Palace to live, it was weird.

The thick stone walls and heavy wooden doors kept out most sound. Unless it was a serious commotion in the hallway itself, Bran never heard anything happening beyond the dormitory door. And the Academy, being toward the back of the Palace grounds, was very far away from an action happening in the city itself.

A thump resonated from somewhere down the hall, breaking the silence. Bran jerked upright. How long had he slept? Without a candle clock or the sun, he couldn't tell, but his neck hurt.

He stumbled to his feet and hoisted the halberd up, holding it against his shoulder.

The hall ahead of him turned to the right before connecting with the main corridor of the building's ground floor. Not being able to see beyond the corner made Bran's mouth go dry with fear.

An unseen door creaked, either open or closed.

Bran flexed his clammy hands on the haft of the weapon. Reflexively, he reached for the itchy passenger in the back of his mind, but it was silent. No feelings telling him what to do came.

He gulped and wondered if banging on the cellar door, screaming for Mistress Olivia, would be a good choice. Or if the other students would just call him a baby.

Movement at the corner.

A scream bubbled up in his chest.

From around the corner came a black cat larger than anything he had ever seen before. Bran was used to the alley cats of the Low Quarters, which were all fangs, fur, and knobby joints. And they weren't that big.

This cat was the size of a horse and black as tar. Its sleek body moved toward Bran with effortless grace. Its lantern yellow eyes glowed.

Bran's heart beat so fast his chest hurt and his breath came in quick pants. Tears filmed his eyes but he rubbed them away.

He hefted the halberd in his hands and cried, "Halt!"

The giant cat stopped and cocked its head.

Some courage warmed Bran's limbs. "You're not allowed here. Go away!"

For a breath, it seemed like the cat would listen. It started forward again.

"I said, go away!" His voice pitched up into a scream.

The cat broke into a lope, crossing the distance between them unbelievably fast. Bran froze as the creature bore down on him. The itch-feeling roared into a blaze in the back of his mind and he jumped out of the way, twisting as he went.

The end of the halberd bit into the cat's shoulder. It roared and bounded back. Blood dampened its fur while it crouched, studying Bran. Tears spilled down the boy's face, and his knees shook, but he didn't move.

King Emmerich, when the riots broke out, wasn't afraid. Bran still remembered helping him into his armor and thought about how brave the King was to go. If the King could be brave, then Bran could be brave, too.

The cellar door opened. The cat took one look and ran off, limping as it went. Bran turned to see Mistress Olivia standing there holding a crossbow with a bolt pulled back.

"Bran," she said, "are you all right?"

"I think so."

"That was very stupid what you did. That cat would have eaten you if I hadn't come up in time. You understand that, yes?"

"Yes, mistress."

"Put the halberd down and come inside."

He leaned it against the hall, feeling sick at seeing the blood on the blade. "I'm sorry, mistress."

"Well." She took his hand. "I think the King would be proud of you."

Bran couldn't have asked for higher praise.

Chapter Twenty-Six

When dawn broke over the mountains, fog clinging to the peaks in thin strands, Thalia found the monsters were gone and the portcullis raised. She watched the dawn and wondered how she was going to tell her other son Alexander, and her husband, about Remus's death. A pain, as sharp as a dagger's edge, sliced through her heart.

There had to have been something she could have done to stop him.

Thalia returned to her daughter, who hadn't moved from her position before the fire after she awoke that morning.

"Dear heart," she said, "the way is clear. You wouldn't happen to have an idea as to where your father would be?"

Clara turned away from the fire. Her eyes held a hollow, haunted expression. She cleared her throat. "We were on the Great Mountain Road just south of Bluebell. We'd only done a day's worth of travel."

"We aren't far from that road, I know that. We should find him easily enough. I rather doubt he would go anywhere without you."

Clara stood, wobbled, and her knees gave out. Thalia caught her by the arm and gently lowered her to the floor.

"The first intentional spirit walk is always the hardest," Thalia said, "and you were gone longer than my mentor would have deemed safe."

"I feel like I could sleep for an age."

"If we were at my home in Tier, I think I would let you."

Clara laughed, a husky and short sound, as if it was something her voice didn't do often. Her face fell back into its usual serious and solemn lines. "We shouldn't detour to take you back to Tier. I'm sorry. They will need me in Bertrand."

"My husband is spending the summer with his courtesan in the Sunstruck Islands. I think he will do fine without me." Thalia patted her on the shoulder. "Do you think you can try to stand again?"

Clara nodded. Thalia stood and held out her hands. The younger woman hesitated a heartbeat before she slid her hands into Thalia's.

"How is he?" Captain Jarrett's eyes felt gritty from no sleep and his feet ached, but he kept his shoulders square and his chin up as he addressed General Asher.

The general gestured at the king's chamber door. "He'll live. When he came around, he was shaken and complained of chest pains. The Master Healer dosed him with something to help with the pain. He wanted to give him a sleeping draught but King Emmerich glared him down."

The mental image of Emmerich scowling down someone from his sick bed made Jarrett smile. "And his attackers?"

"Dead. Eyewitnesses say Lady Clara appeared out of nowhere to warn the King. King Emmerich took care of Captain Percy and she took care of the wizard. Lord Bruin said his name was Harold.

It looks like Percy, Harold, and Valiance were all in a plot with Remus to kill King Emmerich and Lady Clara."

As if saying his name summoned him, the King's chamber door opened and Lord Bruin leaned out. "He's asking for you two," he said.

"Lord Bruin," Jarrett replied, "we were just talking about you."

"All good things, I hope."

"Never."

Bruin huffed a laugh and stepped back, allowing them in.

Jarrett felt uneasy. Lieutenant Valiance had been revealed as one of the traitors and he felt the guilt of that keenly. He'd vouched for the man, left him in charge while he was away, and then didn't demote him when Jarrett heard enough reasons to do so. Valiance could have done a lot more damage and it would have been Jarrett's fault.

King Emmerich was propped up on pillows when they entered. Niall, the aerial, was curled in his lap. A woman healer sat in a chair by the bed.

He waved them closer. "Don't be afraid. The Master Healer says I'm in no condition to kill anyone at the moment. This is Healer Paula. She tended to Niall when his wing was broken. Master Valerian put her in charge of my care."

Paula stood. "I should go. Your Majesty, please try not to tire yourself." She curtsied and left.

Jarrett tried not to watch her go and wondered if her relationship with Emmerich was solely that of healer-patient. For Clara's sake, he hoped so.

Emmerich said, "Lord Bruin was just telling me about what happened with that golem."

Jarrett asked, "Did Lady Clara really climb out of its eye?"

"I saw it myself," Bruin replied.

"Damn."

"I had the same reaction."

Emmerich chuckled. "It sounds like her. Captain Jarrett, have you gone through

Valiance's belongings?"

"Yes, Your Majesty," he replied. "We found nothing to suggest that the traitor's cabal was very large. But we did find a letter from his sister. Apparently, his family have left Bertrand and gone to the Arventi city of Mauvia. If I were to guess, I'd say he took money to clear the family debts and allow them to leave."

"Any idea of how much they knew?"

"None, Your Majesty. Shall I have someone follow them?"

Emmerich shook his head. "I think with the death of Remus and his conspirators, we have little to worry about."

Silence filled the room for a brief moment. Jarrett looked at Asher and Bruin. The other two men said nothing.

Finally, Jarrett said, "Sire, if you wish for me to give my resignation—"

"Oh, shut up," Emmerich replied. "You trusted Valiance because you thought you knew him."

"He almost killed her ladyship."

"Actually," Bruin said, "because she was not in physical form, entirely, there's a good chance that she was never in any danger."

"A good chance?"

"It's better than no chance at all."

Emmerich shifted in his bed, grimacing. "Your men, Captain Jarrett, saved her—despite what her chances might have been—because you trained them well. Because of that alone, I will allow you to continue in your service as Captain of the Guard."

Relief as sweet as sea air swept through Jarrett. He bowed. "Thank you, Your Majesty."

"And as for you two." He fixed Asher and Bruin with an angry stare. "If I ever hear of you two taking chances like those that led to the first fire and the death of aerials, I will have your hides, do you understand?"

"Yes, Your Majesty," they replied.

"Any information either of you might learn will be discussed with Captain Jarrett and each other before action is taken. All three of you are my friends and allies. We need to work together if we hope to make Lorst into a strong kingdom." He settled back into his pillows. "Now, get out. I'm supposed to be resting."

"One more thing, Your Majesty," Asher spoke up.

"Mother Above, help me. Now what?"

"That boy, Bran? He helped to stave off the attack of one of the giant panthers."

Emmerich laughed. "Are you serious?"

"Very. Mistress Olivia saw it herself. She had taken the children into one of the cellars. When she noticed Bran wasn't among them, she went upstairs with a crossbow in time to scare the creature away."

"That boy is very small for all the surprises he holds."

"Yes, Your Majesty. I have a request regarding him."

"I think he's too young to join the army."

Asher smiled. "Actually, I wanted to adopt him."

"Adopt?"

"My sister is moving to Bertrand with her husband and insists that I move out of the barracks to live with her. My sister can be a mother to him."

"And you a father?"

"I hope to be, yes, sire. It's the least I can do for him, after what happened when his mother died."

Emmerich smoothed his coverlet. "There are other orphans as well, General Asher. Are you going to adopt all of them?"

"No, sire. But I can do something for one and I choose that to be Bran. Besides, I've worked with him on the practice fields during his free time. I've grown very fond of him."

"Very well. Have the adoption papers drawn up and I'll be happy to witness their signing. Bran deserves a family."

"Thank you, Your Majesty. Rest well."

The trio left the King, walking together out of the Royal Wing.

"I suppose we're back on his good side," Bruin said.

"It's certainly a nice feeling." Asher scratched at his jaw.

"But not as nice as knowing you'll be a father."

"Yes!" cried Jarrett. "We should buy you drinks tonight."

"I'm afraid I have work—"

"Asher." Bruin stopped. "I'm not a father but I grew up in a large family. As did Captain Jarrett, I believe. You will have precious little free time, between the army and raising a boy willing to stare down a cat six times his size."

Jarrett chuckled. "We're buying you drinks. You'll need the fortification."

Asher laughed.

Epilogue

Thalia and Clara didn't find Egbert until that evening. He hadn't moved from the campsite beside the Great Mountain Road.

"Clarie!" he shouted when the pair came walking up, Clara leaning heavily against her mother. He slid out of the wagon where he sat and hobbled over to them. "I feared t'worst when I woke and you weren't there." They embraced. When he drew back, he squinted at her. "What's wrong? Who is this woman?"

Clara forced a smile that felt more like a grimace. Stubbornness compelled her to try standing on her own and her knees shook. She felt as if she'd suffered for a month under a fever. "I'll tell you later, Da. Da, this is Thalia."

The old man stared. "Thalia?"

"Egbert," Thalia said. "You've gotten old."

"As have ye. It's only made you more the beauty!"

Thalia grinned and, to Clara's surprise,

blushed. "You always had honey for a tongue."

"If memory serves aright, if anyone has the sweeter tongue, it'd be you, love." He winked.

"All right then," Clara said loudly, wanting to be somewhere else in a desperate way. "Shall we have some dinner?"

That night, she watched her parents talk of old times and flirt rather shamelessly. Neither seemed to care about Thalia's marriage to a baron. Though, since Thalia had married Egbert first, perhaps that wasn't an issue at all. Clara felt too exhausted to wonder about that.

The heat from the flames lulled her into a doze, one she barely woke from when Thalia helped her up and onto her pallet. For the first time since she was a small child, Clara was tucked into bed.

The next morning, they started off. The Great Mountain Road was a broader highway used by traders and not the way Clara had taken to Bluebell. Clara's route had taken her along narrow ridges and areas a wagon would not be able to go. The mountain road was easier but slower. It took nearly a month before they reached Candor City.

The oppressive heat of early summer weighed on the city. Men and women both eschewed wool, velvet, and fur for linen and cotton. Despite the heat, the trading and selling that made up Candor City's heart roared on like usual. Since the giant passed the city without bothering it, and because Marduk's creatures had gathered near Bertrand, life continued on as it always had.

Not wishing to make her presence known, and then having to deal with the amorous Lord Candor, Clara took rooms in a hostel in the lower town, near the docks. She worried that Thalia would be offended at staying in such a place.

Her mother didn't appear bothered. Thalia sold one of her gowns and bought plainer clothes, most of her attention split between Egbert and Clara, who still struggled with bouts of fatigue and weakness.

While awaiting a barge to take them down to

Bertrand, Clara wrote a letter to Emmerich. She'd seen him come back to life, so she knew it wasn't a foolish thing to do. However, she couldn't imagine what to write. Finally, she settled on a few terse lines informing him she was on her way back with two guests.

"Are you certain you don't want to say more?" Thalia asked, reading over her shoulder.

Clara just folded the letter, sealing it with wax. "Will you take this to the rookery?"

"Of course, dear heart."

They left on a barge the next day.

The giant's passage had knocked trees across several places in the Lyn Tone River, so a journey that should have only taken a week took nearly two. By the time they passed a pillar announcing they were within a day of the Capital, Clara was more than ready to disembark, if only to get off the water.

She changed into a crimson linen undergown with large, hanging sleeves and a pale yellow silk overgown. Around her hips she tied a belt embroidered with red and yellow flowers.

It was the height of fashion in Candor City when she purchased the clothing. Several merchant wives sniffed when they saw her. What was fashion in Candor was country simplicity to people of Bertrand. Clara ignored them even as she wished for hair long enough to braid, the one part of fashion she really loved.

Thalia took an ivory comb from her baggage and brushed her daughter's hair. "In Pathos, it's not uncommon for unmarried women to wear wigs. Such elaborate hairstyles, it's a wonder they can hold their heads up. The shortness of your hair shows off your beautiful throat and the cut's simplicity brings attention to your eyes. You are beautiful."

The praise warmed Clara and she smiled.

Thalia finished brushing Clara's hair and then adjusted her tunic.

"I've never liked Court," Clara blurted. "I've always felt like the courtiers looked down on me, for having been a slave."

"You also frightened them, I imagine."

Clara made a scornful noise in the back of her throat.

"No, I'm serious. You, my dear, were not born to our position. You earned it and that is an honor which can never be taken from you, while they can be expelled from Court."

"So can I."

"Yes. But you would take your talent and achievements with you and Lorst would be poorer for it. They cannot say the same." Thalia laid a hand on Clara's cheek. "So, when you feel looked down upon, raise your chin and remember: you earned your place."

Clara took her mother's hand and squeezed it. After a heartbeat, she whispered, "I'm sorry about Remus. I tried to stop him."

Sorrow darkened Thalia's eyes, briefly, like clouds skidding across the sun. She smiled thinly. "I know."

They smelled the docks of the Low Quarters before they reached them: smoke and char, decaying corpses and mud. The more fashionable people pressed scented handkerchiefs to their noses. Clara's stomach flipped but she did nothing to alleviate the stench.

Half of the docks were in ruins, broken wooden planks sticking out of the river's bank. Beyond them, many of the warehouses crawled with workmen. A line of barges waiting for unloading backed up for nearly a league. The pilots jeered and shouted at each other.

Clara fanned herself and tried to ignore yet another bout of dizziness. The urge to lie down and sleep nearly overpowered her. The foul smell helped to keep her alert.

Their barge finally slid into a dock. To Clara's surprise, Captain Jarrett with a squad of men waited for them.

"You're in a dress," he said as she stepped off the plank onto the dock. "Thank the Mother. If I presented you to Emmerich while you wore men's clothing, I think he'd have a fit of apoplexy." He grinned. "We have a surprise for you."

"I don't like the sound of that." She considered him. "Emmerich didn't have you killed for returning without me, then?"

Jarret laughed. "There was a moment there I thought was my last." A pause stretched between them. Clara had worried he would be angry. He only appeared to be happy to see her. He continued, "So, your message said you had two guests?"

Clara smiled and stepped aside, gesturing at her parents. "Captain Jarrett, allow me to present to you my mother, Lady Thalia of Tier. And this is my father, Master Egbert of Bluebell."

"Lady. Master." He bowed. "A pleasure to meet you. Lady Thalia, I can see where Lady Clara got her beauty."

Clara rolled her eyes while Thalia preened. Jarrett escorted them to an open top carriage.

Clara settled into the cushions with a sigh. Despite her fatigue, she could feel her gift simmering in the back of her mind, now, as it did before Marduk and his vile touch. There was nothing that kept her from having visions now.

She should have felt joyous at finally being able to be useful and to have her parents with her. Instead, she only wanted to get away from whatever surprise awaited her and find a quiet place with Emmerich. And sleep. Sleeping felt more important now than ever.

Thalia had said it would take time for her to recover her full strength and the traveling wasn't helping. However, Clara felt distressed that she continued to feel weak at times.

As they clattered through the street, Thalia and Egbert stared at the devastation around them. Scaffolds and workmen filled the streets. Everyone seemed to have a task, whether it was sweeping up debris from the road or rebuilding homes. One park had been converted into a small tent city for the homeless.

The further they got away from the Low Quarters, the less devastation. A few buildings were in ruins thanks to the golem but, all in all, it wasn't nearly as bad as the Low Quarters.

The Palace itself appeared untouched. Clara straightened her back.

As the carriage approached the main steps, her brows rose in surprise. Emmerich, with the Council and the High Presbyter, as well as other courtiers, awaited them on the steps. A small aerial, wearing a narrow golden rope around his neck, perched on Emmerich's shoulder with one claw delicately holding onto the King's ear. A boy with a blue box stood beside Asher. It took her a moment, but she recognized the boy as the child she saw in the clearing.

A woman healer in green robes also stood in the crowd. Clara wondered who she was and what she was doing there.

"A hero's welcome!" Egbert cried. He beamed. "Tha's what my Clarie deserves." He reached out and patted her on the knee.

"She does," Thalia agreed, her face warm with pride.

The carriage came to a halt. A footservant

opened the door and put down a small stool.

Clara left the carriage and ascended the steps, trying to ignore all the attention leveled on her. She stopped two steps down from Emmerich and curtsied. Her palms sweated and stomach twisted. Raising her chin, she reminded herself that she earned this welcome.

"Lady Clara," said Emmerich, "you have done Lorst a great service. It is my pleasure to welcome you home."

She croaked, "I only did my duty, sire."

"Unfortunately, we live in a world where duty is easily bought off or ignored."

The back of Clara's neck burned and she could almost hear Jarrett arguing for her to return to Bertrand. If she had done so sooner, would the city be less devastated?

Emmerich continued, "In reward for your service, I bestow upon you the Honor of the Realm." He opened the box Bran held. From it he drew a large opal suspended on a golden chain.

Clara made her legs move to ascend the last

steps. Once she reached him, he slipped the chain over her head. The heavy opal settled between her breasts.

The Honor of the Realm was given only to those who had done some heroic or generous act that benefited the entire country of Lorst. If she remembered her history right, the last time it had been granted was to Prince Marius the Brave three generations ago for slaying a dragon.

Climbing out of a golem's eye apparently also counted.

Unable to speak, Clara curtsied.

"I hope," Emmerich said, "that you will continue to serve Lorst for many years to come."

Silence fell. Clara swallowed hard. "You honor me, Your Majesty, and I can only hope to do what is right. Nothing more or less."

That seemed to satisfy, as everyone clapped. The aerial, alarmed at the sound, half-spread his wings. Emmerich touched it reassuringly before he offered Clara his arm. She took it and that brought an end to the proceedings.

Conversations began among everyone. She hardly paid them any mind as Emmerich led her inside. His arm felt warm and solid. The small part of her that feared she'd dreamed him awakening faded.

"My parents," she began.

"Jarrett will bring them to my parlor. First, you and I need to talk. Should we go to your quarters?"

Clara let him lead the way. They didn't speak until the door to her sitting room closed behind them.

"Off you go," he whispered, shrugging his shoulder. The aerial, crooning, launched into the air and soared to land on the breakfast table.

"Does he have a name?" Clara asked.

"Niall."

"He's lovely."

"Not nearly as lovely as you."

Emmerich pulled her close. Her hands came up to cup his face as his mouth descended on hers.

They kissed until they panted for breath. Emmerich drew her to sit with him on the couch.

They didn't say anything for a long while. Clara quietly reveled in being physically present with Emmerich. All the intrigues of Court and burdens of duty existed far away in those moments, as if another building, another world, another life. Behind them, Niall chirruped and chittered to himself while he explored.

"I'm not the man I was," Emmerich remarked, breaking the quiet as neatly as a dry twig. Dark circles darkened the skin under his eyes and he had the hollow look of someone who feared his dreams.

Clara didn't know what to say, so she didn't reply, only took his hand. Their fingers threaded together.

"And you're not the girl who left me last autumn," Emmerich continued.

"I'm still me," she protested.

"You're more yourself than you were."

Again, she didn't know what to say to that.

"Marry me?" he asked.

"Aye." Clara squeezed his hand.

He barked a laugh. "I expected another argument."

"I was expecting you to ask me to run away with you, like you did last time."

He shook his head. "I shouldn't have asked that. I can't abandon my people for my own desires. I didn't understand that when we last talked."

"You do now?"

"I do but I still think I'm out of my depth in many ways." Emmerich ran a hand through his hair. "You found what you sought."

Clara smiled. "My mother is a witch of some sort from Tier. My father is still living."

"I saw them with you. What of that woman who sold you?"

"She left my father and has gone to terrorize someone else."

"Your real mother, she wouldn't happen to be related to the Tieran Royal Family?"

"No. Why?"

"The Tierans have offered one of their Princesses to me. It's the perfect political marriage and I've been fending the Council off with every argument and reason I can think of. There are those who fear refusing will sour relations with Tier. And no one wants another war."

"So, if I turned up to be some distant relation of the Royal Family, it might soothe the Tieran King?"

"It's a long bowshot."

"My being related or that relation pacifying King Precene?"

"Either." Emmerich shifted so that he faced her. "Men will find any reason to go to war if they want to badly enough, if they think it will win them power or riches."

"Or revenge." Clara raised a brow. When they first met, when Emmerich had been a Rebel General and a suspected murderer, he started a civil war to avenge his family's deaths and the death of a woman he loved.

"Or revenge. As we have gold mines to the North and the sea to the east, his motives would lie more towards wealth."

"If you refuse King Precene, will he start a war?"

"I don't know. I've never met the man. I've only had to deal with his ambassadors. What do you think?"

"I'm too tired to try to see the future, Emmerich."

"I didn't ask that. I asked what you thought."

It was like Jarrett's words thrown back in her face. Emmerich didn't care about whether she could see the future or not. He only cared about her and she felt like an idiot for not realizing sooner.

"I think," she replied slowly, "that King Precene can easily be persuaded that it's in his best interest to remain friendly with us. And surely there has to be another way to solidify relations between our kingdoms."

"My thoughts exactly."

"Then why did you ask?"

"Because I wanted to hear it from you." He kissed her gently.

A question that had been bothering her on and off came back to her. "You said all the aerials had left Bertrand."

"Aye."

"I saw a few during the night of the battle."

"There were reports and Niall grew distressed when some of his brethren were injured. No one is sure what made them return, if it was Niall's presence or you or something else entirely. However, no one has seen them since. It's a mystery best left to scholars and wizards, I think." He released her hand and stood. "I suppose we should go meet our guests. You are beautiful."

Clara rose, smiling, and touched the bodice of her overgown. "Thank you."

He grinned at her and, for a second, he was the arrogant boy with grey eyes who called her a witchling. The grin mellowed into a quieter smile, returning him to the King with hollow, tired eyes.

"There is much to do," he said. "Not only with Tier but rebuilding Bertrand. And dealing with the antics of the Council."

"I know. We will do it together."

He brushed his fingers over her cheek before taking her hand and starting toward the door. "Come along, Niall."

The aerial chirped and flew over, landing neatly on Emmerich's shoulder. He looked down at Clara. She tilted her head to study the brightly colored nestling, sensed a hint of amusement wafting from the creature. It was connected with Emmerich's thinking of it as a "he".

"Emmerich?"

"Yes?" He opened the door.

"I think your Niall is a girl."

"What?"

The look of surprise covering his face provoked a laugh from Clara. Emmerich scowled at her and that only made her laugh harder. The scowled melted away. The sound of their laughter echoed through the halls.

Letter to the Reader

Dear Reader,

Thank you so much for reading my novel. If you liked it, let your friends know! Leave me a review on Amazon or Goodreads or Barnes & Noble or wherever! I wouldn't mind if you wrote it on the wall of a public restroom, as long as you let others know about my work. And if you haven't yet, please check out my other books. To stay up to date on me and future projects, be sure to sign up for my newsletter at suzannalinton.com.

About the Author

Suzanna J. Linton was born in South Carolina and was raised in and around the rural town of Holly Hill. In the summer of 2002, she attended the SC Governor's School for the Arts and Humanities and remembers it as the best summer of her life. She has a Bachelor's in Professional Writing and lives in Florence, SC, with her husband and pets.

Social Media Info

Website: suzannalinton.com

Twitter: twitter.com/suzannalin

Facebook: facebook.com/SuzannaJLinton

Made in the USA
Columbia, SC
30 June 2019